Wallace's War

WALLACE'S WAR

Book 6 in the Lord Edward's Archer series

By Griff Hosker

Wallace's War

Published by Sword Books Ltd 2022

Copyright ©Griff Hosker First Edition

The author has asserted their moral right under the Copyright, Designs and Patents Act, 1988, to be identified as the author of this work.

All Rights reserved. No part of this publication may be reproduced, copied, stored in a retrieval system, or transmitted, in any form or by any means, without the prior written consent of the copyright holder, nor be otherwise circulated in any form of binding or cover other than that in which it is published and without a similar condition being imposed on the subsequent purchaser.

A CIP catalogue record for this title is available from the British Library.

Contents

Prologue 6
Chapter 1 9
Chapter 2 18
Chapter 3 26
Chapter 4 35
Chapter 5 44
Chapter 6 54
Chapter 7 64
Chapter 8 72
Chapter 9 83
Chapter 10 92
Chapter 11 105
Chapter 12 119
Chapter 13 128
Chapter 14 137
Chapter 15 149
Chapter 16 161
Chapter 17 171
Chapter 18 185
Chapter 19 195
Epilogue 205
Glossary 206
Historical Note 206
Other books by Griff Hosker 208

Wallace's War

Real characters mentioned in the novel.

King Edward- King of England and Lord of Aquitaine and Gascony
Queen Eleanor of England
King Alexander of Scotland
Edmund Crouchback, 1st Earl of Lancaster and King Edward's brother
Thomas, 2nd Earl of Lancaster, son of Edmund Crouchback
Henry Lacy- Earl of Lincoln and Constable of Chester
Earl Marshal Roger Bigod- 5th Earl of Norfolk
Humphrey de Bohun -3rd Earl of Hereford
Sir Reginald Grey-1st Baron Grey of Wilton, lord of Castell Rhuthun (Ruthin)
William de Beauchamp- 9th Earl of Warwick
Robert de Brus, 6th Lord of Annandale
John Balliol-Lord of Galloway and Barnard Castle and, latterly, King of Scotland
Antony Bek, Bishop of Durham
Sir John de Warenne- 6th Earl of Surrey and John Balliol's father-in-law
Andrew Murray (Moray)- one of the Scottish leaders of the rebellion against King Edward
William Wallace- one of the Scottish leaders of the rebellion against King Edward
William Heselrig- Sheriff of Lanark
Robert of Béthune- Flemish leader of the attack on Damme
Henry Percy- 1st Baron Percy
Captal de Buch- Gascon mercenary leader
Henry de Beaumont- French Mercenary
Sir John Stewart- Commander of the Scottish bowmen at the Battle of Falkirk
Sir John de Graham- Wallace's second in command at the Battle of Falkirk

England in 1298

Wallace's War

Prologue

Yarpole 1297

I am Sir Gerald Warbow, more commonly known as Lord Edward's archer and. as the new year began my life was good. My line would continue for my daughter, Margaret, had given birth to my first grandson, Gerald Launceston and my son, Hamo, had married Alice, one of the captives we had rescued from the clutches of a Scottish brigand, William Wallace. Her two younger brothers, James and John, also lived with us and when they were old enough, they would become archers. I had been with King Edward when we had first defeated the Welsh in North Wales and then crushed the Scots at the Battle of Dunbar. The captured Scottish nobles who had refused to become loyal subjects of King Edward now languished in either the Tower of London or Chester Castle. Those who had signed were mocked by the people, they called it the Ragman's Roll. With the king back in London and the border not only at peace but gripped by winter, I could enjoy those rarities I had not enjoyed before. My home and peace. My wife was even happier than I was. She hated me being on campaign and as my son was now my lieutenant, she had double the concerns.

I knew that I was unique. I was an archer but I had been knighted by the king and was the lord of a large manor and a smaller one. I could ride and fight as a man at arms. I had never been trained in the arts of jousting and I never considered myself a knight in the true sense of the word. When I fought, I fought with naturally acquired skills and I fought to kill. Knights would not wish to face me on the battlefield. When I had crossed swords with the giant, William Wallace, it had been he who had fled and not me. But I was getting old. I had seen more than fifty summers and lived far longer than I should have.

When Gerald was born, I could not help thinking of my father. It had been the avenging of his murder that had set me on the road to becoming a warrior. His life had been, by comparison with mine, mean and hard. Eking out a living on a small holding in the Clwyd Valley had not been easy. Had he not been murdered he might have died alone but he should not have been killed the way he was and I did not regret the murder of the knight. Now, as I held, somewhat uncomfortably, the swaddled grandson my daughter had borne I thought of my father. He would be amazed to see how far I had travelled. Until Lady Maud of Wigmore castle had died, I had been a favourite of hers who was invited to dine with the great and the good. Great lords deferred to me and King Edward saw me not only as his loyal captain of archers but also as an adviser in all matters military. That I was now shunned by the Mortimers did not worry me although I missed the old lady. She had been a powerful influence in the marches.

Now that Scotland and Wales were safe, I wondered if I would ever have to draw my bow in anger again. I thought that I would become a lord of the manor who hunted and watched his family grow. The thoughts of my father made me even more determined that my children and grandchildren would have a good life and a safe one. That would be my purpose in my final years. Of course, that was not meant to be for higher forces than I were to determine my future and it would not be a peaceful one. I would have to continue to draw my bow for King Edward.

The nagging doubt that sometimes woke me in the night was that King Edward had not completed his task in Scotland. After Dunbar would have been the time to complete his conquest of that land. He had taken the stone of Scone but the vast majority of Scotland was still without the iron grip of English-manned castles. Had King Edward made a rare mistake?

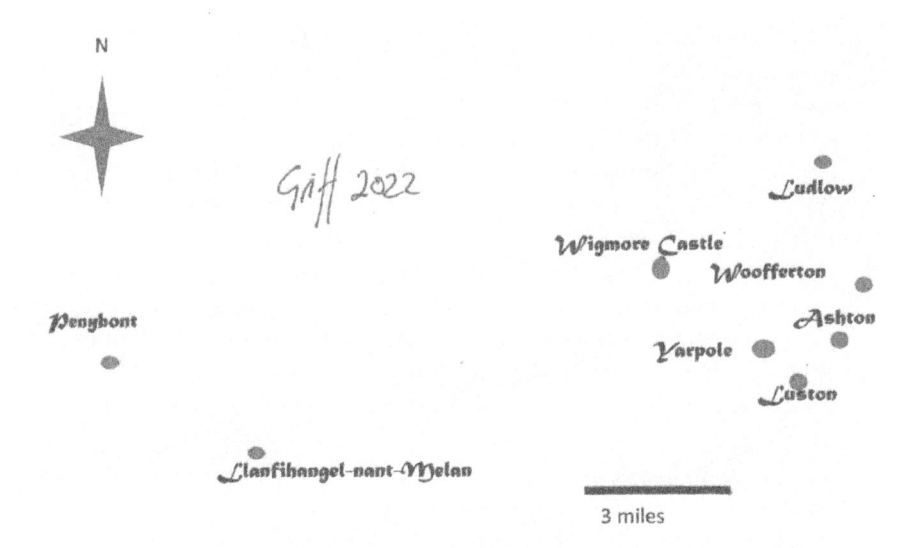

Yarpole and the Welsh borders

Wallace's War

Chapter 1

It might have been winter and the ground might have been bone hard but that did not stop my men and me from training and honing our martial skills. My son had recently married but he left his warm bed each day to come to the butts and to practise. His wife's brothers, James and John, while too small yet to draw a war bow had shorter ones and my archers patiently showed them how to string them. They taught them how to place their fingers and how to pull. Lords who did not use a bow could never understand the complexities of archery. John and James would become archers but it would not take place overnight. Unlike me when I had been the same age my son, Hamo, also practised with a sword. All my archers could use a sword and that marked us as different, that and the fact that we all rode to war. I hoped that Hamo would become as skilled as I was with a sword. An archer's strength, allied with a good sword made for a powerful weapon. When we had captured horses, and being as successful as we were meant we captured horses more frequently than most, we did not sell them but kept them for us to ride to war. It made us the fastest archers in England. We rode to war and reached any battlefield well before other archers. My men were proud of this distinction and we rode every day. I no longer enjoyed riding but I joined my men every day to endure the saddle that, although well oiled by Jack of Malton, still irritated me beyond belief.

Jack was an orphan who had come to us because he had been bullied by the son of a knight whom I had considered a friend. Sir John had been The Lord Edward's squire and we had travelled to the land of the Mongols on a quest for King Edward when he had been but heir to the throne. It had been the harsh treatment of Jack that had resulted in two things, one was the end of our friendship and the other was that my son and I took Jack under our wing and brought him to Yarpole to be raised as a sort of stepson to Mary and me. He had a good frame and he began training as an archer but he was also eager to help and I used him as a squire. He was not, of course. He did not have to wait at tables as other squires did. There were no lessons in French or dancing. He did not have to learn to play the rote and he was not forced to learn of chivalry and honour. I had learned that they were like the fine clothes that some lords affected when they presented themselves at court. They were for show and did not make their wearers any nobler. Jack learned skills from men like me, archers. I knew why I was so fond of Jack. He was the same age as Richard, my dead son, would have been. Taken, not by war but some disease for which the leeches could find no cure he was a loss and a hole in our life. When Jack came to live with us, he seemed to fill the void that the death of my youngest child had caused.

I had surrounded myself with the best of archers. When we travelled, I was always looking for men with the right frame and the marks of a good archer. A truly great archer had a slightly misshapen body. His right side was stronger than his left but even his left side would be far stronger than any normal man. Mordaf, Gwillim, Dick and Ralph the Fletcher were all men who had served me for a long time. Most were married and had boys whom they were training to be archers. William of Ware and his brother Edward were two archers who had fallen on hard times but they now followed my banner. I had many such archers and they all farmed in the manors of Yarpole and Luston in the Welsh Marches. It made my home as secure as any castle for as much as I was honoured by the king, I was still unable to make my home a castle. The anarchy and the wars between Matilda and Stephen had made English kings suspicious of any knight who wished to build a new castle. I had done the next best thing and built high walls with fighting platforms and deep ditches. The last time the Welsh had raided they left just their bleached bones to mark their passing.

I knew I led the finest company of archers in the land and that had little to do with my name. It was our regime. Whilst most archers, even those employed by lords, practised just once a week, on Sunday after church, my archers did so every single day. Their farms were not neglected but they were not tended as often as other farms. We used other agricultural exercises to make us stronger. We made new fields when we hewed down trees and then, rather than using horses to drag the stumps from the ground, used the backs of my archers. We increased the fields we could use as well as creating both timber and kindling. The result was that when my archers did practise with the fyrd on Sunday mornings some of the targets we used were more than three hundred paces away. The ones who did not serve Gerald Warbow as archers, such as the men of Luston, could only stand with dropped jaws as my best archers sent arrow after arrow, without seemingly looking, into the body-shaped wooden target three hundred paces away. I know that it inspired them and even the newest of archers stayed to send arrow after arrow into the targets until the light faded and they had to travel home.

Although Yarpole lay to the south of Scotland and we were far from London, we did receive visitors. Normally they were passing through on their way to Chester or the newly built Welsh castles that fettered the Welsh. It was a mark of my status that they often visited with me. Most times it was just for an hour while they watered their horses, for the castles of the powerful Mortimer family were better suited to accommodating great lords. So it was that when Sir Geoffrey of Burscough travelled to Chester Castle in May to bring news that the Earl of Lincoln was returning from serving in Gascony and to warn Chester castle of his imminent arrival, that we discovered more news of the outside world and the news was disturbing.

I knew Sir Geoffrey from my time in Wales. He had not served in Scotland but was one of the earl's household knights. He was a good if unimaginative warrior. Archers rarely thought well of knights for their world was all show and glorious charges. We archers knew who won battles. For all that I enjoyed his company for he rarely condescended to me.

Hamo and I sat with him in my small drawing room. My wife knew better than to stay and besides since the birth of my grandchild she had other matters with which to occupy her. She and her ladies made clothes for the child. The arrival of Alice, my son's wife, also demanded Mary's time.

"You have a fine home, Gerald."

You can always tell when men have fought alongside each other for they do not bother with titles.

"And I have seen little of it in these last years. Since Hamo and I returned from Scotland we have enjoyed peace not to mention soft beds on which to sleep."

He laughed, "Aye, that is a luxury after campaigning is it not?" He sipped the wine my wife had brought. It was a good one. I might not be a noble but I enjoyed good wine and my service with King Edward had enabled me to enjoy such things. "And Scotland is a place of unrest."

Hamo and I exchanged a look. We had been at Dunbar and the Scots had been soundly beaten. "How so?"

"There are minor infractions and incidents of disorder. Sir Andrew Murray escaped from Chester and hurried north where he began to attack English outposts but the most serious incident was at Lanark where a rebel, William Wallace, murdered the sheriff, William Heselrig and slaughtered the garrison."

My ears pricked up and I leaned forward, "Wallace? The last I heard he was a brigand and I chased him from the forests north of Carlisle."

Sir Geoffrey nodded, "Aye, well now he is now one of the leaders of a rebellion."

"And what does the king do about this?"

Sir Geoffrey looked uncomfortable and shook his head, "Nothing, for it is not one of the claimants to the throne who does this. Wallace

Wallace's War

and Murray are seen as commoners with no claim to the throne. He believes that his lords in the north can deal with the problem."

"Rebellion is rebellion and as we found in Wales, Sir Geoffrey, a single spark can ignite a whole country."

He nodded, "You are right but the king has plans. The Count of Flanders has invited him to help rid his land of the French. We both know that King Edward still bridles at his losses in Aquitaine. His father lost lands he should not have and King Edward would rather fight the French than a few Scottish rebels. I am surprised you have not been summoned to the muster."

I began to become angry, not with the knight but with King Edward, "France is France and King Edward cannot conquer it. He should settle for what he has, Gascony. It produces fine wine and is a rich source of income for him. The French do not threaten it and Flanders is too far to the north to see any gain for England. How many times must Englishmen bleed for what this royal family sees as their rightful inheritance?"

Sir Geoffrey looked uncomfortable, "Gerald, peace. You speak treason."

I shook my head, "I am sorry for my outburst but it is clear from what you have said that the Scots are far from beaten. True there is no longer a figurehead like Comyn or Balliol but this is worse. Every knight whose house was once visited by a Scottish king will swear he has royal blood. If there are enough rebellions then a single leader will emerge. King Edward should take the army he is gathering and head north to quash this Murray and Wallace before they have more success."

He shook his head, "Aye, well, he will not. He and his army are Flanders bound and the Earl of Surrey must quash the rebellion."

After he had gone, I walked my wall to clear my head and to calm myself. Hamo walked with me and our shadow, Jack, followed.

"Is it that bad father? I have never heard of this Murray and Wallace is a bandit whom we bested."

"Aye, but a bandit who has a clever mind. I would be happier if he stuck to banditry."

Hamo shook his head, "My wife and the other ladies we rescued would not think so, father."

Jack asked, "The Earl of Surrey is a good soldier is he not, Sir Gerald?"

"He is but Sir John de Warenne is older than I am and certainly not the warrior that is King Edward. Still, he may have enough skill to thwart a bandit like Wallace."

Wallace's War

I knew Hamo was right but I had served King Henry, King Edward's father and had fought in his French wars. He had handled them badly and all that we retained was Gascony. There was nothing to be gained from fighting in Flanders. Even if we won all that we would be doing would be fighting for the Count of Flanders. The Earl of Surrey had been left in command of Scotland. Whilst not the general that was King Edward, he was no fool. I had to hope that he would stop the rot before it became worse. If he hanged a few of the ringleaders then the sparks of rebellion could be doused.

Sir Geoffrey proved to be a harbinger of war for within a few days of his departure a messenger came with a missive from the king himself. He was not just travelling to visit with me for he had similar letters for the Mortimer family and the de Clare family. When I opened it then my heart sank, it was a summons to the muster. We were summoned to gather on the 1st of August at Winchelsea. If a muster was not bad enough, we had to go about as far south as it was possible to go. I gathered my archers and, with my son, we told them of our task.

"The king commands that I bring forty archers."

Mordaf, the captain of my archers, nodded, "We have sixty, my lord."

"I can count, Mordaf and I am well aware of how many men we have. Choose the single ones first." His eyes flickered to my son, "Hamo will not be coming with us and will command the manor in my absence."

My son, as I knew he would, protested, "But father I am your second in command."

I was tetchy and I knew it but with age comes a little less patience, "And as second in command you will follow my orders." I knew I was being unreasonable and I spoke gently to him, "Hamo, Alice is with child and whilst I do not expect to be away six months, I cannot guarantee it. I do not need a second in command whose heart and mind lie in Yarpole."

Mordaf, who had not been put out by my barbed reply said, "Your father is right, my lord, and this will give us the chance to try out the younger archers. I am centenar and I believe that I can manage without you."

Hamo knew Mordaf's skill and he nodded, "You are right, Mordaf, and no slur was intended but I feel a fraud staying at home."

I shook my head, "Would that I was staying at home. Ralph the Fletcher, you will be at home." The greybeard nodded, "But how stands our supply of arrows?"

"We have been making them since we returned from Dunbar, my lord. We have five thousand."

"That should be enough but keep making them while we are away. From now on we practise at the butts but we need not ride each day. Let us fatten up our animals. It is now almost Midsummer Day. We will need to leave here by the last week in July. You have until then to prepare."

As they left Jack said, meekly, "And me, Sir Gerald? Do I go or do I stay?"

I was torn because he was young but he had proved invaluable in the rescue of the captives, "Would you wish to come?"

"Aye." The joy in his eyes gave me the answer before his reply.

"Then you shall come." I saw James and John, hovering eagerly nearby. "But you two shall stay here." Their faced fell. "Hamo, Jack will need a brigandine and helmet. You must have both in your war chest"

"I do and I have a better short sword than the one you took in Scotland. Come, Jack, you shall be my deputy to my father in Flanders."

My wife was resigned to my leaving. She had been very close to Queen Eleanor and knew King Edward as well as any. As usual, she tried to be positive about the whole thing and look for good reasons for us to go. That was her way and I loved her for it. I did not agree with her arguments but one thing I had learned since we had wed was that I rarely won any argument with her.

"You serve the king and it is only for forty days."

"Aye, forty days from when we sail. That could mean we are in Flanders until the middle of September and then we have another week, at least, to get home."

"And while you are in Flanders then there is no threat to our home. Surely that is a good thing. You would not want Alice to be upset while she expects a child."

I smiled, "And I leave Hamo at home."

My wife was astute and knew how to argue, "Then you moan because you will be made uncomfortable."

"No, wife, I moan because I fear for the north." I was speaking the truth but no one, save me, seemed to hear my words.

In the middle of June, I received two pieces of news. One was welcome and one unwelcome. The welcome news was that Robert Clifford, Keeper of the Marches, and Henry Percy, Warden of Galloway, had marched their armies to Irvin where they had confronted the Bishop of Glasgow, James the Stewart and Robert the Bruce. The three Scottish lords and their men had backed down in the face of the northern lords. The bad news was that the Earl of Surrey had been in London and was only now on his way north. There was no one in command of the king's forces in Scotland.

I rode with Hamo to allow me the chance to speak to him the day before we left for the long march to Winchelsea. "You command the manors and I am confident that you will manage all well." Luston was only two miles away and Hamo would be responsible for ensuring its safety too.

He nodded, "And I am honoured that you trust me with the prosperity of so many."

I looked at the fields full of wheat, barley, oats and beans. It would be a good harvest but with forty men away the ones left to collect the bounty would have to work harder. "I do not think that we will be bothered by the Welsh. They have lost the war and their leaders but you must not relax your vigilance. I know that you must harvest but I want a couple of riders to the west every day."

"I will."

It just so happened that we had reached the end of the ride to the west and as we turned to head back to the hall both of our eyes were looking north. My son and I were close. I liked to think that we were always of one mind and, at that moment, we were for the same thought must have struck us at the same time. "Hamo, if this rebellion flares up do not be tempted to march north. We are not the northern levy. Clifford and Percy would have to have suffered a catastrophic defeat if they were to send to Yarpole for archers."

"Even though Gerald Warbow's men reside there?"

I smiled at the compliment, "They will know that I am in Flanders and, hopefully, the Earl of Surrey will have dampened the embers of discontent."

We rode in silence until Hamo said, "But you do not think that will be the case, do you?"

There could be no secrets between my son and me and I shook my head, "No, Hamo, I do not. If King Edward was heading north then this rebellion would already be over and the leaders in chains awaiting execution but he has made a cardinal error. He has allowed himself to be diverted by France, and that, my son, is a mistake."

I was not looking forward to the campaign and it had nothing to do with its success or failure. I doubted that it would be the latter for King Edward was too canny a general for that, but I knew that my men and I would be called upon to ride and raid. This would be a chevauchée and we would be taking, not from the French lords, but their tenants. We would not be fighting battles to save England but raiding farms to secure a county. I also knew that King Edward and I would have words for I had been with him too long to sit in silence while he made mistakes. As we headed home my spirits plummeted.

Wallace's War

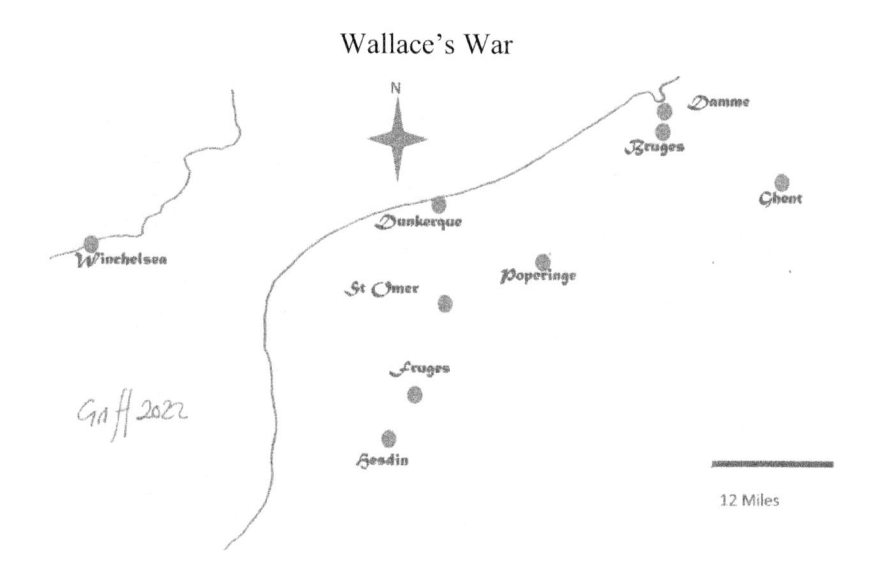

Flanders 1298

Chapter 2

The road south to Winchelsea was, for us, a well-travelled one. Once we had left the quieter roads around Yarpole we joined the Roman Road that began in London and ended in Anglesey. Now that Wales was secured the road was even busier as King Edward's men used it to travel to his ring of castles, Caernarvon, Conwy, Rhuddlan, Flint, Harlech and the newest one, Beaumaris. It had been the capture of Anglesey that had ended the war. The island was the breadbasket of Wales and whoever controlled that island ruled Wales. King Edward had taken it and he would not relinquish his hold upon it. His new castles were like a necklet of stone that could choke Welsh resistance.

As we headed south, I reflected that Scotland was a different prospect and the loss of some of King Edward's newly captured castles already was ominous. The border castles of Norham, Etal, Ford and Bamburgh would not stop an invasion from Scotland but they would make a passage south difficult. Holding on to the castles in our possession was a different matter. Unlike the Welsh castles, the new ones, with the exception of Dunbar, could not be supplied by sea. In a war dominated by men like Wallace then ambush and trickery could swing the tide in their favour. They could wear down the will of the English garrisons and then who knew what the result might be.

I rode with Jack beside me. He had grown since joining us and whilst still a youth was big enough to ride a rouncy. He had been taught well by my men and no longer banged along like a sack of wheat. He rode easily and knew how to control his mount. He had been with me long enough to judge my mood. I was not bantering with Mordaf and my archers and my gaze was on the horizon.

Eventually, he broke the silence, "My lord, you are troubled?"

I turned and smiled, "Aye, Jack. I never enjoy being on campaign abroad nor do I like the muster. We shall not be the first to arrive and those that have will have secured both the best camps and the best grazing. We may well have to cool our heels whilst we await some tardy lord and then we have to load our horses on the cogs that will be there. That is never easy and there is always a risk that we lose a horse or two. While they will be replaced by the king's officers, none of them will be as good as the ones we have. When we do land in Flanders then we will have to use tents or hovels." I leaned over to him, "Jack, I am now an old man who does not like to sleep on the ground. I will be both irritable and unreasonable. I warn you now because I know that I will not be able to control my bad moods. Know that my words will be harsh but they are just a means of venting my anger."

"You are not old, Sir Gerald. You draw a bow as well as the best of your men and I know that any harsh words you use will not be intended to hurt. That is not your way."

I nodded at the compliment, "Aye, I can still bend the yew but I have seen more than fifty summers. I bear wounds that cannot be seen but I feel them. I have served King Edward since I was little more than a youth and I grow weary of martial life. Do not misunderstand me, I am happy to fight England's enemies but this war is about the aggrandisement of King Edward. It is his reputation that we fight for. A little advice, Jack, when we fight, you will just have to watch the horses. While you do so watch out for yourself. Use a shield, a horse, a building, anything that will protect you and if I tell you to run then do so as if the devil was behind you."

I could tell that my words had shocked him, "I would not run, my lord."

Mordaf's voice came from behind us, "Aye, that you will, Jack of Malton, for if that command comes then all is lost and it will be you that will take the message to Master Hamo and Lady Mary for we shall be dead."

The sombre words silenced Jack and we rode without words, the sound of hooves on the cobbles the only noise.

It took five days to reach the port in West Sussex. The length of the journey was determined by two things, the inns that we used and the need to ensure that our horses were not overtaxed before we reached Flanders. As I had expected we had to use a field more than a mile from the port. Luckily, I had ensured that we had plenty of provisions. Being summer we did not use tents and my men made hovels. Mordaf showed Jack how to make mine while I walked the mile to the town and the inn that was being used by King Edward.

The port was packed with the high and the mighty. I smiled when I heard Scottish accents. King Edward had let it be known that the recently captured Scottish knights were expected to fight in Flanders. They might not be happy but they could do little about it. They had to fight and do so without pay. As a senior adviser to the king, his pursuivants and heralds allowed me to enter.

"If you would wait in this chamber, Sir Gerald, there is wine and beer for you. I will tell the king that you have arrived."

I joined a couple of other senior knights. I chose to sit with those alongside whom I had fought in Wales. I nodded, "Sir Richard, Sir Robert, well met."

They were Cheshire knights and I could tell, from their words, that they were as worried about this campaign as I was. "Sir Gerald, you and your archers are welcome news to us. What think you about this venture?"

I kept my voice low but I answered honestly, "Misguided, Sir Richard."

"There may be profit though. The French might be able to walk through Flemish lines but English mail backed by goose flighted arrows is a different prospect."

I smiled. Sir Robert was more optimistic but then he was younger than Sir Richard and me. "I do not doubt that we will succeed, Sir Robert, but will the profit compensate for the expense?"

"The expense?"

"Do you think that we will not lose men and animals? They will need to be replaced. Who will harvest your crops while you and your men serve here? All war costs and any treasure or ransom we take will not make up the deficit. I confess that the forty men I lead, while the most skilled of archers, with the exception of my officers, have yet to fight in battle. I am mitigating the effect of this muster. The benefit I will have is that I will blood my young archers."

Sir Richard laughed, "Your grey hair masks that mind of yours, Sir Gerald. I would hate to play chess against you for you think four moves ahead."

I smiled, "Five."

Just then the pursuivant returned, "Sir Gerald, the king will see you now."

I entered a small room with a table strewn with parchment. Two clerks with ink-stained fingers were scribbling on parchments, copying from wax tablets. He smiled when I entered, "Ah, my good luck charm has arrived. Sit, Warbow, I would use your mind."

My voice was dull when I responded, "Yes, King Edward."

He knew me well and asked, "What is amiss, Warbow?"

"A long journey from the west and a feeling of dread, my lord, about this ill-advised venture." I had said too much. I knew that not only from the king's baleful face but also from the reaction of the clerks and the pursuivant.

The king snapped, "Leave us!" The three men left. The clerks grabbed their wax tablets and the papers they had been working upon. He stared at me, "Do you know to whom you speak?" He shook his head, "Of course you do, and that is why you still retain your head. Be advised, Warbow, that if you dare to question me again then you will be punished."

Wallace's War

I had started my voyage and I continued, "King Edward, you know that there is no more loyal man in your realm than me but Flanders is not where we should take our army but Scotland."

He poured himself a goblet of wine and downed it in one, "You sound like Bigod. You know he is in Parliament now and has persuaded the barons not to allow me the taxes that would pay for this campaign? Am I king or am I not?"

"But Wallace and Murray are causing mischief."

"And if the castellan in Chester had done his job, then there would just be the brigand you allowed to slip through your fingers in Scotland." I felt myself colouring for his criticism was unfair. My priority had been the rescue of captives and not the hanging of a bandit. His words had struck a chord and I did feel guilty. Perhaps the king recognised that for his voice was less carping when he spoke, "Surrey, Clifford and Percy can deal with the bandits. I know that if you and I were there then it would be over in a month and those three might take a year but I have wasted enough time in Scotland. France is the enemy I need to cow and this, Warbow, is the perfect opportunity. We will be raiding France and not weakening Gascony. It is perfect." He took a map from a pile behind him. "We have almost nine hundred knights and more than seven and a half thousand archers and infantry. With the men of Flanders, we will bring the French to battle and defeat King Philip. He will sue for peace quickly enough and then when we have regained some of our lands we will return to England. Six months is all that we need." He sounded enthusiastic and I thought back to the man who had led us so successfully in both Wales and Scotland. Perhaps he was right. He jabbed a finger at Dunkerque, "We land here and I want you and your archers to threaten St Omer while I take the rest of the army to meet with the count at Dunkerque."

St Omer, as I recalled, had a castle and knights. He would not expect my archers to take it but our presence close to it would make the French think we were the scouts of a larger army. I saw the plan immediately, "You are using my archers to disguise your intent."

"I knew that you would see the beauty of the plan. You and your men can be at Fruges within a day of our landing and when you raid the town, they will think it presages an attack by the main army. You will then move on to Hesdin. By that time they should have mustered their army and headed not to the lands around Bruges but further south."

I looked at the map and the scale. "That will leave me and my men more than seventy miles from the main army."

He nodded, "Yet Fruges is less than thirty miles from Dunkerque. The French army is to the north of Paris. By the time news reaches them of your raids and they move towards you then you will have left and be heading to rejoin us at Bruges."

"And we will have to pass through French lands to reach you."

He smiled, "And that is why I give this task to Sir Gerald Warbow and not a young knight eager to impress his king. You will be able to do this, Warbow, and whatever you take will be yours. I will not be asking for my share."

I shook my head, "With due respect, King Edward, we will be lucky to escape to Bruges with our lives. We will not be encumbered with treasure."

"We both know, Warbow, that you and your archers will leave those two towns laden with full purses. Neither town has either a castle or a wall." He nodded, "Despite what you may think I have planned well." He leaned back. Clearly, the interview was over, "Take the map, for you will need it. You and your men will be loaded first. I have allocated two cogs for you and when you land then leave immediately. I want the French as confused as possible. Be ready to leave your camp in an instant." He bellowed, "Geoffrey!"

The pursuivant returned, "Yes, my lord?"

"Go with Sir Gerald and find out where he is camped."

"Yes, my lord."

"Geoffrey will act as a liaison between us."

As we left and pushed our way from the crowded inn my mind was racing. The king's plan and what I intended would have similarities but I would determine the timing. The pursuivant, Geoffrey, was far too polite and I used my archer's bulk to barge through knights whose eyes glared until they recognised me. I had a reputation.

Once clear of the press Geoffrey said, "It is an honour to serve alongside you, my lord." I said nothing, "My father was at Evesham and he spoke of your skill. The king thinks highly of you."

I looked at the pursuivant. He had to have had training as a knight and yet he wore no spurs. "Who was your father?"

"Sir John of Wendover."

I did not remember the knight but then at Evesham, I had been thirty years younger.

As if in way of explanation he said, "We fell upon hard times. The crops failed and we lost the manor. My father had enough money to buy a farm but we lost the title and with it any chance of my becoming a knight. My elder brother inherited the farm and I was lucky enough to be given the position of pursuivant."

We were alone on the road to my camp. I was enjoying the stretching of the legs but I was not sure that Geoffrey was, "And can you fight?"

"My lord?"

"You carry a sword but that does not mean you can use it."

He nodded, "My father had my brother Ralph and I practise at the pel and use the lance. I can fight, my lord." He sounded defensive.

I said, softly, "But you have never fought in battle." He shook his head, "In England, it is unlikely that you will have to do so but when we are in France and Flanders then your fancy livery will draw enemies like flies to a corpse. I would wear a good cloak and keep it fastened and have more than one blade."

He looked down at the royal livery almost seeing it for the first time, "I had not thought of that."

We neared my camp and my men had finished their hovels. Some were already practising either with a bow or sword and I pointed at them. "I have men with me, like you, Geoffrey of Wendover, who have yet to draw blood. The difference between you and them is that they will not be travelling alone. They will have men with them who regard them as brothers. When we are in Flanders you will need the reactions of a cat." I stopped just shy of the entrance to the field, "The king will send you to me with news of our embarkation. Do not be tardy."

I will not, my lord, and thank you for the advice."

"Heed it and you might live."

There was little point in hiding our task from my men and I gathered my vintenars around me, "We have free rein to do as we wish and I intend to ride hard for Fruges when we land."

Gwillim, Mordaf's deputy, looked dubious, "The horses will just have landed after a sea voyage of what might be a couple of days. Will they be ready, my lord?"

"We have at least a week here and we can make them ready. Water them, graze them and groom them. Speed is our only chance. We have to take two villages and take them quickly. The priorities are to lose neither man nor horse and to gather and gain as many horses as we can."

Jack had been listening and he asked, "Why the need for horses, my lord? Surely, we will have to lead them."

Mordaf looked on Jack as a son he might have had and was more patient than I was. He explained, "We deny the French horses and that will delay pursuit as well as news of our presence. Secondly, it gives us animals to take plunder. From what Sir Gerald has said we can take and keep what we like. That part of France is rich and we will take not only purses but goods that can be sold back in England." He smiled at Jack, "Know that we always share amongst the whole company. Sir Gerald here takes the same share as you will, Jack." He looked at me and I nodded. "We will all travel home that much richer than we are leaving."

Gwillim asked, "And when we reach the main army, what will then be our task, my lord?"

I shrugged, "The king did not enlighten me but I suspect we will be used to be the eyes and ears of the army. Are there any of our archers who can speak French or Flemish?"

They shook their heads.

"Pity. We will have to rely on my rusty skills."

Mordaf was quick on the uptake, "And that means you will be in the van, my lord."

I knew what was going through his mind, "And do you think I am too old to be in that position, Mordaf?"

He was not daunted by my glare and smiled, "No, my lord, but if anything should happen to you which of us will have to deliver the news to Lady Mary?"

"I know not why I suffer you! Nothing will happen to me. I am not fated to die in some foreign field in Flanders. When I die it will be in a battle worth remembering." I was not sure I believed my own words but it quietened my officers.

The rest did the horses good and we managed to buy, for we were further from the port, some hams and cheeses from local farmers. We would be taking from the French but the ham and the cheese guaranteed that we would not go hungry and they would keep. When Geoffrey returned, we were ready to leave and broke camp in less than thirty minutes. We rode our horses the mile to the port, passing other men breaking camp and saw the fleet that was gathering just outside the harbour. There were six ships tied up and Geoffrey led us to the nearest two.

"These are your ships, my lord. I am to travel with you and I will be used as a messenger to take the news to the king." He smiled, "I have bought a good, oiled cloak and it will disguise me."

I nodded, "And have you a helmet too?" His face fell and he shook his head. I waved over William of Ware, "William, Geoffrey here needs a helmet. Could you find him one? Your brother will load your horse."

He grinned, "And I am guessing that he will need an arming cap too, my lord. Leave it with me." With that, he disappeared.

Geoffrey said, "He did not ask for money."

Mordaf laughed, "And that is because he will not be paying for it. William of Ware and his brother lived off their wits for many months.

Some soldier will discover that the helmet he laid down to prepare to load the ship will have disappeared."

Geoffrey of Wendover looked as though he had been struck in the face such was his surprise. It would be the first of many such surprises. The loading was laborious as it always was. Our boarding took less time than many of the other ships as we did not use slings but walked our horses up the gangplank. We had learned that if we did this one horse at a time then the wood could take the weight and the horses did not become as stressed as they might be by being swung in a sling. By the time William returned with a fine open-face helmet and arming cap we were almost done. We managed to load both ships at the same time.

Another of King Edward's equerries came over and said, "My lord, the king says that was well done but his ship will be the first to leave the harbour and to land."

I smiled, "Of course." King Edward could be precious about protocol.

We boarded the ship and the first thing we did was to ensure that the horses were securely tethered and that they each had access to food and water. We then dispersed ourselves about the ship. Geoffrey said, "My lord, there is a cabin for you at the forecastle."

"You may have it if you wish. I will endure the same conditions as my men."

"But why, my lord, when you can have a bed?"

"Because, Geoffrey, I am an archer and I need to know what my men can do. If I have not slept in the same manner as my men and eaten the same food then how do I know what they can or cannot do? You may do as you like but until we return to Yarpole then I will be indistinguishable from my men." I could see that he was torn and I smiled, "We will think no less of you if you take the cabin, pursuivant. You are not an archer and your hardest two tasks will be to keep your saddle and avoid death. Ours will be easier, I can assure you."

Chapter 3

The voyage, across the choppy channel, was faster than any of us expected. With winds from the west, we made good time. King Edward and the two ships that contained his leaders and bodyguards led the way but our captains kept close to his stern. Dunkerque was Flemish. Calais would have been a better port for it would have been closer to our target but the County of Boulogne now supported King Philip and not the Count of Flanders. We had to wait while the king's ships disgorged men and horses. It was only when they had completed their task and the standard of the King of England was on Flemish soil that we were allowed to leave our ship. We wasted no time for we had saddled our horses while we waited for the king and with the gangplanks in place, we left our ships far quicker than the first three that had landed. We walked our horses in a long circle to accustom their legs to the land and I smiled as I heard the horse dung being collected. While the ship would stink until the sea and the rain had cleansed it, the sacks of dung would bring a profit to the captain who would sell it to farmers eager to feed their fields.

Geoffrey rode his horse to us, "The king asks why you have not left for your appointed task."

I sighed for I hated having to explain the obvious, "We need our horses to be ready for the ride. When I am satisfied then we will leave." My eyes bored into Geoffrey, "You could, of course, tell the king that had he allowed us to land first we would already be on the road to Fruges."

I saw the fear on his face and he shook his head, "No, my lord. I will give him your explanation. I am to accompany you to Fruges so that I may report back to the king."

He wheeled his horse around and Mordaf laughed, "Scared of his own shadow that one. I pray to God that he does not meet a French soldier."

My horse was ready and so, stopping, I raised my hand and shouted, "Mount." Ten of the archers, the youngest ones, each led a sumpter. If we were successful then it might well be that more than half of my archers would lead a pack animal. The exceptions would be my officers. I had studied the maps enough and with the sun's position to ensure that I took the right road we headed south. The land around Dunkerque was Flemish and I did not expect to be spied upon but the County of Boulogne lay just a few miles south and I intended to cross the border and disappear when it was dark. We had just three hours of daylight left and we would ride for an hour in the dark. We would be heard but not identified. When dawn broke I hoped to be just eight or nine miles from what I hoped would be an unsuspecting town.

We had travelled less than half a mile when the pursuivant caught us up. Jack and Mordaf made space for him to place his horse next to mine. Mindful of Mordaf's views, I did not look at him but spoke words for his ears, "You are to report to the king?"

"As soon as Fruges is taken, my lord."

"Then look at the land through which we travel. I know that it is getting on to night and it is likely that you will be travelling in the dark. Soon we will be on land controlled by the French. My column of archers need fear nothing yet, but a rider alone must be wary. Watch my men and see how they keep looking about them and studying the land for danger."

"I do not understand, my lord."

I sighed. Mordaf was right, Geoffrey of Wendover was like a babe in the woods. "If men lie in ambush there are signs to look for. Too much silence is one and a lack of people is another. If you see either of those things then prepare to draw your sword and kick your horse in the ribs. Your best hope of avoiding death is to ride with your head as close as you can get it to your horse and gallop quickly. Birds suddenly taking flight are a sign to look for." I knew I had no time to give him lessons and I glanced at his horse. "Is your horse a good one?"

"It was my father's and the only thing, apart from his sword, that I have of him. My brother had everything else."

"Then treat the animal well and it may keep you alive. We will skirt St Omer for there is a castle and garrison there. We will use the woods to disguise our movement. Watch and learn from my archers. We pass silently through the land. Your cloak is a start but you now need to acquire the skills of an archer."

The map I carried in my head had certain waypoints and I knew the village of Watten as we passed through it not long before midnight. It lay in a clearing in the small forest. I guessed the forest provided a livelihood for the villagers. That they heard us pass through was obvious but they wisely kept their doors closed. If they had a horse then on the morrow they might send a rider to the nearest castle, at St Omer, but by then it would be too late. We stopped at the even smaller village of Thérouanne just nine miles from Fruges. From the map I had studied I had little idea of the size of the village. When we reached it, I saw that there were just twelve houses and four of those were mean single-room dwellings. We camped at each end of the village and my men made hovels. Jack saw to my horse and I walked along the houses in case any villager poked his head out to see what was amiss. They wisely kept indoors. My vintenars ensured that there were sentries and, after making water, I rolled in my blanket and was asleep in moments.

Just before I dozed off, I heard Geoffrey of Wendover ask, "How can he just fall asleep, like that?"

I heard Gwillim answer, "Because he had us to ensure that all is safe. This village can have at most a dozen men. There are no horses and they are not a threat to us. With men at either end, we are as safe here as in a castle. We will leave before dawn and our visit will keep them talking for a month or more. Once we have strung our bows and released our arrows then the French will know we are abroad and it will be then that we will need to be warier." Then oblivion took me.

William of Ware shook me awake, "Sir Gerald, it will be dawn in an hour. We have hot food and Jack is saddling your horse."

I rose, instantly awake. "Thank you, William. Take your brother and wait four miles down the road. Ensure that there are no surprises."

"Yes, my lord."

After making water, I went to the fire where my men had cooked a hunter's stew enriched with oats. It was a filling breakfast. Looking at the pot I wondered which villager had had it taken from them. They would curse my archers for the sticky stew would take some cleaning. I wiped the wooden bowl with my hand and then licked my fingers. I detected rabbit in the stew and smiled. My archers were natural scavengers and the French bunny had made for a tasty stew. I put the bowl in my saddlebag and mounted my horse. I donned my helmet. I doubted that I would need it but if I did not have it then I would regret the decision. I would not be stringing my bow this day. It would stay in its case and I would use, if I had to, my sword. Mordaf and Gwillim were already mounted and I shouted, "Mount."

My single word would tell the villagers that we were English. If one of them walked to St Omer the eight miles would take them two to three hours. By then Fruges would be ours.

The sun was up by the time we reached William and Edward. "The road is clear, my lord." William was the elder and it was always he who answered.

"String your bows."

They dismounted and the horses took the opportunity to graze on the grass. Geoffrey nudged his horse next to mine, "How does this raid work, my lord?"

"Simple. Mordaf will leave us soon and take half of my archers south of the settlement. The rest will dismount on the edge of the village. We will move in and they will slay any man who opposes us.

We meet in the middle and then we take all that there is to take. You will then take the news to the king but be wary for it may well be that the lord of St Omer has men on the road seeking us."

The magnitude of what he had to do was now clear to the young pursuivant.

With strung bows, my archers headed down the road, riding their horses. When I saw the side road, I waved my left arm and Mordaf led half of my archers to take the road. Gwillim ordered William and Edward forward and we continued on our way. Fruges had no castle but there was a manor house and it looked to be a large village, almost a town. We stopped at the first farm we came to and my men quickly rode into the yard to disarm the men who were there. After tying them up and leaving one archer to guard them, the rest of us galloped along the road. They would hear us and that could only aid Mordaf and his men approaching from the south. The tolling bell in the church told me that they knew we were coming. If there was a lord of the manor then he would be arming himself and his retainers. The crossbow bolt that slammed into the wooden cantle of my saddle told me that they were armed and would resist.

Gwillim shouted, "Dismount!"

I spurred my horse and drew my sword. It was not an act of bravado. I knew that moving faster would make me a harder target and my movement would arrest the attention of those in the village. The crossbowman would now be reloading his infernal machine and as soon as he raised his head to loose a second he would be a dead man. My archers hated crossbows.

The lord of the manor and his squire had emerged from his hall and he was busy shouting orders. He had a coif about his head and he carried a shield and a sword. I rode at him and his squire shouted a warning. The warrior turned and raised his shield. An archer has arms like young oaks and I swung my sword hard at the shield. The speed of the blow and my horse allied to my strength meant that the sword smashed into his shield and knocked him from his feet to land heavily on the ground. Before his squire could react, Geoffrey and Jack had followed me and the squire lay dying in a pool of blood. Their swords and horses had made short work of him. I reined in before the hall and dismounted. Jack rode up to me and grabbed my reins. I saw that his sword had no blood upon it and that meant the pursuivant had been the one to kill the squire. Geoffrey of Wendover was becoming a warrior.

I pushed open the door to the manor house with my foot and an axe sliced down at where my body would have been had I been foolish enough to blindly enter. The swinging axe head told me where the man waited and stepping through the door, I swung backhand. I was rewarded with a grunt of pain. The entrance was gloomy but I saw the man at arms holding his stomach. I had cut through his leather brigandine.

"Surrender for you are hurt," I spoke in French and I knew he had understood when he spat at me. He tried to swing the axe one handed. I simply lunged and my sword's tip gave him a swift death as it entered his throat.

Jack entered and I said, "Guard the door."

Drawing my dagger I walked through the house. I heard movement upstairs but I continued through the house. When I reached the kitchen, I heard the door slam shut and then there was a cry. I opened the door and saw one of the servants, sword in hand lying on the ground with an arrow in their chest. Dick stepped from the shadows. I nodded, "Come with me. There are people upstairs."

We re-entered and Dick placed his bow on the kitchen table. The interior of a hall was the place for swords and not bows. There were just two rooms upstairs and the noises I had heard came from the first one. I opened the door and saw three women, an older one and young maidens. The older woman held a short sword in her hand. Sheathing my sword I said, "You will not be harmed my lady, put down the sword."

"You are English! Why should I trust you?"

"Because I am a knight and I swear you will be unharmed if you obey me. I have never killed a woman and I would not wish to start but I cannot afford to waste time. Put down the sword." There was enough command in my voice for her to obey. "Good. Now dress yourselves and gather enough clothes for a day. We will await you downstairs."

Leaving Dick to collect all of the value from the kitchen I left. Geoffrey was outside looking at the corpse of the squire he had killed. He needed occupation. "Geoffrey, go inside and help Dick. When the women come down then search the bedroom for there will be a chest under the floorboards, bring it."

He looked at me, "How do you know?"

I shrugged, "When you have raided as often as we have you know where to look. Now go."

I walked over to the lord of the manor. He was still unconscious. The blow had smashed the shield into his face and broken his nose. I waved over William of Ware, "Take his weapons and mail from him. Bind his hands. When he wakes then watch him."

"Aye, my lord, that was easy."

"The next one will not be, trust me."

Mordaf rode up, "The village is secure. We lost none and there are ten of the villagers dead."

"Good. Send them up the road to Thérouanne and St Omer and then take a couple of men and clear the first farm we captured. We leave here an hour after the sun reaches its peak."

I took off the helmet and looked around the village. It was a prosperous place. Edward of Ware headed towards me, his brother having secured the lord and bound his head. "You have orders. my lord?"

"Find any horses you can and have the men take all that is of value and load it on the horses."

The lord had awoken and William helped him to his feet, "Who are you and why do you attack my village?"

"We are at war, my friend. I am Sir Gerald Warbow and I serve King Edward. I can see by your mail and weapons that you are a warrior. You know that we could have killed more than we did. This is just war."

Just then the three women ran from the house and saw the bound face of the lord. It was when they saw the squire's body that they reacted and they clung to the lord of the manor.

I pointed north, "We are going to burn this village. Take your people north. I daresay that the lord of St Omer will offer you succour."

With a resigned look, the lord said, "I will remember this and your name, Sir Gerald Warbow."

"Good for if you seek me, I shall not hide."

We had struck so quickly that none had the opportunity to take their treasures and a disconsolate column of villagers headed north. It would take them most of the day to reach St Omer and by then we would have disappeared. My men were efficient at seeking treasure and food that would sustain us. They loaded the horses we had captured and then I ordered them to fire the village.

Geoffrey mounted his horse, "I will take the news to the king. He will be pleased."

I shook my head, "I would wait until we have taken Hesdin."

"The king said I had to tell him when Fruges was taken."

Mordaf said, "Then, Master Geoffrey, I would not use the road we did for the villagers will see you. Take another road."

"Thank you, Mordaf. That is good advice."

With the smoke from the burning village behind us, we headed down the road to Hesdin. That the smoke would alarm the villagers could not be helped but I hoped to be south of Hesdin before dark and we would wait there and make a dawn attack from the south.

As much as I would have enjoyed a more comfortable night of sleep I knew that speed was our best weapon. The French, by the time dawn came, would be beginning to plan where to stop us. Their castles contained mounted men who could hunt us down. The problem that fettered the French had been that they did not know where we could strike next. The raid on Hesdin would tell them and then, like a spider whose web is triggered, they would bring their forces to close around the fly. We had to flee the area before their net could close.

We skirted the village which was about the same size as Fruges. I guessed that it would have a lord of the manor and the smoke in the sky to the north would make him wary. He might, if he had any sense, arm the villagers so that they would be ready to repulse raiders. We skirted the castle at Azincourt. It was only a wooden one and I knew that after we had raided Hesdin then we would have to avoid the knights who would come forth to kill us. We camped in the wood that lay to the north of the village. It was a huge one and criss-crossed with hunters' trails. We saw evidence of deer and wild boar. The lord of Azincourt would enjoy the hunting. With sentries set we ate a cold meal. The men and I had eaten well in Fruges for every house had a pot on with potage and they had baked bread. We had spare loaves and it was no hardship to eat the local cheese and the hams my men had liberated. I sent Mordaf south to find a way for us to move, before dawn, into position and then I slept. Mordaf arrived back while I slept and it was he who woke me an hour before dawn.

"The men are ready and saddled my lord. It is two miles over fields to get to a point where we can attack. They have watchers on the road to the east of this forest. There were four of them and they have a brazier."

I nodded. I had smelled smoke the night before. "Any sentries to the south?"

"No, my lord."

"Then lead off."

As we crossed the road that headed south and west, I saw the sign that told us where the road went. First, it passed through the village of Crécy and ended in the port of Saint Valery-sur Somme. I hoped that by attacking Hesdin they might think we intended to raid the Somme Valley. They would soon realise we had not but by then I hoped we had fooled them. We were just a mile south of the village by dawn. My archers dismounted and strung their bows. We walked our horses across fields and hedge-bound farm roads until we were less than four hundred paces from the edge of the houses. I left Jack and four archers to watch the horses and, after stringing my bow and discarding my helmet and cloak I led my men north. This time there would be no warning. The galloping hooves that had induced such panic in Fruges would be absent.

I had a bodkin in my belt but I chose to loosely nock a war arrow. William of Ware and Dick flanked me. There were no more than four paces between any of us. I was lazy, or perhaps it was my age. While many of my men scrambled over walls and through hedges, I choose paths and the road. So it was that it was I who saw the sentry. Despite my age, I could still move silently and he was not being a particularly good sentry. He was leaning against a tree and his weapons were not in his hands. I drew back and felt the bow fight back. He was less than forty paces from me and the sun was not yet fully up but he was an easy target and I had the luxury of aiming for his weak spot, his Adam's apple. The only sounds that could be heard were the arrow as it whizzed through the air and then the sound of the arrow driving through his neck to sink into the alder tree behind him.

I moved quickly up the road to stand where he had. If any looked from the village they might take me for him. The sun was starting to rise in the east but already the housewives were up as they began to prepare food. I could smell the bread baking in the ovens and hear the low of cows waiting to be milked. The villagers might suspect that raiders were in the area but life went on. It was one of those farmers heading for his barn who sounded the alarm. He spied one of my younger archers. A more experienced warrior would have sent an arrow before the warning could be uttered but the arrow slammed into the farmer a shout too late. Our plan had succeeded in so much as the men who ran from their homes, armed and ready for war, looked north. I sent a war arrow into the back of a man with a spear, helmet, and leather brigandine. As soon as the armed men fell with arrows sent from the south a voice commanded them to form a shield wall and face us. It was the right command but too late. Nocking my bodkin I sent my arrow into the chest of the mailed man. His hauberk and his spurs marked him as a knight. I could not afford to let him live and by killing him I knew that I sucked the life out of the other defenders.

The sun seemed to burst and flare in the east. It made aiming that much harder. My men had less of a problem for they each wore a hat that shaded them slightly from the beams of the sun. I nocked a war arrow and sent it at the farmer with the buckler and spear. He managed to bring up the small shield and sent my arrow spiralling into the air. I suspected it was more luck than good judgement. Dick's arrow found his middle.

The French were falling fast and I wanted no unnecessary slaughter. I shouted, "Surrender, drop your weapons and you shall live. I am a knight and I swear it." We had killed more than fourteen men, including the lord, and the weapons quickly landed on the ground. As we had the previous day, we disarmed the men and told the women to take food and clothes. This time we sent them south, towards Amiens. Our surprise attack had shaken them. Dick reported that two men had taken horses and headed north. That was the only fault I could find. We still took another six horses but the news would reach Azincourt quicker than I wanted.

"Release the animals and drive them into the roads. Take the treasure and then fire the buildings." The last of the villagers was far enough away for me to add, "And then we head east towards Humières. I had no intention of getting anywhere near that village but I needed us to disappear. The flames were just licking the lintels of the door when we left. Every archer, except my officers, led a sumpter. Jack led a sumpter. For that reason, I had Mordaf and Gwillim in the van while Robert and Dick brought up the rear.

We made good time and by noon had covered twenty miles and we rode through the village of Isbergues. It was the first village we had ridden through but our horses needed to be watered and so we stopped. We ate the supplies we had taken from Hesdin and the people stayed in their homes. I sent Mordaf and Gwillim off and then, after giving them the chance to get up the road, we mounted and followed.

We were less than half a mile up the road when I saw Mordaf, he was leading a horse and I recognised it. It was the mount of Geoffrey of Wendover and when he neared me, I saw blood on the saddle. What had happened to the pursuivant?

Chapter 4

It was Gwillim who found the equerry. He had a nose for such things and having found the horse backtracked through the trees until he discovered the king's messenger. My lieutenant of archers emerged from between a pair of beech trees and I saw that the body of Geoffrey of Wendover lay across his horse's neck. "He is alive, my lord, but he has lost blood. There is a bolt in his leg."

I cursed the king. I was honour bound to help Geoffrey and yet it would delay us. You do not simply patch up a wound. You tend it and that takes time. Mordaf was a healer and I said, "Gwillim, take command, lead the men and get as far up the road as you can. Take Jack's sumpter and give it to an archer. Jack, you stay with me. I want a sling rigging up between your horse and Geoffrey's. He cannot ride and I cannot leave him."

Gwillim shook his head, "Let one of the men stay with him, my lord. We cannot risk you."

My eyes narrowed, "And who commands here, Gwillim, you or me?"

Cowed he backed off, "Sorry, my lord."

I softened my tone as I turned to the wounded man, "We will follow as soon as we can."

Mordaf had already cut the hose from Geoffrey's leg and had poured vinegar onto the wound. The shock of the vinegar made Geoffrey open his eyes, "What…?"

"Peace, Geoffrey, Mordaf will take the bolt from your leg."

"I was ambushed and…"

"Lie back and let us do our work. The story can wait."

It was the pulling of the bolt that made the pursuivant pass out and that was a mercy. Mordaf was a strong man and he yanked the bolt through the wound after breaking off the small flights. Blood spurted when it came out and that was also good as the blood would flush out any splinters left in the wound. However, Mordaf carefully examined the blood and wound and only when he was satisfied did he continue. We applied honey and then Mordaf stitched the wound together. They were not pretty stitches but they held the wound together and the young man would have a scar to remember his fight. Mordaf and I lifted the unconscious man onto the sling and we set off. I guessed that we were half an hour behind the main column. I did not know where the border lay but it mattered little for we had to reach the army. We passed a sign that said it was ten miles to Poperinge and I knew that was in Flanders.

Half a mile later we caught up with the column. I wondered why they had halted.

Gwillim rode back. "There are knights ahead, my lord, and they are French. They have with them men at arms and mounted crossbows. There are at least thirty but I could not be certain of the accuracy of that total. I did not want to approach too closely."

I wondered if these were the men who had attacked Geoffrey. "And how were they disported?"

"They had a camp, my lord. It is a crossroads and it seems to me they are there to stop people moving into and out of France."

It was at that moment that Geoffrey awoke. As with all such awakenings he was confused and he sat up. As he did so the horses shifted and his wound sent paroxysms of pain through his body. "Where …"

Jack said, gently, "You are safe, Master Geoffrey. Your wound has been tended."

He saw me and said, "I was passing the crossroads to the south of Poperinge. I saw men at the crossroads and took off across the fields. I thought I had made it when something slammed into my leg. I kept going but then I fell."

Mordaf nodded, "A bolt, my lord sent by an ungodly war machine."

I smiled reassuringly, "You are safe, now Geoffrey and we now have the same men to negotiate."

He tried to move and Jack said, "No, for you are hurt."

Geoffrey was tougher than he looked and he struggled to the ground, despite the pain it caused him. "No Jack, I will not encumber any with my protection. Help me to the back of my horse."

I nodded for if there was a force at the crossroads to stop us then we would need every man we had. As Geoffrey and Jack untangled the rope harness, I waved over Gwillim and Mordaf. "Divide the men in two. I want the best twenty archers with we three. We move through the woods and we use our arrows to disperse them." They both waited for me to elaborate. "My reasoning is thus; if they are there to stop movement then they will only need a couple of mounted men. My guess is that the local lords will have been ordered to stop more men from crossing the border and prevent our escape. There will be a much larger army heading south to take us. The longer we wait the more chance there is of discovery. We have left signs of our passage across the land. Once they reach Hesdin they will know where we are. The rest of the men can lead the horses. When they hear the sounds of battle they are to gallop north. I know they will be encumbered with our horses as well as

Wallace's War

the treasure we took but if they can reach the crossroads then we can mount and, I believe, that north of the crossroads we will be safe."

Gwillim nodded, "And if we have twenty-three archers then we should be able to hit many with three flights of arrows."

Mordaf added, "Unless there are more."

Gwillim and I nodded. That was the unknown and that was the jeopardy we faced. "Let us hurry." I handed my cloak to Jack and began to string my bow. As I did so I explained the plan. "You will need to stop when you see me, Jack. Keep your head down and, if I order it, then leave my horse and flee north. Geoffrey, just get yourself to safety. Where do we find the king?"

"Bruges did not welcome our army and so he headed east to Ghent. They were more hospitable."

I nodded, calculating that the difference added miles to our journey and changed our direction. My bow strung, I took out three arrows, two bodkins and a war arrow. I rammed them into my belt. Gwillim had said mailed men and the only sure way to hurt such a warrior was with a bodkin. I knew that if I, the oldest man in the company, was ready then the rest would be and I moved forward. I headed to the fields to the east of the road. I saw Mordaf wave half of the men to the west of the road where he would hit the enemy. I loosely nocked my arrow and with Gwillim to my left, headed north. We smelled the fire of their camp and heard their chatter before we spied them. It was natural that there would be unsuspecting. Raiders such as we would make noise approaching the crossroads and alert them. We moved warily for as the crossbow bolt to Geoffrey's leg had shown there was danger from hidden scouts.

These were not tended fields through which we passed. At some time it might have been but the conflicts on the border in this part of the world meant that farmers had abandoned them and moved to safer land. The result was that weeds had grown and trees had taken root. A rowan tree can grow very quickly in a short space of time. It meant that what had once been open land with a hedge running around it was now covered with undergrowth and young trees the height of a man. It was a perfect place for hiding. It was Gwillim who saw the first sentry and he drew and released so quickly that I barely had time to take it in before the crossbowman lay dead just thirty paces ahead of us. I had not seen him and knew that he had to have had a good hide. It made me even more cautious and I had only taken another five steps when I saw the flash of white in the bushes ahead. I released the nocked war arrow and was rewarded by a body being thrown backwards. It was unfortunate for he must have knocked something over in his falling and we heard cries from ahead.

Wallace's War

Drawing a bodkin I nocked and, along with the other archers I led, hurried towards the camp before us; its presence marked by a spiral of smoke. A horn from the camp told us that we had awoken the wasp nest but the good news was that we had drawn their attention to us. Mordaf and his men would remain hidden for a few more paces. We had been right and they did have mounted men who were ready to respond to any attack. Half a dozen men rode at the twelve of us. I was already drawing the bodkin arrow back when I found I had a clear sight of the mailed man at arms with a couched lance who rode at me. The spindly trees had hidden him until he was just thirty paces from me. Had I been one of my newer archers then there might have been a problem but I was confident in my own ability and with a bodkin arrow I knew I could kill him. My arrow hit him squarely in the chest and threw him from his horse. His left hand was wound tightly in his reins and in his falling, he jerked the reins to the left and the horse crashed into a blackberry bush. I nocked another bodkin, aware that all the other riders had been unhorsed.

I knew that whoever commanded in the camp would now be either trying to mount their animals or would be trying to form a line of defence. Either way, there was no time to waste and we ran through the dying men and wandering horses. The horses would help us as they would disguise our movement. A hand reached out to try to grab my leg as I passed a man at arms who was not quite dead. I swung the end of my bow to crack him in the face. As I glanced down to make certain he could no longer hurt me a crossbow bolt whizzed across my shoulder. Had I not glanced down then I would be dead. I heard a cry and looking up saw a crossbowman with an arrow in his chest, falling.

We were now at their camp and our attack had surprised them but there were more men than Gwillim had counted. Fortunately, we had killed more than a dozen and when the horses of the rest of my men thundered down the road the remaining defenders took to their mounts and fled for they knew that they were now outwitted and outnumbered. I sent my nocked arrow at a fleeing rider but just hit him in the leg. Other archers were more accurate and another five riders fell from their saddles.

I knew there was no time to lose and as Jack headed over to me, I shouted, "Gather the spare horses. Let us move."

My men, however, were no fools and they began to strip the dead of purses. There had been at least two knights amongst the slain and they always had rings and coins. The result was that it took ten minutes or more to mount our horses and head north. Even my officers and I had to lead a horse. We took all the horses we could to deny their use by the enemy and we knew that to keep mobile we needed as many horses as possible. An hour after the fight I reined in to allow the horses to rest. We had been lucky. Two of my archers had slight wounds but we were whole.

"How is the wound, Geoffrey?"

The pursuivant smiled, "It is a reminder that I am not yet a warrior. Mordaf was right in that but I am alive and I have learned from this wound. Next time I will be more alert. As we waited for you to attack Jack told me how you and your archers use smell and sound to help you. I rode too quickly for I was keen to reach you. It is a lesson learned."

"Aye, and now that we have succeeded and distracted the enemy then there will be no need for you to ride abroad. How far to Ghent?"

"Fifty miles."

I knew that Poperinge lay to the west of us and that we could not make it in one day and so we stayed in the village of Waregem. We had taken enough food to mean that we did not need to impose upon the villagers and we were welcomed. We slept, that night, in barns and outbuildings. The hay and the warm animals made for a better night of sleep for all of us. Before we retired for the night Geoffrey's wound was inspected and it appeared to be healing well. The rough stitches had held. He was pale but Mordaf advised him to eat liver and kidneys when we reached the main army. My archers needed no leeches. They knew remedies for all ailments.

It was late afternoon when we rode into Ghent and while my men found grazing and somewhere to camp, I went with Geoffrey and Jack to the town hall which the king was using for a headquarters. I spied a number of familiar faces and one I did not know. As soon as he saw me, King Edward and the man I did not recognise walked over to me. The smile on the king's face showed relief.

"Warbow, you are well. I am pleased. Your attack worked. The three thousand knights led by Robert of Artois have headed into Picardy to find you. Well done."

Holding out my arm to indicate Geoffrey I said, "And your pursuivant has been hurt in the process. You have a brave man here, King Edward."

I was gently chastising the king as well as reminding him that he owed praise where it was due. I knew that sometimes he was remiss in such matters. When the queen had been alive it had been she who had often prompted him.

The king looked at his pursuivant as though seeing him for the first time, "You were hurt?"

"A crossbow bolt to the leg."

"Then you must see my doctor."

Shaking his head Geoffrey said, "The wound is healing well, my lord, for one of Sir Gerald's archers tended to me."

"Nonetheless we shall need you soon enough." He waved over another equerry, "Take Geoffrey to his chamber and let him rest." As they left the king turned to the man I did not know, "Warbow, this is Robert of Béthune. You will be attached to him. The count has sent him and troops to help us recover Damme and Bruges."

It became clear, as the king spoke, that one reason that Bruges had not welcomed him was that there were French spies who were colluding with the lords of Bruges. It explained why Ghent had been chosen.

The Flemish lord spoke. He did so in French, "The king has told me of your prowess Sir Gerald and I am honoured that you will be with us when we take Damme."

The king waved an arm and said, "I leave you to the planning. My lords and I need to plan how to defeat Robert of Artois and his three thousand knights." He smiled, "At least they will be wearier when they reach us having chased the will o'the wisp that is Gerald Warbow."

The Flemish lord led me from the building, "Come, they have good beer here in Ghent and I know that archers like their ale."

I turned to Jack, "I need you not for a while. Return to our camp and I will find you later."

As we headed to the tavern he said, "He is young to be a squire."

"He is not a squire. I am Sir Gerald but I am not a noble. I am still an archer and Jack just tends my horse at the moment. My men train him to pull the warbow."

We sat at a table and the Flemish warrior rattled off orders. While we chatted about the town, we were served food and beer. It was clear to me that Robert of Béthune was an important man. After we had eaten a little, he said, "The warriors I lead are not a large force. They are a mixture of English, Welsh and Flemish soldiers but there are less than fifteen hundred of us. Your archers will be the only mounted ones and, perforce, we will march to Damme at the speed of foot soldiers. For that reason, I would use you and your mounted archers as scouts. You do not know the land and so I will attach a local man, Guy of Poperinge to act as a translator and guide."

I was relieved as I enjoyed a role free from the reins of others.

"Damme is the port of Bruges and the river Rele connects it to that city. The town relies on water for protection and they have water on all sides. This is how we will take it. They have a citadel in the centre but they have little protection from arrows and bolts otherwise. We will

Wallace's War

make a dawn attack." He gave me a questioning look, "I know you and your men ride to war but can they ford a river?"

"Aye, we can but I am not sure about other archers."

Shaking his head he said, "We do not need them. I want you and your archers to cross the river. There will be a conroi of mounted men at arms, Flemish men, who will cross the river with you. It will be you and your archers who begin the attack and draw their attention to the northwest side of the city. The rest of the English and Welsh archers will rain death on the southeast side. While you send your arrows into the city, we will ford the river and attack."

"Are there no bridges?"

He nodded, "There is one bridge on the west and one on the east but they will be well guarded. The men with you will assault and cross the bridge but the majority will ford the water."

I closed my eyes to visualise the port, "I am guessing that the water is not deep and was originally a moat of some kind."

He nodded, "The land is low lying and tends to flood. The burghers of Bruges and Damme used the natural defences to protect their port." He leaned forward, "If Damme falls then Bruges is cut off from the sea. Whoever controls Damme controls Bruges and whoever controls Bruges is master of this part of Flanders."

I finished off the ale. It was, as he had said, good. "And when do we leave, bearing in mind that my men have had a chevauchée for the last few days?"

He nodded, "We are a week away from the attack. The 1st of September would be time enough. It will only take us a day to march there and with you and your men securing the road we can move more aggressively. I will send Guy of Poperinge to your camp. He will command the Flemish contingent with you. They are all good men." He smiled, "I think that you will like him. He is, like you, a warrior." He leaned in while waving an arm in the direction of King Edward's Headquarters, "There are too many pretty knights with the king. They wear fine mail and have colourful liveries but you and Guy reek of war and they do not."

The men had soon made the camp homely and I waved over Gwillim and Mordaf. While Jack fetched me cloths and water, I told them our task.

Mordaf nodded, "It sounds like our sort of war, my lord and we did well out of the raid. We sold many of the horses we captured for a higher price than they should have brought." He grinned, "Men cannot get enough horseflesh in time of war. We kept the best horses for ourselves and the profit from the raid has been shared out. Jack has yours."

"Thank you. Have our hunters go to the woods to augment our fare."

Gwillim asked, innocently, "And we have permission to hunt, my lord?"

I shrugged, "No one said that we should not. Until I am told to the contrary let the men hunt." I doubted that the Lord of Ghent would be very happy about the finest archers in the land hunting in his woods but we were there at the request of the Count and I deemed that gave me the authority.

Guy of Poperinge arrived the next morning with his squire, Eustace. He was exactly as Robert of Béthune had described. With a scar on his face and powerful muscles, he was a warrior. Wearing a simple surcoat over a mail hauberk, he had a good sword on his belt and I could tell that he knew his business. "Sir Gerald?"

"And you must be Guy of Poperinge." His arm clasp was firm and I approved.

"I am. I have heard of your reputation," he turned to his squire, "Eustace, this Lord Edward's archer. He served the king when he was still heir to the throne and was at the Battle of Evesham." I saw the squire's eyes widen, "And if the stories are true, he travelled to the Empire of the Mongols to enlist their support in the crusades."

His squire shook his head in amazement, "I heard that three men had made such a journey but I put it down to fantasy. Did I hear that one of the warriors married a queen?" His eyes showed his incredulity, "That sounded like a fantasy."

I nodded, "You did, Hamo l'Estrange is a great warrior and I am honoured to call him a friend."

Guy grinned, "Then, when time allows, I look forward to being regaled by these tales but first we have an attack to plan."

He was all business and, after calling over Mordaf and Gwillim we went through all the details. He had with him a hundred men. Ten of them were Flemish knights and the rest were men at arms. He confidently told me that men on horses could easily cross the water to the town. "Unless your men are midgets then they too could easily cross. However, you need not risk a dousing for my men are more than capable of defeating the French within Damme and the traitors who are selling my land to our enemies."

As I learned Guy was fiercely loyal to his count and hated the enemies of his land. I suspect that had we been the aggressor he would have hated us just as much. I enjoyed talking to a warrior who knew his business. I now knew why the king was sending such a small force to make such an important attack. He trusted us to get the job done. As I returned, after the meeting, to our camp, I hoped that the king had also made a wise judgement in the leaders left to quell the Scottish rising. So far, I had not seen a great deal of enthusiasm from the Flemish people for this war. Bruges, a most important port, had defected to the French remarkably quickly. It seemed to me that we might waste time and men here in Flanders fighting a war that would not benefit us and lose Scotland at the same time. I put that from my mind. I had learned, long ago, that I just had to do my job the best that I could and let others worry about the master strategies. I was just glad that Hamo was at home. If the Scottish rebellion flared up and gave hope to the Welsh then my son and my men could defend my home and my family.

Chapter 5

We left Ghent early and it was my company, along with Guy of Poperinge and his men who led. You cannot hide a large army and I knew, without seeing them, that riders would be racing to Damme and to Bruges to warn the garrisons of our advance. The main force we would have to face would be the French. That meant crossbows and as they would be releasing their bolts from behind walls, they would be more accurate than normal. The crossbowmen would also have protection from my archers' arrows. I had discussed this with Mordaf and Gwillim who had a plan for such an eventuality.

"Aye, my lord, they can be protected from the front but as you know, Sir Gerald, we can plunge arrows from on high."

I nodded, "Yes, Mordaf and the crossbowmen might wear helmets."

"They might but the odd arrow which is wasted will not hurt us. King Edward has wisely supplied us with many arrows. They may not be as good as those made by Ralph the Fletcher but we can use them to rain death from the skies. Remember, my lord, that when a crossbow is reloaded then the man who uses it is vulnerable. He has to bend over to pull back the cord and a back is a bigger target than a head."

He was right, of course, and it reminded me that since my elevation to knighthood I had forgotten some of the things that had made me a great archer. I resolved to concentrate in this battle on what I did best, using a bow. Mordaf was right. King Edward had planned well and our sumpters were laden with sheaves of his arrows. They were not bodkins but that mattered not. My archers had their own warbags full of Ralph the Fletcher's arrows and we had bodkin arrowheads in sacks on the sumpters. We could change arrow heads quickly if we were attacked by knights.

The four men who rode with Mordaf and his scouts at the fore were local men and, as we neared the river, they picked a path to take us to the best place to ford the river. The River Rele was not fast flowing, for this part of Flanders was low lying, but the channel was well maintained and deep. We would have to swim our horses across. The scouts, my men, and the Flemish swam first and then my archers strung their bows and awaited us on the far side. We had not seen any defenders, from the port that lay a mile downstream but it paid to be vigilant. The Flemish scouts had chosen well and we had no drop to negotiate. The path enabled us to walk our horses into the shallows and then, as the horses started to swim, we were able to kick our feet from our stirrups and lie across our horses' backs. It made life easier for the horses and our crossing quicker. As soon as my horse's hooves found purchase, I slipped back onto my saddle and climbed to the bank. We all dismounted to empty water from our boots and to check our girths. The hard part had been done and now it was speed that was essential. We rode in two columns across the flat, boggy land of Flanders. We had strung our bows and the men at arms and knights, protected by mail rode to our right but we remained unmolested.

As we were sighted from the citadel, we heard horns and bells sound the alarm. By now Robert of Béthune and the bulk of the army would be in position on the other side of the port and our arrival told them that they were trapped. Mordaf signalled to the four archers who had been assigned to guard the river and they rode to the bank. They would camp there and act as a deterrent to any vessel trying to get to Bruges and warn us of any relief coming from that city. The rest of us rode with Guy of Poperinge to the bridge over the moat. I saw that while there was not a stone wall around the port, they had wooden walls and men were already manning them. The largest part of the army was to the east and I knew we would face fewer men. We set up a camp and Guy placed ten Flemish warriors to watch the bridge in case they tried a sortie. I knew that they wouldn't. The greater part of the French army was still in Picardy and the force that had been invited to Damme was just there to bolster the resolve of the defenders. They would endure all that we might throw at them.

There would be no night attack, not yet anyway, but we lit fires to illuminate the moat and we embedded stakes around the camp in case of a night attack. The signal to attack would be five horn blasts from the main army. We were well provisioned but my ever-optimistic men laid fish lines in the moat. It was connected to the river and there would be fish. They would enjoy whatever they caught, no matter how small.

We breakfasted well and with strung bows and arrows at the ready, we stood behind a wall of Flemish shields and mail. Had they not been there we might have used pavise but the Flemish warriors were reassuring. When the horn sounded, I shouted, "Nock!" I had chosen a war arrow that looked to be the same as most of the others. This first arrow would give me the range and I wanted a missile that would give me an accurate assessment.

"Draw!" There were not a huge number of us but the drawing of the mighty war bows always sent a shiver through my body as they creaked and groaned. A yew war bow was almost a living thing and I knew that many of my men talked to their bows as though alive. I understood that.

"Loose!" There was little point in holding at the draw for it sapped energy. "Loose at will!"

Wallace's War

As the arrows soared, making a whistling noise, we heard the cracks as crossbows sent their bolts back. The range was a little under two hundred paces and close enough for both sets of missile men to be accurate. I heard the bolts as they slammed into the Flemish shields. The warriors were veterans and the shields were held away from their bodies. The crossbowmen, having sent their bolts now had to reload. Our second, third and fourth flights descended onto them before the fastest had managed to reload. We could hear cries as the arrows found the crossbowmen. We sent twenty flights before I deemed we could have a rest. The return of bolts had slowed. Any warrior could use a crossbow but we had killed or wounded many who were the better ones. Their replacements would load more slowly and be less accurate.

"Change strings."

I kept my strings in a purse I wore on my belt. I chose a new one and strung my bow. Most of my men kept them beneath their hats. There is an art to stringing a bow. I remember when I had been in the Holy Land and Hamo L'Estrange had asked if he could string my bow for me. It had been amusing to watch for, strong as he was, the great warrior could not do it until I showed him the technique. He had seen me do it before but it was the explanation I gave that enabled him to do so.

When I had restrung the bow, I walked over to Guy of Poperinge. He was acting as an observer, "How goes it?"

He grinned, "If we had twice the number of archers, we would already be in a position to attack but it will not be long."

I shook my head and cautioned, "We do not attack alone, Guy, and we must wait for the signal."

He nodded glumly, "I prefer to make those decisions myself."

"As do I but as we have yet to lose a man and they must be suffering I am happy to continue to winnow their ranks."

I returned to my archers. This time I chose a good arrow. It was one of King Edward's but had been well made. I nocked it and gave my commands. The short rest and new bow meant that the well-made arrow soared even higher than the others. It would be travelling faster when it struck and would drive through leather, gambeson, flesh and even bone. This time there was an audible series of cries and the cracks of bolts, when they came, were sporadic. We had broken their crossbows. As the cries diminished and the returned bolts ceased, I ordered my archers to stand down. The defenders were now hidden and had protected themselves from arrows. I guessed that they had used shields. A man cannot use a crossbow and a shield. We waited for the orders to attack.

I wondered if the rest of the army was having a harder time than we were. We sent more arrows at unpredictable times and were rewarded with cries showing that we had hit someone. Mordaf even managed to hit a man in one of the citadel towers and as the range was over three hundred paces it was a prodigious effort.

The horn, when it sounded, came three hours after the sun had reached its zenith. The Flemish warriors mounted their horses and while we showered the defenders with arrows, they crossed. We brought up our horses but half of the archers sent arrows at targets who obligingly stepped from their defences to attack the Flemish men at arms and knights. When the horsemen disappeared into the port, we mounted our horses and crossed the moat. The water only came up to our horses' hocks but we looked for buried stakes; there were none. On the other side, we hammered stakes into the ground and tethered them. The men we had left to watch the river, having heard the signal, had now rejoined us and they and Jack would guard our horses.

As we neared the houses, we heard the cries of battle and saw the results of the Flemish attack. French bodies littered the ground. We had loosely nocked arrows and were vigilant. When the crossbowman on the tower stood to loose a bolt at us William of Ware sent an arrow to knock him from the fighting platform and he crashed to the ground below. We went at a steady pace. There was no reason for haste as the horsemen were faster than we were and our task was to ensure that Guy and his men were not ambushed.

When we reached the citadel, we found Guy and the men who had attacked from the other side sheltering by the buildings for the last of the defenders had retreated to the stone citadel. All our attackers were protected by the houses and businesses of Damme. I saw the bolts in the walls of the buildings. A citadel was the perfect place for a crossbowman to release his deadly bolts. He could rest the weapon on the walls and would be protected when he reloaded. We would be able to do little about the ones behind arrow slits. Robert of Béthune nodded as he approached me, "Sir Guy has told me of your success. How do we deal with this? I am loath to lose men in a frontal attack."

"Send the captains of the Welsh and English archers to me. We will burn them out."

As he sent a man to fetch the captains, I turned to Mordaf, "Have the men make fire arrows. The walls might be stone but the floors and beams are wooden."

Fire arrows were notoriously hard to use for men could douse them. My hope was to use so many that one or two would ignite and once the fire took hold then the citadel must fall.

I only knew one or two of the captains but they all knew me and my reputation. All were happy to follow my orders.

"Have your men make fire arrows. We release on my order. I want half of the archers to send fire arrows at the tower and the other half will release war arrows. My aim is to make the top of the tower uninhabitable. Once it is set alight, they will surrender. I want one in four archers watching for their crossbows. I do not intend to lose any men in this attack." I had men find a brazier and light it.

My leaders assigned the best men to the tasks. I relied on the other leaders to do the same. Fire arrows were hard to aim and to loose. The flaming head made the flight of the arrow more unpredictable. As soon as we were ready, I said, "Send in the arrows to clear the platform." I took a prepared fire arrow and stood ready to ignite it.

The half who were assigned to send war arrows simply ran from the shelter of the buildings to stand and draw in one. The shower was a ragged one but it kept down the heads of those on the top of the walls. The archers would continue to send arrows but they each moved to a different position first. The reasons were two-fold. The men loosing from the arrow slits would target them and we needed to get into position to send our fire arrows.

"Light the arrows."

I dipped my arrow into the brazier and it flared. Making sure that the head did not set fire to the arrow I hurried to the open area. Bolts were sent in our direction but we bore charmed lives. I reached the open area and drew and released in one. I watched the flight for this was the first fire arrow I had used in a long time. It arched and then dropped with the other arrows. They looked like stars. I knew mine had hit and I ran back to get a second. By the time I had sent three fire arrows my clothes were singed and my bow was hot to the touch but the top of the tower was on fire. I spied five archers who had yet to loose their fire arrows.

"Send them at the door!"

They all knew me and obeyed my command. The door to the citadel, the height of a man above the floor was a much easier target and all five arrows slammed into the solid wooden door. The unpredictability of the fire arrow was shown when two fizzled out but the other three took and flames began to lick at the dry wood of the door. It would take time for the door to burn but, inexorably, the fire grew. There had to be men behind the door and they would know what we had done. It did not take long for a French voice to shout from the top, "We surrender! We yield! Let us leave before we are roasted.

Robert of Béthune stepped out and shouted, "Drop your weapons when you reach the door and throw out your crossbows now."

The clatter and crash of crossbows being thrown to the ground were followed quickly by the opening of the door and men rushing out. My archers were the closest troops to the French and we all nocked a war arrow in case of treachery. The defenders obeyed the command and the weapons were dropped as the men ran to safety. One man who came out was weaponless for he was almost a human torch. His clothes were afire. Mordaf and Edward of Ware were close to him and they hurled him to the ground and used their hands and cloaks to put out the fire. As they helped him to his feet, I saw that his beard had caught fire and he would be marked for life.

"Thank you! I swear that I will give up a life of war and join a monastery for I thought I was dead."

I was not sure that Mordaf and Edward understood the man's French but they recognised the gesture of a proffered arm and took it. I knew why the man had made his decision. Fire killed nine times out of ten and survival would be a moment akin to the Road from Damascus, told in the Bible. I had never been that close to death but I knew that when The Lord Edward had endured the poisoned blade in the Holy Land he had changed. A king cannot give up his life and become a monk but the near-death experience made a better leader of the king.

Robert of Béthune sent his men to the citadel with water from the river to douse the fire. It took until dark to completely put out the flames. He saved the tower but it would take a great deal of work to repair it.

Our work was done but a message came, two days later, for us to stay in Damme in case the French or the rebels tried to retake it. The English and Welsh contingents had little to do except to sleep more than we had and to talk of the campaign. The Flemish men were the ones who were vigilant. They sent men to Bruges to demand its surrender. Robert of Béthune was there most of the time. Guy of Poperinge also left after swearing undying friendship to my men and to me.

"You all have great skill. I can see the advantage, now, of a bow over a crossbow. I shall train men in the art."

I shook my head, "You do not become an archer overnight. It is like the growing of an oak tree. You have to begin almost as soon as the acorn has sent its roots out and begun to grow. You train your boys and make their bodies as deformed as ours. If you start now then your sons will lead archers into battle."

With my sobering words in his head, he left. The English and Welsh would guard the town until relief came. The French were disarmed and the nobles were sent under Flemish escort to Ghent where they would be ransomed. The ordinary soldiers, just one hundred of them remained, were freed. They had the whole of Flanders to cross before they reached their homeland. Although their wounds had been treated, I was not certain just how many would make it successfully.

It was the twentieth of September when the English cog sailed, somewhat nervously, up the river. I was the most senior lord there and it was my standard, along with that of Flanders which flew above the port. I later learned that it was the sight of my flag that induced the captain to risk landing. The captain himself came ashore to speak to me. He had, in his hand, a sealed parchment and I recognised the seal of the Earl of Surrey. The captain spoke quietly to me, "My lord, there has been a disaster. The Earl of Surrey was defeated by Sir Andrew Murray at the battle of Stirling Bridge. One hundred knights and five thousand archers and spearmen fell. The earl barely made it out with his life. I took him to London, along with Sir Henry Percy and he told me to deliver this to the king."

My mind was filled with a range of emotions. I was shocked that the Scots had beaten an English army. Such a thing was unheard of. I was angry for my predictions had been correct and I was befuddled. Why would the earl and Percy go to London and abandon the north?

"When was this?"

"The battle was nine days ago, my lord. I did not sail up the Thames but dropped the lords at Dover where they took horses. We had heard that Damme had fallen and then been recaptured but I was not sure if it was safe."

"You may tell other captains that Damme is safe but I beg that you stay here until I return from the king. He may need your cog." He nodded and I took the letter, "You have done your duty and I will now complete the task." As the captain returned to his ship, I summoned Mordaf and Gwillim. "I have to get to the king quickly. I will take Jack and William and Edward."

"Will that be enough, my lord?"

"It should be for I want to be there as soon as we can." Taking a spare horse each we rode like the wind to Ghent, arriving well after dark. We had completed the twenty-seven-mile journey in half a day. The horses were exhausted.

Leaving my three companions to find us rooms and to see to the animals I was taken directly to the king. He had just finished eating and his face creased into a frown when he saw me. "Your clothes bespeak a hard and rapid journey and is that the seal of Surrey on that missive?"

"Yes, my lord. He has been badly beaten by the Scots."

Wallace's War

The knights with whom he was dining all erupted. I heard cries of 'Impossible!' and 'A mistake' along with other expressions of shock.

The king held up his hand for silence and then took out a knife to slice through the seal, "Peace! Let me read and get Sir Gerald a goblet of wine. Sit, Warbow."

I did as I was commanded and was handed a goblet of wine by a servant. I was close enough to the king to see his eyes widen as he read the letter. He seemed to read it twice and then putting it down he folded his hands together, almost as though in prayer. I knew it was a sign he was planning. The news had shocked him but he was ready to do something about it.

He gave a thin smile, "It seems that Sir Andrew Murray and the brigand called Wallace managed to trap our men at Stirling Bridge. The fates conspired to give victory to the Scots and the earl and his men barely made Berwick. Sir Hugh Cressingham fell in the battle along with many more brave knights." He turned to me. "As ever, Warbow, you were proved right. However, the Earl of Surrey is confident that the Scots will not take our castles. There is no need for me to rush back to England. If I did so then the Count of Flanders would feel I had abandoned him and the French would take heart. The taking of Damme and the imminent surrender of Bruges are victories we must exploit."

"But, my lord, what of the people of the north? The Scots will devastate their land. Why did the earl and Percy not stay in the north?"

His eyes narrowed and then he smiled, "We would speak in private with Sir Gerald. Leave us." When we were alone he topped up our goblets and then said, "My wife, the late queen, thought you the most valuable man in my land and for that reason, I tolerate you and your questions. Do not risk censure, Warbow." I nodded and he continued, "Surrey and Northumberland have gone to London. Sir Roger Bigod, the Earl of Norfolk and Humphrey de Bohun, the Earl of Hereford have conspired to turn Parliament against me. Surrey and Northumberland go to secure Parliament and to raise an army to return north. The harvest has passed and while the Scots may cause great mischief in the north, they cannot take our land. In the spring I will return with our army and we will crush this rebellion and display the heads of the rebels on London's walls." He drank from his goblet, "I will write my orders for the earl and you and your men shall deliver it. If you feel so strongly about the Scots and, bearing in mind that you know this giant, I give you a commission to take your retinue and go to Durham. Until I join you I would have you be my eyes and ears in the north. I know that you will give me a truthful interpretation of the situation. You will leave in the morning and the letter will be ready for you. I will pay you and your men for each day of service from now until Murray and Wallace are defeated. The payment starts now. Your manors will not suffer."

I stood and nodded, "I urge you, King Edward, to come to England sooner rather than later. You are the king who can quench this rebellious fire. All I can do is to slow it down."

He smiled, "Yet, Warbow, I have more confidence in you and your bow than in five hundred knights and I will be there as soon as I have fulfilled my promise to Flanders."

The captain was relieved when I returned but unhappy that he had to carry, at his own expense, my men and horses back to England. The royal warrant brooked no refusal. The second cog that arrived with supplies was even more unhappy but I was in no mood for an argument and, two days after I had returned from Ghent, we boarded the ships and headed back to England. I did feel sorry for the two captains and so I allowed them to land us at Dover and save them the long journey up the Thames. They would have the detritus of our horses to clean from their ships. We rode the eighty four miles and stopped at Rochester to break our journey. Rochester castle had been badly damaged in the rebellion led by Simon de Montfort. Although the keep had not fallen the outer walls and the buildings had been badly damaged. The result was that the constable, John of Cobham had been given permission to pull down the damaged buildings. It was a sorry sight.

He did, however, have good news for me, "The earl sent a message, my lord, London is secure and the two truculent earls returned to their lands. He is to be found in the tower."

I was relieved. I did not want to stumble into the start of a civil war. When we reached the mighty fortress that dominated London it took some time for us to be admitted and took the arrival at the barbican of the earl himself. While my men were housed in the warrior halls Jack and I were taken to the tower itself where Henry Percy was sitting, poring over maps. He looked up and smiled. I had been there at Dunbar when King Edward himself had knighted him and I could tell he was pleased to see me.

"Sir Gerald, does your arrival presage that of the king?"

The earl waved me to a seat and I shook my head. I handed the letter to the earl and, as Jack poured me some wine, he was learning skills he had never expected to learn, I explained, "I understand that the king will return in the spring or, perhaps the summer. I have been given a commission to travel north to Durham when I have collected my retinue and try to prevent the Scots from causing too much mischief."

The young knight looked at the map he was studying, "I confess that Topcliffe is far from the border else I would aid you." He nodded to the earl, "My grandfather was unlucky at the battle, you know."

"You were there?"

Shaking his head he said, "I was in the west at Irvine. I joined my grandfather as soon as I could. Murray was wounded, you know, badly I believe."

"And Wallace?"

"The giant?" I nodded, "He leads the rebellion now while Murray recovers. I hear you met him?"

"I did but then he was but a brigand, now, it seems, he has elevated himself. I would not underestimate him, my lord."

"But he has not an ounce of noble blood in his veins."

I emptied my goblet for the earl had finished reading the letter, "Neither have I, my lord, but I think that my enemies still fear me."

The old earl smiled, "Aye, Warbow, you are a loyal friend and a fierce enemy as de Montfort discovered. I will write my own letter to the Bishop of Durham. It is too late in the year to muster an army. I will join you in the spring." He tapped the letter, "I think that the King is right, you and your mounted archers are the best deterrents to raiding Scotsmen."

My heart sank for the north was being abandoned by the lords who lived in the south. I was a border warrior and knew the parlous existence of the ordinary folk who lived close to enemies. I would be the only hope until King Edward arrived. The Earl of Surrey had been beaten and the Scots would not fear him but Edward Longshanks was a different matter. His execution of those who had bared their buttocks at him had shown the Scots that King Edward was a king to be feared.

Henry Percy was a likeable young man, "I will be taking my mounted men and joining the garrison at Carlisle. If this brigand thinks he can use that as a gateway to England, then we will show him otherwise." I admired his spirit.

Chapter 6

We reached Yarpole at the start of October. The fields were now cleared and the winter barley had barely begun to grow. The sheep and the pigs were clearing the other fields of stubble and my manor was preparing for winter. I knew that my arrival and my new orders would not be welcomed but I would do my duty. All the way north I had ruminated about my enemies. Murray, it seemed, was not long for this world and I had questioned the earl and his grandson about Wallace. I had known from our first encounters that he was a warrior but had he the ability to lead the rebellion? There had been more than a little luck involved in the defeat but I also suspected that the Earl of Surrey was simply too old to lead the king's army. King Edward was not a young man but had he led the army then I suspect he would not have lost. Wallace had been knighted after the battle and had been appointed the Guardian of Scotland. That made him, effectively, the leader of the Scottish army. As I rode into my yard, I put those thoughts from me.

Dismounting I said to my leaders, "The men can have six days and then we ride again."

Mordaf and the others were as unhappy as I was about this burden we had been asked to carry but the resolute looks on their faces told me that they would do as I had asked. It was my wife and Hamo who opened the door to me. I frowned, "Alice?"

Mary smiled, "She is well but being with child, she needs to lie down now and then. Do you not remember when I carried Hamo?"

I was relieved, "Of course." I hugged and kissed her.

"You are back sooner than we expected, father." I saw the real question in Hamo's eyes. He knew my early arrival had to have something to so with the disaster at Stirling Bridge. All the way home it had been the sole topic of conversation in the alehouses we had used.

"And we leave in six days, all of us." I felt my wife stiffen in my arms. "The Scottish victory at Stirling Bridge means that the north is in danger. We have been commissioned to go to Durham and offer Prince Bishop Antony Bek our bows to limit the damage that the Scots do." We were about to enter the room where Alice waited. "Hamo, you will not be here to see your child born."

I saw him nod, "Father, I am your son and just as I know you have had to make sacrifices to serve King Edward so I am prepared to do the same."

"We will not speak about this until tomorrow. For tonight let us enjoy each other's company." I turned to Jack, "Fetch the presents we brought and then you are free to do as you will. We will not need you to wait at table this night."

When we had retaken Damme, Guy of Poperinge had found the warehouse of a merchant who had died in the fighting. We shared the contents and I had some beautiful lace for the women in my family. We also had weapons we had taken but they could wait to be shared. Alice and Mary, not to mention my daughter Joan, were delighted. Margaret lived in Launceston and would have to wait for her gift. We did not mention our departure but all wanted to know how the war in Flanders fared. They were all genuinely pleased that none of our men had been hurt but, like me, could not understand why the king bothered with a war that could not really benefit England.

I believed I knew the king better than any. I had first served him in Gascony when we had both been young men, "King Edward has enjoyed great success on this island. He has defeated de Montfort and his baronial enemies. He has curbed both the Welsh and the Scots but beyond this island, he has done little. The crusade," I touched my wife's hand, "did not bring him the victory that would ensure his name, like that of his grandsire, King Richard the Lionheart, would echo through history." I smiled and kissed the back of Mary's hand, "I, for one, was glad of that adventure for it brought me the greatest of treasures."

Mary smiled, "Then perhaps this Flanders venture may prove as fortuitous for England too."

I was not sure. After Dunbar, I had thought the Scots had been cowed and leaderless. As King Edward had found when he had fought Llewelyn, all it took was one charismatic leader and rebellion could take hold.

It was good to sleep in my own bed again and I vowed to enjoy the six nights I would have to wallow in its comfort. Mary lay snuggled in my arms and I told her what I had to do. We both had grey hairs but the nights together were the same as they had been when we had first met. "Do not worry about Alice, Gerald, for she thought when she was taken by the Scots that her life was over and she had resigned herself to be a slave. She expected that she would be used and abused by the barbarians from the north. More than anyone she will understand why you have to do what you will do. She would not want others to suffer as she did. I am just sorry that you will be dragged hence once more. You are missing the sight of young Gerald growing. Margaret brings him over once a month to see me and each time I swear he has grown. He will be a giant."

"And tomorrow I shall ride to see my daughter and grandson. You are right. I do miss the chance to see my grandchild. Mayhap, when I return there will be another." I felt her tense in my arms, "What is it, my love?"

"I have not mentioned Joan yet."

"I thought that she was both quiet and distracted."

I felt the sigh on my chest, "She is being courted by Ralph Fitzalan."

I searched my memory for the name seemed familiar, "Is he related to Lady Isabella, married to John Fitzalan?" Lady Isabella was the daughter of Lady Maud and Baron Mortimer.

"The second son. He came to stay at Wigmore Castle and passed through the manor when you were in Scotland. I did not think to mention it but there must have been sparks between them for he came again not long after you had departed for Flanders. He visited every day and Joan confided in me that she was enamoured of the young man. He said he would visit again when you returned so that he could speak with you. He seems an earnest young man."

I liked Isabella who was very much like her mother Lady Maud. It was only when that great lady died that relations with the Mortimer family became strained. Perhaps this was a good thing and was meant to be. I had been sad when Isabella had died six years earlier. "I trust that you will ensure that all is done well, my love."

She elbowed me in the ribs, "I do not need lessons in civilised behaviour from you, my love!"

I laughed, "Aye, the title of Sir Gerald still does not sit well for me and even the king still calls me Warbow."

"And why not for that is the most honourable of titles?"

Before I left to visit my daughter, son-in-law, and grandson, I took Joan to one side. My younger daughter had grown into a beauty and I had not even noticed. To me, she was still my lively daughter, Joan. Now I saw her as a potential bride for another. I had known Margaret's husband but this Ralph Fitzalan was just a name, "Your mother tells me that you are being courted."

She looked fearful, "I am sorry that I did not speak of it, father, but you have been away so much."

I smiled and hugged her, "And for that, I apologise. Do not be fearful, my child, I am not angry but I am your father and would have you happy when you are wed. Hamo and Margaret are content and before I give my approval, I must meet this young man. I knew his mother and she was a fine lady but you should know that I will be away this winter in the north." She looked crestfallen. "I do not say that you cannot meet, of course you can, but your mother will see that all is done well. That he has no title is good for that means we do not need to seek a licence to wed but you must be patient."

"It will be hard, father, for I love him."

"And when I met your mother in the Mongol camp, we knew that we were meant for each other but we waited until we reached Yarpole to wed and that was a longer wait than you will have. Be patient."

The smile I loved reappeared on her lips and she reached up to kiss my cheek, "I will and know that you are the best of fathers. Take care when you are away, serving the king."

"Do not worry, I will. I hope to have a host of grandchildren to bore with tales of my youth."

The first two days were joyous as I saw my family once more. My wife was right and Gerald had grown much since I had last seen him. He now smiled rather than bringing forth wind. He grabbed hold of my fingers and hair. I played and let him wrestle my hands filled with the joy only a grandfather can know. I was sad to part from my daughter and grandson but the sadness was mitigated by my being with my larger family. I looked at Joan more fondly, knowing that I would lose her to another man soon. Alice had blossomed and bloomed in her pregnancy and that boded well. The captive who had been full of fear had grown thanks to the tender ministrations of my son. All was good and then I had to choose the men who would come with me. I spent the last few days at Yarpole with Hamo, Gwillim and Mordaf as we made lists of what we would need.

I had no intention of leaving my manor unguarded from the Welsh. We had captured many weapons in Flanders and they were not weapons that were needed by my mounted archers. Every man who remained, young and old, was given a weapon. In many cases, we were able to supply a brigandine and helmet. As the crops had been harvested, I mustered every man for a day of training with their new weapons. I would be leaving forty men to watch my manor. A dozen or so were warriors, like Ralph the Fletcher, who were too old to go to war. Some might argue that I fell into that category but none would give the thought utterance. There were eighteen or so likely lads who were not yet ready for war but could use a sling and a sword or spear. Then there were the rest of the men. These were my farmers who knew how to fight but never ventured forth on campaign. I made Ralph the Fletcher their captain and at the end of the day, I was confident that if the church bells were sounded then all knew to bring their families to the manor. Luston was also provided with weapons and Henry the Steward there was put in charge of its defence. James and John, Alice's brothers, had the disappointment of being left behind lessened by being given weapons and told to aid Ralph the Fletcher.

That left me with sixty men in addition to Jack, Hamo and myself. We had ten sumpters with tents and spare sheaves of arrows. I had the King's Commission and that meant I was entitled to food and lodgings from religious houses and royal residences along our route. That meant a journey that would take us to Chester and thence to Craven and Ripon before arriving at the Palatinate. What we did not have was intelligence about the Scots. I had no idea what Wallace was up to.

Mordaf was philosophical about the whole thing, "My lord, no news is good news. If the Scots had crossed the Tyne, then we would have heard. I know that it is hard to be in the dark but we cannot move any faster. It is but two days and then we can leave and in a week from now we will know all."

He was right. As soon as we reached Ripon, on the east side of the mountains, then we would have news. The Bishop of Ripon would be able to give us up-to-date information.

Our last meal was a mixture of happiness, for we were all together, my daughter and her family had travelled to visit with us and our table was full. Yet there was sadness. I caught Alice looking tearfully at my son. As soon as she knew I was looking the sadness was replaced by a false smile. Mary kept touching my hand and chose my favourite food from the fine array we had on our laden table to tempt me with morsels. Joan too was more solicitous than I had ever known. She was a woman and knew that she might soon exchange a husband for a father. Such was life.

The tears came in the morning as we left. Mary hid her tears but I knew that when she was alone, she would weep. I was stoically silent as I led my line of archers north to Chester. The heads of my married archers turned to catch the last glimpse of their homes and families while the single ones bantered. Jack and Hamo rode next to me and aware of my mood neither said a word.

Fate sometimes has more of a hand in our lives than we realise. Our route took us through Oswestry. Lady Isabella had lived there and, as it was getting late in the day, I headed there to seek shelter. The Constable welcomed us for the news of sixty extra archers would be spread to the west and make the Welsh wary.

"Is Baron Edmund not here, Constable?"

The old warrior shook his head, "He keeps us victualled my lord but he spends more time at Wigmore. The land there brings in more coin but we hold the Welsh here."

Wallace's War

He invited Hamo and me to dine with him and the subject of Lady Isabella's children came up. I was not prying but the constable held the Lady of Clun and Oswestry in high regard. "Her elder son, Richard is a fine knight. I often sparred with him when he was younger."

"And Ralph?"

"He was younger but a keen boy who was desperate to be like his grandfather."

The youth went up in my estimation for Roger Mortimer had been a good warrior and like me a bastion against both de Montfort and Llewelyn. When we left the next day, I was looking forward to meeting the grandson of Baron Mortimer of Wigmore.

It was after we spoke to the Lord of Craven at Skipton Castle that we learned that the Scots were rampaging through Northumberland. The castles of Norham, Berwick, Bamburgh, Ford and Alnwick were too strong for the Scots to take but there were not enough horsemen there to deter them and, as I had suspected, it was not the lords who suffered but the ordinary folk, the farmers and the like. The army had headed down the Tynedale Valley and ravaged Hexham and Corbridge. The monks at Hexham had been forced to pay gold to the Scots to avoid their abbey being ransacked. We could not get to Durham soon enough.

I had known Antony Bek but that had been in the Holy Land when he had been a lowly clerk serving King Edward. Our paths had rarely crossed for at that time he was not a warrior and I was busy fighting the enemies of Christendom. He had done well in the service of King Edward and had been rewarded with the Palatinate. It made him the second most powerful man in England and as the guardian of the north vital to King Edward's plans. Durham Castle, nestled in a large loop on the Wear was a powerful castle and with just one bridge across the river was unlikely to fall. My troop of horsemen was a welcome sight and as we rode through the town, up the hill to the cathedral and castle, we were greeted with cheers. I was not as well known in this part of the world but my exploits rescuing the captives the previous year had made my name and livery better known.

While Jack saw to my horse and Mordaf and Gwillim found beds for my men, Hamo and I were welcomed by the bishop. He grinned when he saw me, "We have both moved on since last we saw each other, Warbow."

"Indeed we have, Your Grace."

"None of that, Warbow, I am Antony. You were kind to me in the Holy Land and there were other warriors who disparaged me. You and Hamo L'Estrange did not."

I nodded, "And this is my son, Hamo, named after that great warrior."

"It is good to meet you, Hamo. I do not envy you for you have much to live up to."

Shaking my head I said, "A man has his own path to follow. I cannot see Hamo having to travel deep into Mongol lands. He is a good archer, a fine husband and I am proud of him. That is enough. He does not need to be burdened with the Warbow legend. Now... Antony, what do we do about this Wallace?"

He had read the missive from the king while we had been served wine and he patted the parchment, "You know the man, I believe?"

"He held my son's wife and other captives hostage in the west, north of Carlisle, but then he was a brigand. He has risen higher since then."

"You and your mounted archers are the only weapons we have save a handful of knights. Many of the Palatinate knights fell at Stirling and others were captured. I can let you have twenty knights, no more."

I shook my head, "I think we will be better employed acting as Wallace did. We ambush and we hunt. His army is largely afoot and we can use speed. He is at Carlisle I believe?"

"He is but Henry Percy is there and with him are many knights. It will not fall."

"Then we will ride tomorrow to Carlisle and turn the tables on him. While he attacks the walls, we shall attack his camp."

"But you have had a hard ride from Yarpole!"

"We brought good horses and it is but seventy miles to Carlisle. Perhaps the sight of my archers will bring heart to those who have had their lives and livelihoods ruined by these Scots. If you could supply me with four or five riders to act as messengers then it would help. I would keep you well informed about the intentions of the Scots so that you can be prepared. I am surprised that he did not try to take Durham or Newcastle."

"We are too big a morsel but you are right, Newcastle is not yet a strong castle and it could fall if it was attacked. I believe that he just followed the Tyne Valley as there are few castles there. Barnard, Bowes and Brougham are all powerful castles but there is nothing west of Prudhoe to stop the Scots."

"Then prepare yourself for a siege. If we succeed then he will look for another victory before winter sets in."

Hamo and I shared a chamber and we spoke as we prepared for sleep. Jack had the luxury of a cot in which to sleep and he was already in the land of dreams while we discussed the raid.

Wallace's War

"He will outnumber us by more than twenty to one, father."

"Aye, and if he could pin us down then he could squash us like a fly. We do not go to give battle, we go to make him bleed. We attack him while he sleeps and when he sends horsemen to take us we ambush them. He will tire of it and then he might be more dangerous. If he leaves Carlisle, where will he go? If he goes north to his home in Galloway then we have won. If he comes east then there are many rich prizes for him to take but, equally, there are many places we could use for an ambush. Winter will be our ally. It comes earlier in the north. We have to annoy him until December and then, I think, he will slink back to Scotland."

"And we can go home?"

"No, my son, we are likely to be here for six months no matter what the Scots do. We are here until King Edward returns for as Bishop Bek said, we are the only potent force that can deter the Scots. We cannot beat him but we can restrict him. It is not glorious and men will not write of it but it is the right thing to do." I saw the disappointment on his face, "If the bishop lets us go earlier then that will be good but do not count on it.

As we had discovered when we had rescued the captives there were many ways to cross the great divide. Although I did not think that the Scots were organised to have watchers, we avoided the main routes and, riding hard reached Bowes Castle before dark. It was a cold hard ride and we were glad of the walls as they protected us from the harsh east wind. The castle belonged to the earl of Richmond but this was not a luxurious palace and I doubted that the earl had even visited it. A constable and thirty men were its only defence. Compared with nearby Barnard Castle it was tiny but I knew its value.

Many of my men had to stay in the stables as accommodation was limited but the constable, John of Kirkby, fed us well. Hamo and I dined with him. He confirmed what we had been told, "No, my lord, the Scots did not come this way. There is little of value for them on this road. The Romans built the road to enable them to cross the land quickly but they avoided verdant valleys. Betwixt here and Brougham there are less than thirty families. The Tyne Valley had more to offer him."

Hamo nodded as he tucked into the hogget that had been prepared for us, "Then this castle is safe from attack?"

"I would not say that. If an enemy wished to raid the Tees Valley or York, even Durham or Newcastle then this route is the quickest and we can be avoided. From what I have heard this Scottish army is largely on foot." He waved an arm toward the walls, "They could simply cross the

Wallace's War

moors and then rejoin the road further east. I doubt that they would waste time trying to reduce these walls for there is nothing for them, now Carlisle is a different matter. Take that and the west coast comes under threat, Craven, the Forest of Bowland, Lancaster, are all places the Scots could raid and take great riches,"

The next day, as we headed towards Carlisle, I told Hamo my innermost fears, "This William Wallace is unpredictable. We found that when we hunted him. He has a natural cunning and, it seems to me he has the ability to use the land as an ally. The king should be here. We cannot stop Wallace. All we can do is annoy him. We poke him with a stick and hope we can get out of his way when he reacts."

Hamo nodded, "And I pray that Robert of Carlisle is safe."

That had been one of my worries. The captain of the guard at Carlisle had been reunited with the love of his life on our return from Galloway. The constable, Robert de Brus, had left the castle in his hands and I feared that the old warrior might not be up to a long defence of his home. The arrival of Henry Percy would have helped but Percy was young. It was another reason I had ridden so hard. Once they knew that help was outside then any wavering resolve would disappear. Henry Percy knew that I had been tasked with helping the Bishop of Durham and our arrows would be the best messenger we could send to the beleaguered garrison.

We knew the Eden Valley well and we left the road to Carlisle long before we reached the town and castle. We stopped five miles from the castle in the forest that nestled close to the River Peveril. The river was barely more than a stream but it would give us water and some protection. The river was easily fordable and we would not be trapped. The nearest settlement was the tiny hamlet of Engelthwaite and we could avoid it. The reason for that was that I did not want the villagers to be harmed if the Scots came for us. While the men made camp, I rode with Hamo and Mordaf to view the siege lines.

It was dark when we reached the Scottish camps but their fires, which ringed the castle, were light enough to see that this was a huge army. They had already done much mischief and many buildings had been destroyed. The smell of roasting meat told us that they had captured and slaughtered many animals. This part of England would have a lean winter.

Hamo said, "Now would be a good time to attack them, father. They are eating and will not expect us."

Shaking my head I said, "There is too much risk. We have ridden our horses hard and the men have not eaten. We have seen enough. We go back to our camp, eat and sleep until terces. Then we return and shower them with arrows."

Mordaf said, "Many will be safe in houses they have commandeered."

I smiled, "We poke the beast. This poking may not be enough to rouse it but if we do it often enough, it will."

We reached the camp and ate a cold supper. With four men on watch we slept. The four watchers would remain at the camp and sleep while we raided. I left Jack at the camp too. He was annoyed until I told him that I needed him to command the four men I left. "We need our sumpters to be guarded and you, Jack of Malton, are the one for the job."

When we had scouted the previous night, we had watched from a row of four derelict cottages. The Scots had already ransacked them and I prayed that the occupants had made Carlisle's walls. We tethered our horses there and with full sheaves of arrows headed close to their camps. They had no sentries and that was a mark of their confidence. Since the battle, they had raided with impunity and no one had raised a finger against them.

We were so close that we could hear the sounds of sleep. Men snoring, breaking wind and the like. The greatest danger would be men rising to make water. For that reason, we strung our bows quickly and nocked a silent arrow. The creak of our yew bows might make light sleepers wonder what woke them but once the missiles descended then they would know for sure that they were under attack. I released and then it was as though a flock of birds had taken flight. I nocked another and sent it high. I had just chosen my third arrow when we heard the screams from the camp as men were struck by the falling arrows. By the tenth arrow, commands could be heard coming from the camp.

I said to Hamo on one side of me, "Tell the men five more flights and we leave." I turned to repeat the instruction to the archer on my left, Peter Warbow. Hamo and the men on my right turned to leave. I waited until the ones on my left had turned before I sent one last arrow. It was specially chosen for this one had feathers that were stained red with cochineal. I was leaving a message.

Chapter 7

We reached our camp without incident and, before we ate, drew lots to see who would have the first watch. I was included in the draw but I was not chosen. Mordaf and Gwillim were. My men understood the fairness of the system and we rarely had anyone complaining about such duties. After we had eaten most of the men went to sleep but I sat with Hamo and Jack to plan the next part of our strategy. "I will sleep but four hours and then I want to be awakened. I will take twenty archers, the ones who are awake, and we will follow the river. I intend to find somewhere to attack them. You, Hamo will command the camp in my absence."

"In daylight, father, is that not risky?"

"It is but I need our enemy to know that I am here."

Jack was clever and he nodded, "You want him to hunt us."

"I do and when he does then we will ambush him. If he is hunting us then he cannot assault the walls with as many men. We will attack again, this night but from a different place. However, I know that he will have men watching for us. We have to be unpredictable. Tonight will be the attack that makes them set sentries and sleep with one ear open. They will lose sleep and not we."

Hamo nodded, "And if you are to ride again in four hours then you must sleep now. I will tell Mordaf and Gwillim what we have planned."

I fell asleep quickly, despite the hard ground and it seemed but moments before I was shaken awake by Jack. "I have food, my lord." I sniffed the air. Jack grinned, "Fear not, my lord, we lit no fires." Woodsmoke would give us away and my men were willing to endure cold food to avoid our camp being discovered.

There were twenty men preparing their arrow bags and horses. Jack had already gone to fetch my horse. After eating I mounted and, as I did so, said to Hamo, "Ensure that the men rest for a tired man makes mistakes."

William of Ware and his brother Edward were amongst the men I led. Since joining us they had proved to be good scouts and the most reliable of men. We followed the path that led along the river. I knew that eventually, we would reach the castle and the siege lines. The river gave us the chance to escape if we were pursued. We could swim across the river. A mile or so down the river we spied a peel tower on the other bank. I had heard that the Salkeld had built such a defence but I could not tell if it was occupied or not. It had clearly not been slighted. The trees through which we passed began to thin and I heard the sound of hammering. We reined in and tethered our horses. We were too few to have horse holders. I strung my bow and hung my cloak from the back of my horse. Winter was coming and it had been too chilly to ride without a cloak. Now I was warmed up and did not need the encumbrance of a cloak. With four arrows in my left hand, I led my men towards the sound of hammering.

Archers can move easily, silently and invisibly through trees and scrubland. We are all natural hunters and that was what we were doing, hunting men. We stopped when we saw their camp. They were building a ram. It was simple enough to construct. The hardest part would have been making the wheels. They would have either hewn down a tree and cut rounds or more likely reused ones taken from a farm wagon. There were about twenty men making the ram. They were one hundred paces from us and clearly oblivious to danger. They had not set sentries. I could see that a hundred and fifty paces closer to the walls, were the bulk of the men on this section of the siege lines. Their archers and slingers, as well as a handful of crossbowmen, were sending missiles at the walls. They looked to be having little effect. The Scots cheered whenever an arrow made a defender duck and the men on the walls jeered back at the Scots. Insults flew and, allied to the hammering made a noise that would allow us to close with the Scots. We had not attacked this part of the camp the previous night and so these Scots had not yet suffered a wound. That was about to change.

Using hand signals I instructed the men. They knew what they had to do for they were well trained. We nocked arrows and chose our targets. If was not a question of whether our arrows would strike a target but where? My half circle of archers did not stand until the last moment. I rose and drew at the same time and sent my arrow into the back of the Scot who was about to hammer a plank into the side of the ram. The force was such that it pinned him to the weapon. I nocked another and moved forward. All the builders were hit. One or two even managed a cry but those at the siege lines did not turn. Perhaps there had been cries before when accidents had occurred or more likely the noise of the siege hid the death cries. There was a fire close to the ram and food was cooking on it.

"Edward, set fire to the ram. The rest of you kill as many of the attackers as you can and then fall back on my command."

The burning of the ram would do two things. It would undo their work and that would demoralise them but it would also provide cover as we fled. We moved to within one hundred and twenty paces of the attackers and began to send our arrows into the attackers. I chose a bodkin to send at the mailed man who was clearly shouting orders. The arrow slammed into his back. As others fell the attackers looked at the walls and I managed to send two more arrows before they realised where we were. The crackling and burning ram also made them turn.

We had done enough and I shouted, "Back!" I sent one more arrow and then ran. We had less than three hundred paces to run but I was no longer a young man. My archers could have reached the horses quicker than me but they slowed to enable us all to reach our horses together. The result was that some of the Scots were within a hundred paces of us as we reached our animals. We turned, nocked and drew, sending our arrows to hit at least ten and make the others take cover. It bought just enough time for us to mount and I led us into the river. Here the Eden was fast flowing and the current would take us downstream. It was a foolish man who wasted energy fighting such a force and so we crossed the river diagonally. I knew that the Scots would assume we were heading for our camp and if they sought us would be looking in the wrong place. Using the river would hide where we left the river. On reaching the other side we stopped and looked back. The cloud of smoke from the ram told us that they had doused the flames. The ram might be repaired but it would not be used for some time. We headed back down the river towards our camp. When I spied a narrow part, we crossed and soon arrived back in our camp.

While Jack saw to my horse, I told Hamo, Mordaf and Gwillim what we had seen. Using a stick I drew a map in the mud where one of the horses had relieved itself. "Here is the castle." I put an x on the eastern side. "We attacked here today and escaped north across the river. I am hoping that if they seek us, they will look to the north." I put a second x on the southern side. "Last night we attacked here and tonight I want us to go the west. Here." I put a third x on the western side."

Mordaf was chewing a twig and he used it to point, "A good plan, my lord but this Wallace is no fool. Tomorrow, he will hunt us."

I smiled, "I know and if he does then he cannot attack Carlisle." I pointed to the grey skies above our heads, "Winter is coming and the Scots if they have not made a dent in Carlisle's walls, will have to go home."

Mordaf nodded, "Then when we return from this night attack, we must make traps in the woods to give us warning."

My men were all capable leaders and Mordaf had read my mind.

I rested, wrapped in my cloak and I even managed to sleep. I knew that some of my older warriors at Yarpole, the ones who no longer went to war, often enjoyed, when they could, an afternoon sleep. I wondered if my need for such a nap was a sign of my age. When Jack roused me, I felt refreshed. "Tonight, Jack, I leave you here again with William and Edward. I have a task for you. I want the three of you to cut brambles and ivy. When we return, we make our camp a fortress of sorts."

"We will do as you command my lord. I have filled your arrow bag. I did not put bodkins in."

I smiled, "Good, you are learning to be an archer."

Jack was not yet ready to stand with my archers but the daily practice with his bow, smaller than ours, was already making him broader and more muscled. He could send an arrow at an enemy and would probably hit whatever he aimed at but he would not yet be able to send a war arrow through a brigandine and into flesh.

We headed due west, keeping well south of the siege lines. Wallace would have men watching for us. I did not think that we would be able to attack his defences and find his men sleeping. There would be sentries. Before we had left, I had instructed my men. The sentries would have to die and then we would repeat our night attack. The attack in the east had shown me that the Scottish camps there were hovels. They would not afford protection from plunging arrows. We forded the River Caldew. Whilst larger than the River Peveril it was not an obstacle and we made it across easily.

It soon became clear that there was less cover on this side of the town. We would have to use the wrecked and ransacked houses and that meant moving in smaller groups. Our training paid off and, after tethering our horses to the few trees we found, Hamo, Mordaf, Gwillim and I led our four groups of men towards the Scottish lines. A coordinated attack would be impossible and we would have to react quickly to whatever came our way. I was not wearing my cloak and I felt the cold. It was a damp cold that presaged rain. We could still send arrows when it rained but our range would be shortened.

My group of archers moved in a half circle, flanking me. We each had a loosely nocked arrow and used the cover of a burnt-out farm and outbuildings. I could see the edge of the town to our right but ahead looked to be open to the river. Harold was the archer who had the fastest reactions. As the face of a Scottish sentry rose, just twenty paces from us, his arrow slammed into the Scotsman's face. The sound of his falling was not loud but it told us that we were close to their sentries. Having seen one we were able to predict the next ones. An arrow sent from a range of twenty paces never misses and my men were skilled enough to ensure that the sentries died silently. We moved closer to their camp and I saw the glow of the fires they had used to cook their food. The residual heat would make the air closer to their hovels a little warmer. The arrows we sent at the camp were loosed to rise high in the air. It was Mordaf's men who sent the first ones; they were to my left and this time the men who were hit made a noise as arrows fell from the air.

"Alarm! We are under attack!"

The Scots had prepared themselves for another night of attack. I had told my men that we would just send ten flights before falling back. As we started to move back, I wondered if that had been optimistic for we heard, coming from our right, the sound of hooves. We did not panic nor did we shout. We just moved as quickly as we could back to our horses. Nocking an arrow I turned as I heard approaching hooves. My men and I were exposed for our horses were still eighty paces from us and I was at the rear. Some of my younger archers were already waiting with the horses. The rider who rode at me was on the back of a pony and with him were another twenty or so riders. I drew back and my arrow knocked him from the back of his mount. I had another arrow nocked and sent at the second rider in a heartbeat. When the rest of the men with me sent an arrow at the riders it slowed the attack dramatically.

Hamo shouted, "Father, back to the horses. I spy mailed men following these riders." My son was mounted and from his elevated position could see what I could not. I ran and threw myself onto the back of my horse. We had planned for a quick escape and we headed due south. Mailed men would be slower than my archers but we would leave a clear trail. We crossed the Caldew and then waited in the trees on the far side of the river. We heard the horsemen as they approached. Gwillim's men dismounted and each of them nocked an arrow. As the horsemen galloped along the clear trail that we had left the fifteen archers began to draw. We were using war arrows and Gwillim's men would target the horses. The arrows struck flesh and as the horses veered to the side or fell so their riders were thrown from their backs.

"Mount."

The wounded horses and dismounted riders would take some time to organize and to be able to follow, we headed along a trail that led to a road. At night they would find it hard to decide if we had headed to the north or the south. It was dawn when we rode into our camp.

"Before we rest, and I know that you all both deserve and need rest, let us make the camp more defensible."

We all set to making barriers of branches, brambles and ivy. Vines were strung between trees and when all was done and after setting sentries we slept. I drew a lot which marked me for sentry duty. I went into the trees and squatted by an old hoary hornbeam. I took off my used string and found a new one. I did not string my bow but I was ready to do so. I watched. At noon Jack came with food.

"Your watch is over, my lord, Robert son of William is here to relieve you."

I saw the archer walking towards me and I shook my head, "Have him relieve someone else. I am awake and do not feel the need to sleep. Fetch me half a dozen bodkins." Neither my apprentice nor my archer was willing to argue with me and I was left. I knew that Wallace would not rest until he had found my camp. We had made three unanswered attacks. Some of the mailed men we had unhorsed would be hurt and they were the men Wallace needed. The ones we had slain in the camp were not specialists. His mailed men were. Jack returned with the bodkins and I saw that he had brought his war bow.

"May I watch with you, lord?"

"Of course, but no words. A sentry used his eyes, ears and nose."

The first of the traps were less than ten paces from Jack and me but it was the smell of the Scottish scouts further away that alerted us. Men sweat and if they do not regularly bathe then they stink. It was the stink that warned me of an approaching enemy. I said nothing but as soon as I began to string my bow then Jack knew to string his smaller bow. I nocked a war arrow and listened. It was barely discernible but I heard the movement of at least two Scottish scouts as they drew nearer to us. The traps we had set would not stop a determined enemy but they would slow one down and, in removing them, tell us where they were. The Scottish scout did not cry out when his hand was ripped by the bramble thorns but I heard the noise and drew back. I spied his face, twelve paces from me as he tried to negotiate the barrier. The arrow killed him instantly. His companion had been either luckier or more careful. Even as I nocked another arrow he appeared from my right, just ten paces from me. I was still drawing back my arrow when Jack's arrow struck his skull. There were more cries now and so I shouted, "Alarm! Alarm!"

The horses' hooves told me that they had mounted men with the scouts and as I drew a bodkin I said, "Tell Hamo we break camp and flee. Have the horses saddled."

Nodding, he ran. We had planned for discovery and while half the men waited with nocked arrows the other half would hold the reins of the horses. Thirty odd arrows would slow down an attack and allow my men to cross the river and escape. The mailed man who came at me was forty paces away and he had a spear. I drew back and my bodkin hit his chest, splitting the mail links and driving through his gambeson and into his chest. I had a second nocked while I was taking three steps back.

The second horseman brought up his shield. I sent my bodkin into his leg. The range was short enough that the arrow also went into the flank of his horse and the animal reared and threw the wounded rider. I nocked another arrow and moved five paces closer to my camp. When the crossbow bolt thudded into the tree next to me, I knew that I had to risk running. I ran and heard Jack's voice, "Here, my lord."

I veered to my right and barely avoided an arrow sent by a Scottish archer. There was a sound like a flock of birds rising in the air and thirty arrows fell behind me as my men loosed almost blindly to fall upon the Scots who were eager to get at us. I mounted my horse and saw that there was just Robert son of William to mount. I saw him and then watched in horror as the crossbow bolt hit him squarely in the back and he fell.

We would mourn him later but Hamo took command, "Mount and cross the river."

We turned and headed into the river. I was able to walk my horse through the shallow water and once we had climbed the bank we dug our heels into our horses and rode them hard. We had the advantage over our pursuers that we knew where we were going but they had to be careful as they were expecting an ambush. In addition, we were all mounted and they were not.

We stopped at Warwick on Eden. It was just three miles from our camp but there was a wooden bridge over the Eden. We stopped to rest our horses and to change the strings on our bows.

"Thank you, Jack, I owe you a life."

He smiled, "I had not the time to think if I could kill a man or not, my lord. he was there and I just reacted."

"You are becoming a warrior."

There appeared to be no pursuit but I feared an ambush. We made camp by the river and enjoyed our first hot food. We bought ale from the village alewife and we toasted Robert son of William. He had been our only loss but even the loss of one man was one too many. My men insisted that I slept and I did in the luxury of a barn.

I sent Dick to spy on the Scots. It was a risk but one archer could evade pursuit.

I woke up early and went to the bridge. William of Ware was on duty with his brother, "Any sign of pursuit?"

He shook his head, "Perhaps we blooded their noses."

"Perhaps."

Dick galloped in an hour before noon, "The Scots are breaking camp, my lord. The siege is over."

"Well done, Dick, get some food for we will soon be leaving. I want to know which road they take. Do they head home or follow us?"

It was noon when we spied the Scots but this was not a pursuit. Their whole army was marching towards the bridge. They had given up the siege but were not heading home. They were heading east. I had poked the bear but the result was not what I wanted.

"Rouse the camp. Edward, have men pull down the bridge. It will slow them down."

"Aye, my lord."

Ropes were attached to the wooden posts in the river and then the posts were hacked with axes. The bridge tumbled into the river. The Scots could cross but first, they would have to clear the wreckage from the water and their journey would be slower.

We now had to play a tricky game. We had to keep ahead of the Scots but we also had to anticipate in which direction they would go. They had taken all of value from Tynedale and therefore they would take the road through Penrith. Would their destination be the Tees? It could be the Tyne or even York. I found myself admiring William Wallace. He was decisive. Winter was not yet upon us. he could still cross the high passes and raid the east. Tynedale was ravaged. Would other places suffer the same fate?

Chapter 8

Until Bowes, there was but one route and we kept ahead of him. His scouts rode ponies but they did not risk our arrows. We stayed for one night in Brougham at the fine castle over the river and there the constable ordered the villagers and their animals within the walls of the castle. If he stopped to besiege Brougham then he would be able to reduce it but winter was coming and I thought he wanted a bigger prize. The question was what was the prize? As we left the next day, we endured a shower that was more sleet than rain. He would not want to waste time on somewhere as insignificant as Brougham. He had defeated the English and needed to build on that success.

We reached Bowes and were able to give a warning to the constable, John of Kirkby. "I will fetch the villagers inside our walls. I am grateful for your bows. I shall send a rider to warn Barnard Castle."

Since John Balliol had been stripped of his crown the castle had a skeleton garrison but early warning would allow the townsfolk to get within its walls.

"And I will send a man to warn the Bishop of Durham and the Lord of Stockton Castle."

That night as we ate in the castle, we discussed our plans. "I would not be trapped in here, Constable, but I cannot abandon you. If he tries to besiege us then I will stay but if he heads north, south or east then I shall stay ahead of him."

John of Kirkby waved a hand, "We are surrounded by moors, my lord. Unless it suddenly snows then men on horses can easily outrun men on foot. This Roman Road is the only way an army laden with loot can travel."

I was reassured by his words. I had been charged with limiting the scope of Wallace's mischief. Thus far I had succeeded but one slip could lose King Edward the north.

The Scots arrived the next day at noon and their arrival coincided with the winter snow. It was not the sleet we had endured at Brougham, it was a blizzard. We were safe within the walls of Bowes but Wallace and his army were trapped outside. It was a storm that raged for the better part of two days and we had to keep a good watch on the walls as we could barely see fifty paces from the wall and had no idea what the Scots were doing. When the storm ceased and we looked to the west there was no sign of the Scottish army. It was as though the storm had swallowed them up. I did not think we were lucky enough for that to happen. I ordered my men to mount their horses for we had to find the

Wallace's War

Scots and I did not want to impose upon the good offices of the constable. We had eaten too many of his supplies as it was.

We found their trail half a mile from the castle. They were headed east and we were now behind them. What we needed was for us to get ahead of them so that we could warn whichever town or castle they chose to attack. It was clear to me that they were not going home. The shortest route would have been north from Carlisle to Galloway and the Wallace heartland. It soon became obvious that the worst of the snow had been to the north of us. The road to Durham was blocked and his army could not move there. That left three choices, York, Stockton, or Newcastle. Until we found the ravaged village of Middleton Tyas, we did not know where they were headed but their bloody trail was clear. They were going north. Stockton had been warned and Durham but not Newcastle. We did what we could for the survivors of the attack and it delayed our pursuit but we could not leave them without giving them some aid.

We were now a day behind the raiders but, being mounted, we could overtake them before they reached the Tees. We spied them as they forded the Tees and we just watched. Wallace had left a sizeable force of more than a hundred mounted men as a rearguard. I guessed he had as many with his vanguard. The horsemen waited on the south side of the ford as their bulky baggage train crossed the river. We waited patiently. We could have used our arrows to thin their numbers but little would have been gained. As soon as the horsemen left, we crossed and I took my men north and east towards Sadberge. If the Scots were headed for Stockton, then we would be ahead of them but I believed that the Tyne was their target. It was as we entered the village that we spied a rider heading west. It was Dick the rider I had sent to Durham and Stockton. He looked relieved to see us.

"I have delivered the message, my lord. It was lucky that I went to Durham first. The blizzard chased me all the way from Bowes and harried me on the road to Stockton. I had to spend two nights in Stockton but the constable is now prepared."

"And there is no sign of them closer to Stockton?"

"No, my lord."

I turned to my men, "Dismount and string your bows. If their vanguard comes this way, we will bloody their nose and then ride to Stockton. Mordaf, send to scouts down the road to give us warning of their approach."

When the scouts returned, two hours later it was with the news that the Scots were still heading north and east. Newcastle would be their likely target. It made sense for it was a royal castle and if it fell it would

Wallace's War

be a further insult to King Edward. If the castle was taken then only Bamburgh and Berwick would remain as King Edward's royal bastions in the north.

We had rested our horses and we still had two hours of daylight left. We reached the village of Segges Field before the Scots and were able to warn the villagers of the approaching horde. There was no castle and so they all packed their belongings in carts and drove their animals south to Thorpe and Grindon. We camped in the deserted village and waited. The land to the west was still thick with snow and another snow flurry in the night had hidden our tracks. Wallace was not heading for Durham. It was not because he did not want to but nature was against him and as Dick had discovered, an army could not pass along the snow-clogged roads. It was the ninth hour of the day when the Scottish vanguard appeared. This time I decided that we would engage them if only to give the folks from Segges Field more time to get to safety. We tethered our horses and then formed a single line across the road north. My men had good buskins but, even so, standing in the snow was not comfortable. The hot breakfast we had enjoyed had been invaluable but the sooner we could leave and head the twenty odd miles to Newcastle the better.

The Scottish horsemen saw and recognised us. There were more than I had expected, almost three hundred of them and they formed two lines. Wallace stood head and shoulders above the others and I saw that the handful of knights he had with him formed a ring around him. That told me that he was the clear leader of this rebellion and explained why so many men had stayed with him. The Scottish army was visible in the distance as they headed north through a white world.

"As before we give them ten arrows and then stop. I want them to think that we will flee. When they charge, we give a second flight of ten arrows and then we flee."

My men cheered. I hoped that the Scots would hear and fear the cheer. They would have expected my handful of men to run when they approached. They began their charge but Wallace had miscalculated. The thick snow slowed him more than he had expected. Some horses were clearly suffering from the conditions and the line was soon a ragged one rather than a continuous wall of steel. We released our arrows at two hundred and fifty paces and using our bodkins meant that every arrow that struck caused death or a wound. Holes appeared in their line and when we stopped, I saw that Wallace's horse had been hit and he was on the ground. The snow had given him a softer landing than he might have expected. Even at a range of one hundred and fifty paces, I heard his voice as he demanded another horse and he ordered his line to form again. I nodded and drew back my bow. Even before Wallace had mounted our arrows fell amongst stationary riders and we emptied even more saddles. We had done enough and I gave the order to mount. We had no need to rush as his vanguard was in tatters. We rode north at a steady pace and reached Newcastle by dark. The crossing of the river was well upstream from the castle and town. The old Roman Bridge had been allowed to fall into disrepair and the Scots would have to do as we were doing and approach the castle from the west and north.

The wall around the town had only been finished a few years earlier and it looked reassuringly solid. My name gained us admittance and as we passed through the west gate I warned, "There is a Scottish army heading here. We will inform the constable but it will be your eyes that will spy them. Have those who dwell beyond the walls seek the safety of the castle."

The men of Northumberland were dour men and did not fear the Scots. He nodded, "No fear, my lord, we have chased them from these walls each time they have come and I do not doubt that we shall do so again. Still, your archers will add to our defence, eh, my lord?"

Ever since Eustace de Vesci had led knights to capture King William of Scotland after one of his attempts to retake Northumberland, the castle had been a thorn in the Scottish side. Perhaps Wallace hoped to garner even more glory by taking it.

While Mordaf and Gwillim saw to the housing of the men I went with Hamo to speak to the constable. I did not know him but I learned that Geoffrey de Blaydon was a good warrior. Like his sentry, he was not put out by the news of the imminent arrival of a Scottish army. "We will order those who live to the north and east of our walls to enter as you did with those to the west. We have plenty of food in our granaries and the weather aids us. I am pleased to have you and your archers with us." I nodded. "Does the Bishop of Durham know the situation?"

"He does but as Durham is cut off by the snow, he can do little about it. We have to hold."

"And hold we shall."

I had the luxury of a bed and no need to stand a watch. I took advantage of both and slept longer than I had since Yarpole. Hamo had risen before me and just Jack waited to help me dress. "The ones who were outside the walls are now within, my lord and the Scots have been seen approaching from the north and the west."

"The river is still ours?"

"Aye, ferries can cross to the south and we can send messages hence. The constable has sent one to Stockton and a second to

Durham." I raised my head and Jack said, "If he cannot get through to Durham, he will return but he felt honour bound to tell the bishop that we were under attack."

I joined the others in the hall where we breakfasted. The bread ovens were far enough from the keep to remain in use and we enjoyed good bread. There is something about the smell of freshly baked bread that gives a man an appetite and we ate well. The constable allowed us to finish our butter-slathered bread and ham before he invited Hamo and me to join him on a walk around the defences.

Wrapped in my cloak we left the castle through a mighty barbican which had two towers that could hold off a determined attack. The castle was not old, as its name suggested and that meant its defences were the best. We headed to the west gate where two towers would allow my archers to rain arrows upon the attackers. When we reached the wall the constable pointed to the exterior base of the wall, "You cannot see it, Sir Gerald but there is a ditch and it is well maintained. The snow hides it."

"And that helps us although I think that our opponent is clever enough to find some way to cross the ditch. At Carlisle, they tried to build a ram."

"There are trees, my lord, further to the west."

I pointed to the black clouds in the skies above us, "The weather means that he will attack sooner rather than later. The supplies he took from the Tynedale will be almost consumed. There was little for him to take on his passage north. Middleton Tyas was the only place he managed to take food and his large army needs some feeding." I looked down the length of the wall. "Constable, I will place my archers here for this gate will, in all likelihood, be the place that they will attack. How many archers do you have?"

"Forty, my lord and forty crossbowmen."

I laughed, "You know how archers feel about crossbowmen, even friendly ones." He smiled and nodded, "Have the crossbows on the rest of the walls."

"My men at arms?"

"Will be of more use at the barbican and the curtain wall. If they breach the walls then the gate will need to be held long enough for the townsfolk to pass through. If I have the horn sounded five times then we need help to repel attackers. Use your own judgement to decide how many men to send. You must hold the castle and the keep." What I did not add was that if the walls fell then it would mean that all my archers were dead. "I will speak with my men. We will act as sentries. Hamo, divide them into three watches."

The men had also enjoyed a warm night and a good breakfast. They were ready to fight. Our flight north had not pleased them.

"Captain Mordaf will divide you into three watches. Mordaf and Gwillim will command two and my son and I the third. We divide the day into three. We know that Wallace has a clever mind and may well try to emulate our trick of a nighttime attack. While only one-third of us will be on the walls the rest will sleep with buskins on and bow cases to hand. When Hamo has divided the men, then you, Mordaf, will take the first watch. Hamo and I will take the night one."

Being a royal castle Newcastle had a good armoury and was well supplied with arrows. While my men marched to the west and north wall Hamo and I went with Gwillim to choose the best arrows for us to use. By noon a messenger had come from the north gate to tell us that the Scots had their siege lines in place and they could hear the sound of hammering. I went with the constable to the top of the keep to see the lines. The Scots stood out quite clearly against the snow-covered ground. Soon the snow would be turned to a muddy mush by the constant tramping of their feet. We could not see clearly enough to identify what they were building.

The constable said, "If they build a trebuchet then we are in trouble."

I laughed, "If they are building a trebuchet then they will not attack before Christmas and by then hunger will have defeated them. No, Constable, they are not siege engineers. The ram we destroyed at Carlisle was crudely built and little more than a covered log and badly made wheels. I think they are building ladders. When I was at the walls this morning, I did not see braziers to heat oil and water nor stones."

The constable nodded, "I was remiss. I will have both sent."

"Aye, but do not light the braziers yet."

"Will your men not need the warmth they provide?"

"They can stamp their feet. A brazier ruins night vision and draws men, even good ones, to them for warmth."

Hamo said, "You think it will be a night attack."

I nodded, "He knows how many archers we brought and will do all that he can to minimise the effect of our arrows. Night means we have to loosely blindly until they are close. They will advance with shields over them so that blindly loosed arrows will have little effect."

The Constable smiled, "And that is why you have taken the night watch."

"Aye and now I will enjoy a couple of hours of sleep."

Neither Mordaf nor Gwillim had to string their bows for the Scottish warriors were occupied at their camps. The news they did report was that a line of pavise shields had been erected so that they could not be observed from the walls. The pavise, I knew, would be used at night to allow the Scots to advance, unmolested. As the hammering had continued throughout the day then I guessed that they were using ladders. Gwillim took me down the fighting platform when we changed archers, "There are stones as well as oil. There is kindling to light the braziers. Mordaf sent men out when he arrived and they marked the range." He pointed to some cleared snow. It would disappear once the attack began but it served as a marker for my archers.

"Good, enjoy your sleep but be ready if you hear my horn sound."

Jack had taken the horn from the archer in Gwillim's company and it would be his task to sound it stridently three times if help was needed. After Gwillim had left I went along one wall and Hamo the other to ensure that our archers were spread out and knew what they were about. Four men were in each of the four towers that guarded the two gates. Hamo was one of the four at the north gate and I was one of the four at the west gate. That left just twelve men to walk the walls. The four towers rose above the walls and we would have the better view but if the Scots took out my archers on the walls, then we were in trouble.

I had long ago discovered that just sitting and watching was a recipe for disaster. The best way to watch was to move regularly. In my case it helped me as sitting for long periods did nothing for my knees which ached if I did not move them regularly. As I passed each archer, I spoke to him. It was partly to ensure they were awake but a more important reason was that it showed the archer that I, too, was enduring the watch. It was Peter Green Arrow who gave me warning of danger, "Sir Gerald, there was movement in the distance." He pointed to the west. "I am sure that the pavise shields are closer than they were."

"You have good eyes. Pass the word to string bows."

It was like a bat flying in the night as the sibilant sound of the command was passed left and right. I headed back to the tower and told the men there that danger was approaching.

"Do I sound the horn, Sir Gerald?"

"No, Jack, for it may just be that they are closing with the wall and may not plan an attack yet. If this is not the attack then we unstring the bows and our fellows enjoy undisturbed sleep."

With my bow strung I chose four arrows and held three of them in my left hand while I nocked the fourth. It was cold at the top of the tower. Rafe was the other archer in the tower with me and he had younger eyes. He hissed, "My lord, the pavise are moving."

Wallace's War

I stared and saw, eventually, what Peter and Rafe had both seen. The Scots were moving their shields closer to the wall. The black line in the snow marked the range for us. They were still forty paces shy of it. I was still unsure if this was an attack or if they were taking advantage of the darkness to get as close to our walls as they could. I turned to Jack, "Take a drink, Jack, and then if you have to sound the horn you will not have a dry mouth." It was more to give Jack something to do. I had smiled when he had strung his bow. Since he had come to my aid in the woods, he had strung his bow each time I had ordered my men to do so. He was becoming an archer. I remembered when Hamo had been his age. Hamo had enjoyed better food when he was younger and he had developed an archer's frame quickly but Jack was catching up. He would be a good archer.

It was the Scots themselves who precipitated the attack. They were within range of our bows and I knew that every one of my archers would be waiting for the command when the pavise stopped moving and the fifty or so crossbows poked over the top. I knew that my men would have seen the threat and the moment they heard the distinctive crack of a bolt being released then they would duck. Being on the top of the towers gave me a slight advantage. An archer could drop an arrow down but a crossbow had to be incredibly accurate if he was to hit one of the three of us. The snapping of the crossbows was like a ripple of stones hitting a wall. We dropped our heads and the bolts clattered against the walls and the wooden hoardings that protected the top.

"Sound the horn! Release when you have a target."

I stood and drew. They had archers too and Wallace must have mixed them with his crossbows so that while his crossbows were reloaded his archers could hit the sentries. I saw a face above the pavise and I sent my arrow toward it. The range was less than two hundred paces and even though I had seen more than forty summers as an archer I had not lost my skill. I hit the Scottish archer a heartbeat before he had reached full draw and the arrow and bow fell from lifeless hands. Jack had picked up his bow and he joined Rafe and me as we sent our arrows, not blindly, but carefully whenever we saw a target. As my other archers joined us so the number of missiles increased. The result was that some of the Scots were hit by two or even three arrows. It mattered not for we had plenty of arrows. Three more archers climbed up the ladder to the top of the tower.

A Scottish horn sounded and the pavise began to march forward. The garrison archers had also joined us and we had the walls fully manned. The Scots were taking casualties but fewer, the closer they came to the walls. The reason was simple. Their archers and crossbowmen were not risking death. They were getting as close as they could to the walls. They stopped just shy of where the ditch lay beneath its covering of snow. When a Scottish horn sounded again, I knew that something was going to happen.

Rafe shouted, "My lord, more men with shields."

I saw the second line of huge wooden shields appear in the distance. I knew what it meant. They had ladders and were about to attack the walls. The Scottish archers and crossbowmen rose as one and sent their missiles at us. We were ready and in the deadly duel we came off better. Wallace had sacrificed fifty or so men so that his men carrying ladders could get closer without impairment. When the double wall of pavise and shields stopped the duel ended, albeit briefly.

I shouted, "They will use ladders. Use the stones to break them."

If the ladders were shattered then they would have to make new ones. All of that would take time and I knew that the Scots could not endure a long siege. I estimated that we had sent twenty arrows apiece at the enemy. Soon we would have to change strings but I was loath to do so yet. The Scots must have been given a spoken command for the pavise and shield wall suddenly opened and the archers and crossbowmen who remained sent another flight of bolts and arrows at us as men ran with ladders towards the wall. I estimated that there were more than thirty ladders, each one carried by four men. Behind came mailed men. Until we switched to bodkins then they would be safe. One ladder collapsed when the men carrying it were all slain while another fell when the men tripped into the ditch. Others, however, were pushed against the wall. It had cost the Scots and the bodies of the brave men carrying them were a testament to their courage.

"Jack, sound the horn five times. We need aid."

I selected a bodkin and sent it into the body of the mailed man holding a shield above his head as he ascended the ladder to my right. His shield protected most of him but his leg was exposed and my bodkin drove through his chaussee and threw him into the ditch. I put down my bow and picked up a large stone. I threw it at the exposed ladder. It did not break it but the loud crack told me that it was damaged and that was confirmed when the next mailed man who tried to ascend fell as the ladder broke.

There were now four men in the tower and I said, "Rafe, take command. Jack come with me and we will assess the damage." I descended the ladder and saw that we had taken casualties. Two of my archers were at the base of the wall having their wounds tended to. Three of the garrison archers lay dead, their bodies covered by cloaks. Some of my archers were doing as I had done and were hurling rocks to break the ladders. The wisdom of building a wall eight paces high was now clearly to be seen. The ladders that the Scots were using could not cope with the weight of mailed men and were breaking under the weight.

Jack had quick reactions and, twenty paces from our tower he raised his bow and sent an arrow into the face of the mailed man about to clamber over the battlements. It was a war arrow he used but that was sufficient and the man fell. By the time we reached the North Gate, I could see that our walls were holding and the men at arms and spearmen led by the constable were already climbing to the fighting platform.

Hamo turned and grinned when I arrived, "Persistent aren't they?"

I nodded, "And the night is not yet half over. I believe he will attack until dawn. How are you for arrows?"

"We have plenty." He pointed, "But they are bringing fire."

We saw the burning brands in the distance. They were more of a glow and that suggested that they were protected by shields. The brands became visible only when they had to cross an obstacle. "They mean to burn the gates. I will head back to my gate."

As I hurried back down the fighting platform I said, to the archers I passed, "Keep up the arrows and try to hit the men bearing fire."

The constable was at the West Gate. On my journey along the wall, I had ascertained that the main attack was on the West Gate. While Wallace might send kindling and fire to both gates, he would send his best men to our gate. "They mean to burn the gates, constable."

He nodded, "I have the townsfolk using water to damp them." One advantage of the castle was the proximity to the river. Water was not in short supply.

The Scots had been making many shields and pavise. A wall of them walked towards the ditch. The ladders which had fallen had made a crude bridge over the ditch. There were bodies in the ditch and that too would make life easier when they tried to cross it. So long as the Scots advanced behind the shields then we could do nothing. The weak parts of the defences of the two gates were the two bridges over the ditches. They were needed to allow easy access during times of peace but now they were a weakness. I laid down my bow and picked up a huge rock as the pavise neared the bridge. I hurled it as a bolt flew over my right shoulder. It hit a pavise and the man holding it tumbled. As he did so he was exposed and Rafe killed him. The constable and his men emulated me and they too hurled stones. I picked up my bow and as the stones shattered the shell-like shields the men carrying the kindling and brands were easier targets for my archers. When the brands hissed into the ditch to splutter and die, the handful of survivors headed back to their own lines. I looked towards the North Gate. I did not see flames. Hamo had held.

Dawn was just an hour or so away when the Scottish horn sounded and Wallace called off his first attack. He had failed but he would have learned from his failure. Already he would be planning a second attack.

Chapter 9

We left just the garrison archers and spearmen to watch the Scots while we went for food. The townsfolk cheered us as we marched back to the castle. "Mordaf, assess the wounded archers. If they cannot draw a bow, they can stay in the castle to defend its walls."

"They will not like that, my lord."

"I care not. I will not risk losing a valuable archer."

Jack said, somewhat optimistically, "The Scots lost many men today, my lord."

Mordaf grunted, "Not enough. Still, we winnowed their archers and crossbowmen." Like me, Mordaf knew that if we eliminated those who sent arrows and bolts then we had a chance of withstanding a sustained attack.

Food had been prepared and after a night in the cold allied to the drawing of the bow meant we were ravenous. We ate in the hall assigned to the garrison and I shouted, as my archers ate and spoke of each arrow they had released, "Those who had the night shift and the afternoon watch can sleep. The day watch can sleep at noon."

Hamo asked, "Do you think they will come again this night?"

Shaking my head I said, "I doubt it. Just as we need food and rest so will they but Wallace will be chafing at the bit. He will be planning something to catch us off guard. I am guessing that he will try again at dawn on the morrow. By then he will have made new ladders and this time they will be stronger. If he has any sense, he will have pots filled with fire and use those to hurl at the gates. It is a safer and more reliable method." I sensed that some of my men were low in spirits at the thought of night after night of attacks and raised my voice so that they could all hear my words. "It is my belief, Hamo, that we will have to endure but a few more days before he gives up. He will not have enough food to feed his army and the last thing he needs is for his army to bleed away in dribs and drabs. He will seek a victory of some sort before he returns to Scotland."

The constable had decided to use the townsfolk on Newcastle's walls. My archers added experience but the constable, quite rightly, thought that it would make Wallace think we had more warriors than we had. It also was good that they defended their own homes. My men were too full of the battle to sleep and I sat with them while they spoke of arrows that had killed and others that had wounded. They shared the techniques they had used. We had rarely had to defend castle walls and it was not the same as sending arrows on an open battlefield. It was noon before I retired, along with Hamo and Jack, in our tower chamber. The keep was spacious and the constable had offered me his bed chamber. I had, of course, refused and taken instead a chamber in one of the smaller towers at the corner of the keep. We were disturbed by men going on duty as they climbed the spiral staircase outside our door but that was a small price to pay for a cosy chamber.

I suppose I was woken by my bladder and I rose to use the garderobe. Hamo and Jack slept blissfully on. After opening the shutter I peered out of the arrow slit and, spying the moon, estimated that it was close to eleven. We would be roused at midnight. I would stay up as I knew I would not enjoy an hour of sleep. We had slept well already and I hurried to use the garderobe in the corner. The others needed to be woken soon as we were due on duty by midnight and it would not do for the leader and his son to be late.

I shook Hamo and then Jack, "Wake, it is late." Lowering my hose I sat on the wood over the garderobe.

Seeing that the garderobe was in use my son and Jack left the chamber to ascend to the top of the tower and use the ones intended for the sentries. I heard their feet on the stone as they climbed. There they could relieve themselves but I had a relatively cosy chamber while they would have to endure the cold of a December night. When I had finished and cleaned myself, I donned my buskins, put on my brigandine and fastened my baldric around my waist. It was then I heard feet thundering down the stone staircase.

The door opened and Hamo said, "The Scots have used the river. They have climbed the curtain wall."

"Jack, sound the horn."

I was dressed while the other two needed to arm themselves. Placing a helmet on my head, I ran along the corridor shouting, "Alarm!" as Jack sounded the horn continuously. The constable was not in his chamber. I ran to the small gate that led to the curtain wall and fighting platform. As I opened it, I saw the body of the sentry and a pair of Scottish warriors walking purposefully toward me with swords in their hands. I drew my dagger and blocked the door with my body. Behind them, I saw more Scottish warriors but the only way into the keep on this side was through my gate. The constable and the rest of the defenders needed time to get into position. There would be fifty or more of my archers rushing to the walls not to mention the men at arms and spearmen. I needed to buy them time.

Wallace had discovered that I was a skilful swordsman and his two men were about to be given the same lesson. One took a small hatchet from his belt while the other drew a dirk. They each wanted two weapons. The advantage I had was that to my left were the crenulations of the curtain wall. The Scot there could not swing his sword in any other direction than down. The other would be swinging at me with his dirk. Stepping onto my right foot I swung my sword in a wide arc while raising my dagger to block the sword strike of the other. It was not needed as he swung too low and his sword scraped and scratched along the stone battlements. The one on my right was bringing his sword down from above when my sword sliced into his right arm and struck the bone. His dirk fell from his hand and the sword did not connect. I drew my blade back and ripped through an artery. The blood spurted and dropping his sword he used his right hand to try to stem the bleeding. His companion was splattered with blood and I lunged with my dagger to tear into his throat.

Behind me, I heard the door open and I whipped around. It was Hamo and Jack. Hamo said, "The guards from the tower have gone along the other fighting platform." He looked down at the bodies for the wounded warrior had already fallen. "I see you have been busy."

Nodding, I pointed with my sword to the bailey where I could see my archers flooding from the keep, "Our archers are down there. We will clear this walkway and ensure that no others are climbing up."

As we moved down the platform, we saw men falling from the fighting platform ahead, struck by arrows. The ones who survived were heading for the corner tower. There they would be protected from the arrows of my men and they could reach the sally port. If they could open another gate then the hordes of Scotsman I knew were waiting could pour in. The sounds of fighting from the west told me that they were assaulting the West Gate. As I glanced down the walls to the river below, I saw Wallace's plan. In the short time he had been there he must have observed our routines and knew that one shift of men was coming to the end of their duty. By attacking when he did, he hoped to catch sentries unawares. The use of the river was clever as an army could not attack there but determined men could scale the walls and open the gates from within. These Scots were not as skilful as the assassins who had so nearly ended the life of The Lord Edward in Acre but they did not need to be. The crossbow bolt in the head of the dead sentry told me how they had almost succeeded. With just four men in the towers on the keep and one patrolling each section of the wall the odds were in Scottish favour.

I saw that more men were climbing the ropes that had been attached to the battlements by the ones who had first ascended. "Cut the ropes and then use the rocks."

While Hamo and Jack ran ahead I used the hatchet from the dead Scot to chop through the nearest rope. The man who was halfway up fell screaming to his death. I picked up one of the rocks that lay neatly piled along the wall and dropped it. Although it was pitch black beneath me, I was lucky and rewarded by a cry of pain. Although the fighting platform was now unguarded, I knew that the Scots would not be able to exploit it. Running down the platform I worked out that they had used agile men to climb, like spiders, the stone walls of the castle. It would not be easy but I knew there were men who could do that. The ropes they carried would then enable less skilled men to ascend. By the time I reached the tower all eight ropes had been severed on the castle walls that faced the river.

"I will lead." Hamo looked as though he was ready to argue with me when I gave the command, "I have fought in castles before and there is a skill to it."

The spiral staircase was so built as to give the advantage to a defender. Descending with my sword held before me I went down the stairs that were lit by just two brands, one at the top and one at the bottom. We made sounds as we moved down and one of the Scots must have decided to stop the pursuit. As I turned a corner, I saw him waiting for me. Had he lunged at my legs with a straight thrust he might have hit me but he forgot about the stone to his right. His blade made sparks in the dark as it hit while my sword found flesh and his body tumbled down to the guard room at the bottom. We could hear shouts from both the guard room and the bailey beyond. As we reached the guard room the five survivors of the attack were taking shelter from the open door. Seeing us, three of them ran at us. One made the mistake of passing the open door and he never reached us as an arrow sent from the bailey slammed into him. I blocked the Scottish sword with my sword and drove my dagger up under the ribs of the warrior. Hamo's opponent was using both weapons. This was no place for honour or fairness and I slit the man's throat with my sword. Even as the other two risked the deadly passage past the open door, arrows flew through the opening and they fell.

I shouted, for the benefit of my archers who were loosing arrows at shadows in the dark, "It is Sir Gerald. All inside are dead."

William of Ware shouted, "Come then, my lord, the rest of the attackers lie dead."

We emerged into the bailey and I saw that there were thirty or so Scots dead and already the off-duty garrison warriors were ensuring that the Scots were dead. It had been known for them to play dead.

"My archers, come with me to the walls. The rest of you, check the dead and man the walls." It was just twenty-three paces from the keep to the gate and I shouted, as I neared the gate, "Open it and when my archers and I are through close it."

"Yes, my lord."

Hamo and I had no bows but that mattered not. There were stones we could throw. I saw the dead and wounded defenders lying in the lee of the north wall. We ascended the wall and found the constable.

"They almost caught us out. Had I not been walking the walls before retiring I might not have seen them sneaking along in the dark." He looked beyond me, "The keep?"

"Is ours, my son and Jack saw men on the fighting platform and your men have secured it." I looked along the wall and saw smoke rising.

The constable said, "Aye, they tried to fire the gates. We have just doused the flames here but the West Gate…"

"We will deal with that." I turned to the men with me, "Archers, spread yourselves out. Dick, bring ten with my son and me."

We ran along the fighting platform and passed archers who were releasing arrows as fast as they could. The spearmen and men at arms from the garrison were hurling darts and dropping rocks. The smoke from the gatehouse was thick and that suggested that the damp wood was slowing down the fire. Upon reaching the gate I saw how they had managed to start the fire. They had not made a ram but they made a shelter using animal hides and that had allowed them to get close to the gate and start the fire.

Gwillim shook his head, "Sorry, my lord. There was a mist and it allowed them to bring the shelter for the fire. It has almost taken hold."

"Jack, I spied a grappling hook in the other gatehouse. Fetch it." He ran off. "Gwillim, you and the archers keep the gate clear of Scots. Hamo, find spearmen. Let us drop rocks onto the shelter."

"It looks well made, father."

I snarled, "Then let us just stand here and do nothing, eh?" I picked up the largest rock I could see and, ignoring the bolts which flew in my direction, hurled it to crash onto the roof of the shelter which protected the men feeding the fire.

"Sorry, father. You men, grab rocks and do as Sir Gerald commands."

Although my rock did not break the roof it weakened it and as the other stones fell the weakness became a split and when Hamo dropped a huge stone it broke and revealed the men beneath. The range was less than eight paces and my already angry archers did not miss. I could see the kindling amidst their bodies.

Jack returned with the grappling hook. Whirling it around my head I threw it into the shelter and then commanded, "Now pull it into the ditch." My men grabbed the rope and we walked backwards together, pulling the ram with us. The bodies within made it awkward to move but eventually, it was cleared and we could see the fire that they had started. The next part would be harder. The falling ram had torn the grappling hook and roped free. I coiled the rope and leaned out between two of the crenulations. Bolts cracked into the wall and an arrow hit my helmet.

Gwillim shouted, "Kill those Scots!"

I swung the rope back and forth, lowering it a little more each time. I would have to time this well. I caught the fire on a back swing and then shouted, "Hamo, pull!"

The two of us managed to pull the bulk of the fire and it landed on the ram, kindling and bodies. The flames began to lick up the walls. Newcastle would have blackened walls but the gate would be safe. "Throw water on the embers by the gate." The spearmen obeyed and I stared at the Scottish lines.

"Gwillim, have the archers release in volleys. Let us make life hard for those waiting to attack. The fire below will deter a further attack here."

"Aye, my lord."

The fire had melted all the snow and it would be a muddy morass that the Scots had to cross. As the fire on the gate was doused the smoke from the burning shelter began to drift down the wall. The wind was a swirling one and it took the stench of burning flesh back towards the Scots. They continued attacking for another half hour or so but when I heard the Scottish horns, I knew that we had defeated the attack. As dawn broke we saw the bodies that the Scots had not managed to recover.

I took off my helmet, "We were lucky Hamo. They almost succeeded."

He nodded, "It was Jack who saw them. He did not use the garderobe but stood to pee into the river."

I ruffled his hair, "Jack of Malton, it was a good day when Sir John asked me to watch over you and raise you as an archer. You are a lucky charm."

By the time the sun had fully risen a pair of Scottish knights approached under a flag of truce, "We would speak with the commander of the castle."

Wallace's War

I sent Jack for the constable and said, "Until the constable arrives you may speak with me, Sir Gerald Warbow."

The looks they exchanged told me that they had heard of me. "We would recover our dead for burial."

I nodded and pointed to the ditch, "I fear that many will be unrecognisable but why should I show you such mercy? You attacked Middleton Tyas and many other places on your way here. What is our motivation?"

The older of the two said, "We go home. The siege is over and, to be truthful, Sir Gerald, you are spoken of as an honourable man."

The constable arrived and I said, loudly enough for the two Scots to hear, "They would take their dead and depart hence. What say you?"

"Aye."

I nodded, "But tell Wallace that I will follow you with my archers as far as the border. If you so much as take one fowl from a farmer then we will rain death upon you."

"Fear not, we would be home and enjoy Christmas with our families."

"Then gather your dead."

They left the next day and my men and I trailed them all the way to the Tweed. They crossed by Jedburgh and my warning had been dire enough that they obeyed and took nothing. Their passage was marked by the graves they dug for wounded who fell on the cold march north. Men succumbed to wounds or the cold. Newcastle had dented Wallace's ambition but he had enough men with him to suggest that he would be back and as he and his rebel army controlled Scotland, we would have to await the arrival of the king. Until then our work was done.

At the Tweed, we waited until the last Scottish warrior crossed into what had been Scotland until the battle of Dunbar. It was far enough for us to turn around. The last four showed their derision by baring their buttocks at us. The same act had angered King Edward at Dunbar but I just smiled. I was about to order the men to turn and head south when Jack said, "Sir Gerald, it is Wallace."

I saw the Scottish giant riding the horse that he made look like a pony towards the edge of the river. He wished to speak. Some of my men took out their bow cases. "Peace, he means to talk."

Wallace wore no helmet and his long sword hung from his saddle. He shook his head, "Are you ever destined to be my Nemesis, Warbow? Your king does not deserve your service, you know. He allows you and your men to suffer the privations of winter while he enjoys the pleasures of the Flanders court."

Wallace's War

That told me a couple of things. He had good intelligence about King Edward's movements but he did not know the king. King Edward had many faults but he was not dallying at the court of the Count of Flanders.

"Wallace, you are a brigand and a bandit. That your warband has grown does not change that. You do not seek to free Scotland from English rule for the Battle of Stirling Bridge achieved that. Your raid along the Tyndale tells me what you are, a bandit and a brigand. Enjoy the little time you have left for when the king comes, and come he will, then your temporary victory will evaporate like morning mist."

I could see that my words had hit home for he became angry and stood in his saddle. His horse looked like it was ready to collapse, "Know this, Warbow, when you come north with your king then look for me on the battlefield for I shall look for you and these insults will be answered."

"Good, for I shall not hide."

I whirled my horse's head around and having had the last word, led my men back to Newcastle. Pulling the cowl of my cloak above my head and watching my mount's breath vaporise before him I thought about Wallace's words. In one respect he was right. King Edward did not deserve the army he led. I thought about the army slaughtered at Stirling Bridge. The lords, the knights, and even the clerics would all have their names remembered. If I had been there and fallen then, as a knight, my death would have been recorded. The spearmen, and for me, more importantly, the archers, would have no grave and the only marker for their passing would be that their families would have lost the man who brought coins into their homes. I knew that many archers with whom I had served would lie dead, probably unburied. I would not know who they were until the army was mustered again. Perhaps, even then, I would not know who they were. My father had been an archer who had been abandoned when he was too old to go to war and he had been killed by a tyrant. That was the difference between King Edward and me. There was a huge gap between us in terms of class and social standing but we were both good warriors. That was not the real disparity between us but our natures. I cared for every archer who served me. Every man who raised a weapon in my defence was important. To King Edward, they were pawns to be used. If they died then he would not have to pay for their service and he would hire new men. When my men fell, I provided for their families. Wallace was a brigand and a bandit but I suspected that he too would mourn the death of his men. King Edward would not.

I turned to Hamo, "We have done what the Earl of Surrey asked us and more. We have relieved the siege of Carlisle and driven Wallace home. We will visit with Bishop Bek and then return home to Yarpole. We may not make it in time for Christmas but we will try. Tell the men."

As the word was passed down the column, their cheers told me their approval. I smiled and that small act made me happier and more content.

Chapter 10

The road to Durham was now open and when we reached the castle Bishop Bek fully understood my reasons, "You have helped to save both the Palatinate and Northumberland. The constable sent a rider to tell me that the threat had gone and he was fulsome in his praise of you." I nodded. "You will be with King Edward when he returns from Flanders?" His voice was almost pleading.

I smiled, "I have ever heeded my king's commands. I shall be here with my mounted archers but you should know, Bishop Bek, that there were no desertions from the Scots as they retreated."

The bishop was a soldier and knew what I meant. A retreating army haemorrhaged men. Wallace's had not. He sighed, "Aye, I have heard that the man inspires loyalty but I cannot understand why.

The bishop was a noble and I was not. I explained, "Wallace is not of noble blood. To the men he draws to him he is one of them. he puts himself at the fore of the fighting while their lords, men like de Brus, can change sides and benefit from the changing of sides. I think Wallace is a man to be feared and when he summons men to fight King Edward, it will be an even larger army. I believe that with King Edward leading us we can win but it will take every man that the north and the king can muster." The bishop nodded, "I know I was commissioned to stay until the spring but we both know that the threat from Scotland has now gone. Have I your permission to return to Yarpole?"

"Of course."

"Then I shall see you again when the king comes and we end this war."

It took seven days of hard riding to reach Yarpole. We were lucky that the snow was confined to the north. The pass at Stainmore was open and by the time we reached Craven the weather was just cold and the air filled with wintery sleet and rain. It was not comfortable but we were not slowed on our journey home. That my family was both surprised and pleased to see me was an understatement. We arrived at my hall on Christmas Eve and that seemed appropriate somehow. After a hug from my wife which threatened to crush the air from my lungs, she and her women began to add to the food they were preparing for the Christmas feast. The men who had been left behind to watch my home had used their patrols to hunt in my woods. A deer was fetched from the larder to augment the ducks that had been readied. More vegetables were brought from the store and prepared. None of the food would be wasted. My wife knew that it was better to prepare too much than have too little. By the twelfth night, all the food would have been consumed and we would not need to venture beyond the wall around my home. I was content.

That night, as she lay in my arms, she asked me about the campaign. Mary was not an ordinary wife. She had lived at the Mongol court and served Queen Eleanor. She understood that war was sometimes necessary. Our wild ride to Acre had shown her my abilities and she had an informed mind. I told her all.

It was dark and I could not see her face but I knew that she smiled when she said, "And I am pleased that Jack is growing so much. He endured a harder life than he should with Sir John and your kind act has reaped a fine harvest."

"Aye, Hamo is my son and of my blood but Jack feels like he is a younger son. I have tried to be as a father to him."

She paused and her next words told me that she had been thinking about this matter for some time, "We should adopt him."

"What?"

"We should make him part of this family so that when you die, he will be protected in law. Hamo, Margaret and Joan will not mind. They are all fond of him."

"But when I die, all will pass to you."

She was silent for a moment, "I am aware, Gerald, of my own mortality. When you were away, Agnes, the wife of Ralph the Fletcher succumbed to the winter sickness. I am not of this land and was brought up in a warmer clime. I am not a fool and know that each spring that I see may be my last. Let us adopt him and then write your will. I do not believe that God has you marked for death yet but your profession is one which is parlous, to say the least. Do this for me."

I leaned over and kissed her, "I love you so much and while your words score wounds that you cannot see, you are right and I will do as you say."

"Thank you."

"You know that if I asked the king, he would give me a manor in Gascony? There the climate is more suited to a longer life than the borders are."

"This is our home and our people. I am content. Fate threw us together and I will not abandon Yarpole. We will stay here on the Welsh borders and see if I have lived a good enough life for God to allow me to see Joan have children."

I had not had much to do with clerics and so I consulted my son-in-law Richard of Launceston. I chose a pleasant, although chilly morning to ride to Launceston. My daughter had been the one who had alerted me to Jack's predicament when she had stayed in Malton and when I explained what I needed she was enthusiastic. I dangled my grandson on my knee as Richard took me through what I would need to do.

"I have a clerk who works for me, Henry, who is studying to be a lawyer and I will send him to you. All that you need to do is tell him what you wish and he will put it into legal language. He will return here and write the will out properly so that you and Lady Mary can sign it." I nodded and he added, "I think that this is wise Sir Gerald. Your profession is one that is riddled with danger and I have seen first-hand how war can pluck one man from a saddle and leave another whole. You have been lucky thus far."

My daughter clucked, "Richard! My father came for advice not so that you could give such dire warnings."

I smiled and handed my grandson to her. He had made an alarming noise from his rear end and I knew not what to do, "Your husband is right, Margaret. I have been lucky and men have stood alongside me and died. As Richard knows a man must do all that he can to protect his family in this life and do the same if he can when he is in a better place. You know that your sister has set her eyes on a young man?"

She smiled as she began to unwrap Gerald's clothes. The smell that rose told me that my decision to hand him over had been a wise one. "She told me when last I visited. You should know, father, that she is not struck by some romantic thought; she does love the young man. As I know from Richard, such things are possible. I knew that I would wed Richard from the moment I saw him and she knows so too. However, I will be happier when we get to meet him. I trust my sister's judgement but…"

I nodded. My elder daughter was like her mother and wise. My grandson was in good hands.

We did not tell Jack what we intended straight away. I wanted to save that news until after the document was prepared. I did tell Hamo, Alice and Joan for Jack would be given land that they had a claim to. As I expected he was more than happy for us to do so. I told my son and his wife first.

"I know why you do this, father, and your reasons are understandable but you have many years ahead of you. I have no doubt that King Edward will reward you for your services and that your lands will grow but even if they do not you have two manors, Luston and Yarpole. Either would suit your heirs."

Alice came from the Eden valley and knew little of lords and titles. She asked, innocently, "What of Margaret and Joan? Will they not have a claim upon your lands?"

I nodded, "I can see your confusion, Alice. Margaret needs not my lands, for her husband has his own and he is a rich man. As for Joan, I will make provision for her until she weds but it will be in the form of money. She will be well taken care of and when your child is born both he and Gerald will not be forgotten."

Hamo put his arm around his wife who was blossoming with her unborn child, "And when I am head of this family, wife, I shall take care of my sisters should anything untoward happen to their husbands." He smiled, "Whoever they are." Alice nodded, "And your brothers too, whilst still not yet youths will be given land and money when they are old enough. My father has taught us well."

I knew then that Mary and I had brought our son up well. Sadness pricked me as I thought of my dead son, Richard. He would have become just as fine a young man as his elder brother. As I stood my hand went to my cross and I said a prayer in my head for my dead son.

Henry came and the studious young man with the inky fingers took me patiently through what I ought to say in my will. Mary sat with us and offered advice. By the end of the morning, he was satisfied that he knew my intentions. "I have other work to do for my master but I will return in a week with the completed document. How many copies would you like, my lord?"

"Just two will do. I will keep one and the other can be lodged at my son-in-law's."

My second grandson, James, was born two days after Henry's departure. He was healthy and had a fine set of lungs on him. "We were going to name him Gerald, father, after you," Hamo shook his head, "but then we realised that you already have another grandson called Gerald and we know how confused you get with names."

The others in the chamber, Jack, James, John, Mary and Joan all laughed. I often shouted John when I meant Jack or Jack when I meant Hamo. I nodded, "Aye, I am an old man who needs others to watch out for him."

Mary kissed me, "But we love you anyway."

Hamo smiled, "Anyway James was the name of Alice's father so all is well."

Joan was beaming, "And he is beautiful. Tell me, brother, that I shall be his godmother."

Alice answered as my grandson greedily sucked at her breast, "Of course, Joan, and we would have Jack as godfather."

It was the first time that Jack began to realise that he did not just serve me. He was part of the family. I knew that when I told him of the will, he would fully realise that he was secure, here in Yarpole.

Wallace's War

The will was returned in the first week of February and it was then we heard that Stirling Castle had finally fallen to the Scots. Wallace had made his own victory. Perhaps he had learned from his encounters with us at Carlisle and Newcastle but whatever the reason there were now no English-held castles of any size left in Scotland. I put that thought from my mind as I gathered my family in my hall for the signing of the will. Alice's brothers were there too. Although I had not named either in the will, they were part of our family and deserved to hear all. The parish priest Father Michael attended as did Mordaf. They would witness the document. That Mordaf was proud of my decision was clear for he came to my hall dressed in his finest clothes.

"Lady Mary and I have decided that we need a will," I smiled, "I need a will. Know that all those who live on my lands will receive monies when I die. We have been prudent and there is gold and silver enough for all. The two most important parts relate to the manors of Yarpole and Luston. The king will have to approve the will."

Hamo said, "Not Baron Mortimer?"

I smiled, "I believe that King Edward outranks the baron and when he returns, God willing it shall be soon, then I will ask for his approval." I wanted nothing to stand in the way of my decisions and using the king seemed the best way to do so. "You, Hamo, will inherit Yarpole and Jack of Malton, who will now be known as Jack of Luston, will inherit Luston." We all smiled as the affable young man's jaw dropped. He was speechless. Although rapidly approaching my size he ran to me and buried his face in my chest. I put my left arm around him and I saw Mary's eyes well with tears. Mordaf nodded his approval and that meant much to me.

We celebrated and the joy that my words brought to all made me wonder why I had not done so before. That it was a popular decision with my men was clear. Jack was as much their stepson as he was mine. Now that he was one of my heirs Mary had clothes made for him which showed his new status.

Life was good and as the weather began to improve so my men and I threw ourselves into the hard work that resulted in good archers. Alice's two brothers were now old enough to begin training but more importantly, one day they would come to war and that necessitated their learning what they had to do. Jack showed his increasing maturity by giving them all the advice he could. He showed them how to saddle horses, tether horses, and ride leading a string of animals. He told them how they would be expected when we fought to fetch bundles of arrows. He showed them how to change an arrowhead from barbed tip to bodkin. He did all of this happily not only because of his new status but because Mordaf, when we had our practice in early March, told him that as he could now hit the furthest mark, he could join my archers. Hamo had been the same and Jack knew that despite the fact that one day he would be master of Luston, until I died he would still be an archer who would be ordered around by vintenars and centenars. It had made Hamo the good leader he had become.

I did not recognise the rider who entered my manor in the third week of March but Joan did. She had been helping my wife and the women to fold the sheets that had been washed and dried in the windy yard. She squealed with delight and then, as my wife gave her a glare, covered her mouth. He was a smartly dressed young man and wore the livery of King Edward. He was a pursuivant.

He dismounted and gave a slight bow, "My lord, I am Ralph Fitzalan and I have been sent here by King Edward." He handed me a sealed parchment. "This is for you, my lord."

This was the young man whom Joan had set her heart upon. Now I understood the squeal. I did not open the letter but stared at the young man, "And is it a coincidence that the young man who wishes to court my daughter should arrive dressed as a pursuivant?"

He blushed and gabbled, "My lord, I am he but the reason I was sent was that my brother John has been knighted by the king and serves as one of his household knights. He told the king that I know this land and mentioned my interest in your daughter. The king…" his voice trailed off and I could not help but smile. Many people only saw the hard king that was King Edward. I had seen the romantic king. That had been the effect of his wife, Queen Eleanor.

I nodded, "Just so. Then when I have read the letter you and I shall talk. For now, you should stable your horse. I daresay that you will require a room for the night?"

He looked embarrassed, "My lord, the king asked me to stay with you and your men." He nodded towards the letter, "If you read the letter, my lord, then all will be revealed."

I sat alone to read the letter. When I had visited Richard of Launceston, I had heard of the Earl of Surrey's march north to relive both Roxburgh and Berwick. I had also heard that the bulk of his army had been released from service. King Edward's letter was, in effect, a summons of service. It promised payment for service for me and one hundred archers. As I read that I frowned. It meant we would be taking all but a handful of my men to fight far from Yarpole. It also hinted that there would be more than ten thousand Welshmen or border archers and spearmen joining the king. However, while they were to join the king at Roxburgh by way of Carlisle, I was to meet him at York and I had to be in that city by the middle of May. That was some consolation. It gave me more than a month to ensure that my family was well prepared. The king concluded by asking that I take Ralph Fitzalan under my wing, so that he could be used to communicate with King Edward. I hoped he would not be placed in as great a danger as had his predecessor, Geoffrey of Wendover. Then I realised that my success in Flanders and the pursuivant's success had led to the king asking me to do the same for Ralph. The romantic side of King Edward must have also had a bearing. He was acting as a matchmaker. The letter had given me a great deal of information but I knew that Ralph could supply more. I went to my door and shouted, "Hamo, Jack, find the pursuivant and fetch him hither. Steward, wine for four!"

I heard the acknowledgements and prepared myself for chastisement from Mary later on. She hated when I bellowed commands. I had changed in many ways since Mary had married me but when war was on the horizon, I always reverted to being Gerald Warbow, Captain of Archers.

A servant brought in four goblets and a large jug of wine. John, my steward, knew me well. A second servant brought in a ham, a round of cheese and fresh bread. A pot of butter was also there as well as hot, freshly made mustard. The two of them arranged the chairs so that we could all reach the refreshments and talk. John had trained them well.

Ralph Fitzalan arrived first and looked unsure of what to do, "Sit and pour the wine."

"Yes, my lord."

It was on the tip of my tongue to ask him to call me Gerald when something told me to keep the formality for now. Jack and Hamo arrived and their ease was in direct contrast to the man who would be Joan's husband.

Hamo grinned, "Ham and cheese, John is a fine steward, father."

"Aye and he knows what I like." I stood and sliced some ham before smearing butter on a hunk of bread and then, after putting the ham on the bread, liberally covering the ham with the mustard. I took the goblet that Ralph had filled and sat. My son and stepson emulated me and the three of us sat and began to eat. Ralph stood with a goblet of wine in his hand. I cocked an eye at him, "Are you not hungry or do you not like such simple fare?"

"No, my lord, I was waiting …"

Hamo laughed and a few flecks of ham flew from his mouth, "That does not do around here, Ralph. Take food and then sit. You look like the spectre at the feast."

Wallace's War

Ralph did as he was bid as Jack nodded to the letter which still lay on the table, "The king needs us?"

I swallowed and, after drinking wine said, "Aye, as we knew he would. While the rest of the archers will march to Carlisle, as we are mounted the king wants us with him. We meet him in May at York and then accompany him to the muster at Roxburgh." I glanced at Ralph who had now taken food and was eating it. I would save my questions until after he had eaten. "Do not worry, this will not be a horse-killing ride. The muster at Roxburgh is not until midsummer. We ride with the knights. From what I can gather there are more than two thousand of them."

Hamo's eyes widened, "That is more than the king had in Flanders."

"Aye, well it is easier to send a summons of service for wars within these lands than abroad. If things do not go well then knights can always get home quicker than if they were across the sea."

Ralph could not help himself, "My lord, is that fair? Would knights abandon the king?"

I could not help but nod, "In a heartbeat, Fitzalan. How many knights were killed at Stirling Bridge and how many archers and spearmen?"

He shook his head, "I know not."

"Less than one hundred knights fell yet five thousand English foot soldiers perished." I could see from his face that he had not realised that. "So, pursuivant, who is with the king? His letter did not name them but you must know their names."

"Yes, my lord. There are eleven earls in the army including Sir Roger, the Earl Marshal. Bishop Bek will lead one battle and we shall muster with him at Durham."

I nodded to Hamo, "The king, it seems, is now taking the Scots seriously. The ten thousand Welshmen who march to join us will be a hard enemy for Wallace to defeat."

"That is true but it means that we will be away once more and this time we will all miss the harvest."

"In that case, the women and children will have to work harder." I turned to Ralph, "And is there any other news you can give us?"

"My lord, the king said that if I impressed during this campaign there might be spurs for me."

I leaned forward. Kings and nobles often tempted young men with the lure of knighthood, "Do not be reckless. My daughter is fond of you and I would not have you try to win the war and get yourself killed. Spurs are not a reason to throw your life away."

"But the king knighted you, my lord, did he not?"

"He did but I had to wait many years and the knighthood did not change me."

I saw the sceptical look on his face and Jack said, "Sir Gerald is right and if you ask any of the archers, they will confirm that Gerald Warbow is the same man he always has been."

"You two, when you have eaten, can tell Mordaf and Gwillim our orders. We have time and it will allow those who are married," I glanced at Ralph, "or who wish to be married, to put their affairs in order."

Hamo shoved a large piece of ham in his mouth and emptied his goblet, "Come, Jack, we have much to do."

As they left Ralph asked, "Much to do, my lord?"

I nodded and drank some more of my wine, "Aye, for many of the archers live a few miles away. Each of my archers has a small holding either in Yarpole or Luston. It will take some hours for the two of them to visit with them all." Putting my goblet on the table I folded my arms and leaned back in the chair. "And now, Ralph Fitzalan, what is it that you wish to ask me?"

I was deliberately intimidating him. If he wished to marry my daughter then he had to earn that right; I watched him summon up the courage to speak and he sat straighter in the chair, "Joan and I love each other and would be wed."

"And have you acted honourably?"

He stiffened in his chair, "My lord, I find that question offensive. Of course, I have."

I hid my smile. I knew my daughter and my wife. When he had visited before there would have been no time for anything dishonourable to have taken place. "And so you wish to wed?"

"Yes, my lord."

"You know that even if, and I emphasise, if, I agree to the marriage as you are now his pursuivant then you need the approval of the king as well as that of your eldest brother, the Earl of Arundel."

He nodded, "I know but I need your approval first."

It was a good answer and I warmed to the youth, "And what are your prospects?"

"Prospects, my lord?"

I sighed and refilled my goblet, "Ralph, you serve the king. If he makes you a knight then you may well do as your brother does and serve him. Is that how you see your future?"

I could see that he had not thought of that. Shaking his head he said, "I do not think so.

"Then have you land?"

"There is a small manor, left to me by my mother, Shawbury. It is tiny with just a church a one-storey hall and five farms. It provides me with an income."

I closed my eyes as I tried to picture a map of the area. "It is a few miles northeast of Shrewsbury?"

"It is, my lord."

"And therefore close to the Welsh Marches."

"My mother was, as you know, Sir Gerald, vigilant in her role as Lady of Clun and Oswestry. Shrewsbury is a strong castle."

I waved a hand, "We know the dangers of living so close to the Welsh, Ralph, but what I need to know is how my daughter would be protected if you were called away to war, supposing that you win your spurs."

"As yet, I have neither men at arms nor archers but, when I am knighted then I will hire such men."

I had made my decision sometime earlier and I now decided to put him out of his misery for I could see that he was sweating profusely and clearly nervous.

"Then I give to you, my approval. When you are knighted and have hired men then you may marry my daughter."

The joy that filled his face was dashed when he realised that his knighthood might be months or even years away. My eyes bored into his and he eventually nodded, "Thank you, my lord. Might I be given permission to tell Joan?"

"So long as her mother is close by then aye."

He left and I finished the bread and the wine. John entered, "All done, my lord, or would you like more wine?"

"No, John, you may clear the table. I am guessing that Lady Mary has a feast planned and you will need to organise the room."

"Yes, my lord."

"Then I shall leave you to it."

I heard the squeal of joy from the sitting room where Joan and her mother were sewing. Mary would be happy. I went out to the yard and headed for the stables. Most of my archers kept their horses at their homes but we had the sumpters and the rest of the horses at my stables. William was the man who looked after my horses. Had we been a grand castle then he might have been called the horse master. We did not bother with such titles.

"William, you should know that we go to war with the Scots in midsummer. How stands our stock of horses?"

He rubbed his beard and shook his head, "You will need a new mount, my lord. The winter did little for Caesar. He is an old horse already. He has a heart as big as any but I know that you need a horse that can be relied upon. That is no longer Caesar."

I nodded for I knew that he was right. I did not need a war horse but I needed a horse that could carry me and my mail and would be fast enough to get me out of trouble. "Then have you a replacement?"

"Brutus was sired by Caesar. He is four years old and while that is a little young I have schooled him well. When do you leave, Sir Gerald?"

By the middle of May."

"Then if you ride him every day the bond should be made and you can decide for yourself if I have done my work as well as I think I have."

I smiled, "I do not doubt that you have for you are too modest. Saddle him now and I will enjoy a ride in the afternoon."

Brutus looked so similar to Caesar that they could have been twins. The main difference was the blaze. Caesar had none but Brutus did. I took to him straight away. I did not push him, as I rode but tried to get to know him. He had, indeed, been schooled well and responded to my knees, the shift of weight and my hands almost as though he was reading my mind. I knew that was William's skill. I enjoyed the ride so much that it was late afternoon when I arrived back in my yard and I saw my wife watching anxiously for me.

I dismounted and handed the reins to William, "You have schooled him well, William. He is perfect."

"Thank you, my lord." He led the horse away and Mary approached, "You were away a long time, husband."

"And you missed me, how touching."

She laughed, "No but as you are no longer a young man, I feared you might have fallen from your horse, especially as he is a new one. You shouldn't ride alone."

I snorted, "The day I fall from a horse, any horse, is the day I cease riding." I kissed her on the forehead, "So Ralph told you the news?"

She nodded, "Joan wants the wedding sooner rather than later but when I pointed out that you were quite right and that the king's permission was needed, she calmed down. It will be hard for them, Gerald."

"And we had it easy?"

She laughed, "No we did not but you would not wish to inflict that upon our daughter, would you?"

I leaned in and said in her ear, "The campaign will be over before All Saints and I will speak to the king. They can be wed before Christmas but do not tell her that."

She took my arm and, as we entered the hall said, "And you are the best of fathers."

Wallace's War

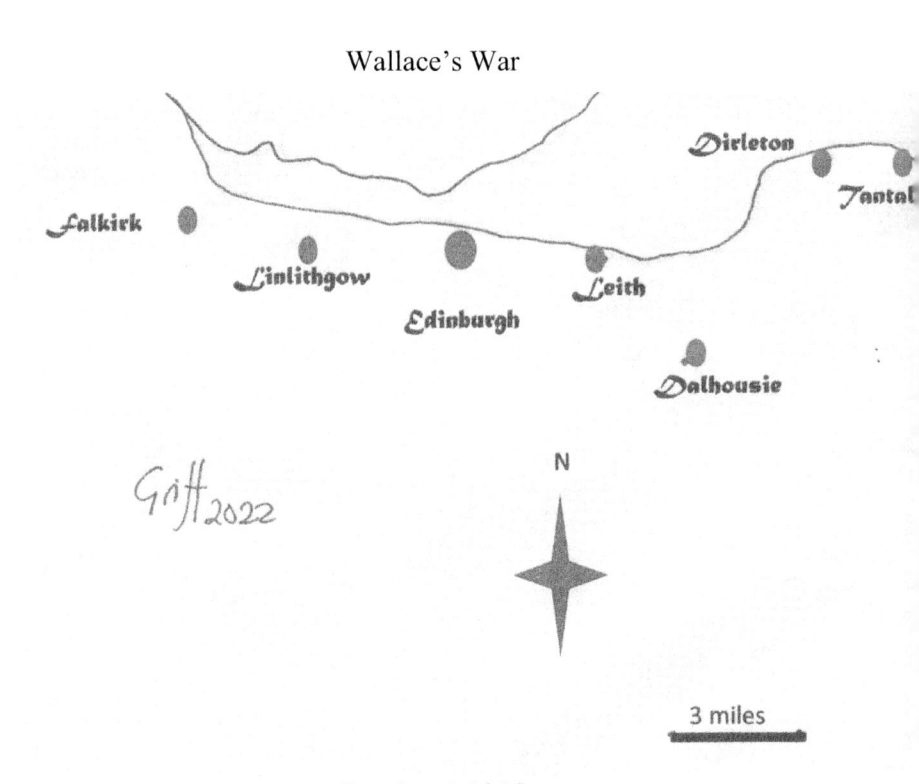

Falkirk Dirleton Tantal
Linlithgow Leith
Edinburgh
Dalhousie

Griff 2022

N

3 miles

Scotland 1298

Chapter 11

We left for York on the third day of May. We were well mounted and we took just five days to cover the one hundred and seventy miles. We could have done it in four but we had no need to thrash our horses and, besides, it suited our journey for we had royal castles we could use along the way. It meant we reached York relatively fresh. The sheriff found accommodation for our men while Ralph, Jack, Hamo and I were accommodated in the King's Tower. James and John would have to stay with my archers. I knew that Mordaf would watch over them. Already the other archers had taken to Alice's little brothers. When I asked the castellan if we would have to move out when the king arrived, I was told that the king's hall was in the bailey and was more comfortable for the king. He smiled, "King Henry found his tower at the top of the motte a little tiring for him. He did not like the stairs."

It suited us and although we had to share a room it was a well-apportioned one. The castle was a strongly made one. That had been the work of King Edward's father. With a moat around the King's Tower and the rivers that ran around the castle, it was almost impregnable. Allied to the Roman walls which still ran around the city, York was a bastion against incursions from the north. Even better was the fact that it could be kept supplied by sea. As it was a port there were many goods available in their markets and my men took advantage of the situation. They went to buy those things that they might not find at home. The married men, especially, bought Whitby jet for the stone was much prized. Others bought amber jewellery from the Baltic. I bought nothing for I knew that when this war was over, we would have to pass through York again.

What I did do was to go with Ralph, Hamo and Jack to walk part of the walls and then to pray at the Minster. Mary's words that night, when she had first asked me to write a will had weighed heavily on me. I wondered if there was some illness that she was concealing. I remembered the death of Queen Eleanor. She had seemed hale and hearty yet her last weeks had seen her become almost a walking skeleton. I prayed for Mary first and lit a candle. I also prayed, as all warriors do, that we would emerge whole from this campaign. Death was always a possibility as many archers and spearmen had discovered at Stirling Bridge and so warriors devoutly prayed whenever they could. York Minster was a magnificent edifice and I felt sure that God would be more likely to look kindly upon my prayers in such a monument to His greatness.

Wallace's War

King Edward and his household knights arrived on the 26th of May. The constable had ensured that the new King's Hall was well prepared for the royal visitor. He had also laid in supplies of food for a feast having been prepared for the king's arrival by messengers. I made myself available for him and Ralph, as his pursuivant, went to greet the king as soon as he arrived. My future son-in-law soon returned, "The King would see you, Sir Gerald. He would meet you on the barbican at the river gate."

The barbican was almost like a keep and was one of the strongest I had ever seen. Looking out of the river it afforded a good view of the town. I reached it before he did. The sentries had come to know us in the time we had been at the castle and they moved to the side when I told them that the king approached. I had left Hamo and Jack with the rest of our men for King Edward was always precise in his instructions. He had said he wished to speak to me and that meant I would be alone. He came with Ralph and a knight whose face was so similar to Ralph's that he could only be his brother.

The king smiled, "It is good to see you again Warbow. You two stand on the other side of the tower and take the sentries with you. I would have words with Warbow in private." He nodded to Ralph, "Fear not Fitzalan, I will come to your request in the fullness of time." When we were alone, he led me to the corner of the tower. We were young men no longer and we both pulled our cloaks tighter. "It is always cold up here."

I nodded, "And the land of the Scots even more so, my lord."

"Aye. Thank you for what you did at Carlisle and Newcastle. That you left earlier than you might, was understandable." I took the gentile chastisement with a nod. "You were right about this Wallace, it seems. You know that he has been made Guardian of Scotland?"

"I had heard a rumour."

"That means the Scots accept him as a leader. I confess that when his name first came up, I thought him merely a brigand."

"And that he might be, my lord." I knew then that the king and those who advised him thought that a man who was not noble-born did not pose a real threat.

"He has been knighted." I had heard that too. "We muster at Durham at Midsummer. My intention is to first relieve Roxburgh and Berwick and then bring this Scottish rabble to battle. This time we shall choose the battleground and I will bring so many men that I crush the rebellion and snuff out the last sparks of opposition to our rule. You and your mounted archers, when we cross the Tweed, will become our eyes and ears. It is clear you have the measure of this giant and I would use that knowledge to our advantage."

Shaking my head I said, "He is clever, my lord, and being, as I am, lowly born, perhaps his mind works in a different way. I have been lucky thus far."

"Then let us use that luck."

"And when the threat is gone, my lord, what then?" I knew King Edward's mind. He would want Scotland firmly in his grasp. I did not mind being away from my family to end the threat to England's borders but I did not relish a long campaign.

"When Wallace is dead and Scotland is once more under my control then the campaign will be over." He was shrewd, "I know why you ask, Warbow. I am using Parliament's money to pay for men like Captal de Busch and his Gascon mercenaries not to mention the Welsh. I know that some will criticise me for using mercenaries but the losses at Stirling Bridge leave me with little choice. When I no longer need you and your archers you may return to Yarpole. Is that good enough?"

I smiled, "It is, my lord."

Shaking his head he said, "You are allowed liberties that I give to no other man!" He too smiled, "Eleanor always said you were the best man in the land and you have yet to let me down. You annoy me at times but I know that I can rely on you." He turned and gestured to the Fitzalan brothers. They came towards us. "Their mother was a rock against the Welsh, you know, and I was sad when she died. What think you of Ralph?"

"He seems earnest, my lord and my daughter loves him. Such matters are important."

His smile was sadder as he said, "Aye, I know that for I was lucky as were you. Let us see if we can make life easier for him."

"I hope, however, that he does not do something reckless and foolish to earn the spurs."

The king just nodded.

The two brothers reached us and stood expectantly waiting. The king looked from one to the other.

Sir John Fitzalan said, "My lord?"

"Ralph, when you were at Windsor and your brother was knighted, I promised you the chance of spurs."

"Yes, my lord, and I heeded your words. I will do all that I can to earn them."

"Hmn, when I said earn them, I did not mean by some ridiculously brave act such as taking an enemy standard, I meant by showing the sort of courage your mother showed when she kept the Welsh Marches safe." I saw the look of surprise on both their faces. "Warbow and I have seen bravery on the battlefield and also the courage of women who did not fight but had to show great courage." The two brothers knew not how to react and I suspect only I truly understood his words. "When we have brought the Scots to battle and, I pray to God, defeated them, then you shall have your spurs. To that end, the manor of Woofferton, to the north of Yarpole is now vacant. The lord of the manor foolishly chose to side with the de Montfort brothers rather than siring children and when he died it was left to the crown. It is not a rich manor but is safer than the one you inherited which lies closer to the Welsh. When you are knighted then it will be yours."

Ralph's face lit up, "My lord, I am speechless."

"Good for I am being more than generous in memory of your mother and you, Warbow, shall have the manor of Ashton which also belonged to the unfortunate lord of Woofferton. It is time you were better rewarded. Heaven knows you have done more for England than some who have received greater gifts. Tomorrow, we ride to Beverley to collect the standard of St John of Beverley. Warbow you and your son shall accompany us."

As he was in such a good mood, I chose to bring up Jack. "King Edward there is a boon I would ask."

"Another?"

"I took under my wing, some time ago, a boy, Jack of Malton. He is close to my wife and I and has become a stepson of sorts. I would have him join Hamo as my heir. I have written my will and left him the manor of Luston. Have I your permission to do so?"

He laughed, "Another commoner with a manor?" I nodded. "Then if he is half as loyal as you, he will be a great lord. You have my permission. Have a copy of the will sent to Windsor. Now let us go indoors and eat for this wind is a lazy one." I saw Sir John frown and the king smiled, "It cannot be bothered to go around a man and cuts right through him." He laughed at his own joke and I could see that he was in good spirits. I was pleased for since the death of Queen Eleanor he had been more inclined to frown rather than smile. Perhaps the kind acts of which his late wife would have approved made him happier or more content, at least.

Hamo, Jack and I looked plain next to the peacocks of the king's retinue. That none looked down on us was simple enough. They all knew of my reputation and that I had served the king since he had been but a youth. They might not yet know of our skill on the battlefield but knowing that the king did was enough. Ralph looked splendid in his pursuivant livery. He spent most of the journey just listening. Hamo,

Jack and I had ridden together so often that there was an easy manner to us that he was not part of.

Hamo asked, "Why do we seek this standard, father? I have never heard of St John of Beverley."

We were not far from Malton and Jack answered for me, "St John was Bishop of York in the time that the Vikings raided. He was a friend of the great Bede. Archbishop Thurstan had a banner made and he carried it in battle at the Battle of the Standards when the Scots came more than a century ago." I smiled at his words.

Hamo was dumbfounded, "How do you know all of that, Jack?"

Jack waved a hand, "I grew up around here and the Scots were always seen as a threat. The story of how an ancient archbishop used the standards of John of Beverley and St Cuthbert to defeat the Scots is often told around fires in the middle of winter."

I had heard the tales and I said, "And I think embellished. The thought of an old archbishop riding a war horse and carrying a standard into battle may be a slight exaggeration."

Jack looked hurt, "But the archbishop led the army at the Battle of the Standards, Sir Gerald."

I nodded, "But it was a knight who commanded the men and made the military decisions. When we fight the Scots, I do not think that King Edward will be at the fore with St John's standard in his hand. It will be held, perhaps, by your brother, Ralph, but it will not be placed in danger. The household knights are not with us to go into battle but to protect the king and his standards."

Ralph asked, "Then who will do the fighting?" He shook his head, "I have never been in battle and while I have read and heard of battles, I do not know the reality."

I nodded to Hamo who said, "The knights who will meet with us at Durham will be the ones who fight sword to sword with the Scots. From what I heard the Earl of Surrey made the mistake at Stirling Bridge of trying to defeat the Scots using spearmen and archers. From what my father has told me that combination of arms can work but Stirling was not the place to try it. King Edward will try to bring the Scots to battle where we, the archers, can thin their ranks and then the horsemen can try to drive their knights from the field."

I saw Ralph as he processed that information, "Then the Scots, if they have any sense, will choose somewhere that we cannot do that."

"As they did at Stirling Bridge. King Edward, Ralph, is a better leader than the old earl. John de Warenne will be on the battlefield and lead his own battle but the plan will be King Edward's."

Wallace's War

"You know him well, Sir Gerald. I could tell that from our conversation yesterday."

"I was with him in Gascony when his father took me on and I was known as Lord Edward's archer. Some men still call me that and for me is a nobler title than Sir Gerald for a man cannot change his heart. I am an archer as is Hamo and as is, I hope, Jack. You, Ralph, will be a knight. Do not try to change that. Your mother's blood has royal connections. My family had common blood. We are content."

After we had collected the standard we returned to York.

We left York for Durham a couple of days later. James and John had become proficient riders and they had made themselves useful. When we stopped, they held the reins of our horses and were happy to fetch and carry when we rested. With their short swords and dirks in their belts, they felt like warriors. I would ensure that no harm came to them. When we fought, and I knew that we would, then they would stay with the horses.

We passed through Wilton, Kirkham and stopped at Northallerton where the king visited the site of the Battle of the Standards. Such was the fame of the battle that a stone had been erected. As we ate in the Great Hall of the fortified palace Jack told us the story of the Battle of the Standards and how, with three holy banners a small English force had destroyed the army of King David of Scotland, chasing his son, the Prince of Cumberland, all the way back to Carlisle which was then held by the Scots.

Hamo nodded, "Then I can see why we came here. King Edward is doing all that he can to bring the past to life."

I nodded, "The standard of St Wilfred of Ripon was brought here so that the king can take it." I waved my hand at the tapestries on the wall. "King Henry the Second built this palace after the Scots destroyed the old town. Northallerton stands as a reminder to the Scots that even when they had success, we still stopped them."

We reached Durham on the 12th of June and the other horsemen of the retinues of the earls and bannerets were there already, camped outside the city walls. The northern knights under Prince Bishop Bek had arrived as had the Earl of Surrey and his battle. A messenger arrived to tell us that the Earl of Lincoln would arrive within a day or so bringing the last of the knights. We were seated at a lowly table and I was surprised that we had been invited for not every banneret had been chosen to dine with the king. King Edward and Prince Bishop Bek had arranged troubadours and musicians to entertain us with songs and tales about battles past. All of them, of course, told of victories against the

Scots. It was too soon for one to have been composed about Dunbar but, no doubt, the king was planning for one to be written.

It was while we were there that Baron Mortimer arrived. Sir Edmund did not like me. I think he resented me for many reasons. I was not noble born, I had been given a rich manor and his parents had been as fond of me as though I was a member of their family. When the king was in earshot he was politeness personified but when he caught me with no witness save my family he was vitriolic, "I know not why the king allows you to rub shoulders with those men who are destined to rule this land." He turned to Ralph, "And you, cuz, disappoint me. You can do better in marriage than the daughter of an archer."

I had been willing to endure personal insults but not those aimed at my family, "Have a care, Sir Edmund. If you insult my family again then my gauntlet will be out and we shall see if this rough archer can wield a sword. What say you?"

There was a heavy threat in my voice and I saw the fear in his eyes. I had a reputation as a fighter and as he stared at me he saw, seemingly for the first time, my frame. He shook his head, "A man cannot have a civilised conversation with the likes of you. Luckily I shall be with the knights when we go to war and I will not have to endure your company." He turned and left.

Ralph looked on in disbelief, "But, Sir Gerald, the king speaks to you as a friend."

I nodded, "And that is why many lords dislike me so. He listens to me. So, Ralph, do you still wish to join my family?"

He grinned, "More than ever!"

We now had an army of almost fifteen thousand men and the majority, the retinues of the lords, were on foot. It would have made for painfully slow progress to Newcastle had not the king planned for this and sent the foot soldiers directly to Roxburgh where they would join the Welsh contingent. The mounted men reached Newcastle on the 20th of June. While the army camped on the moor to the north of the town I went with the king, prince bishop, the earls, Captal de Buch and Henry de Beaumont into the town to meet with the constable and gather the latest intelligence. My plain attire marked me out and I was recognised. There were cheers for the king as we passed through the West Gate. I was embarrassed when the cheers for me, coming behind the others, was as loud if not louder. I saw the king turn and his scowl turned to a shake of the head as he realised the cheers were for me. The Novocastrians recognised my service to the town and castle. Baron Mortimer was also close to the king and the scowl he gave me made the cheers seem sweeter.

As we entered the castle, I also spied Geoffrey of Wendover. He was still a pursuivant and while we waited for our turn to enter, I spoke to him, "You still serve the king, I see."

"Yes, my lord but thanks to you and your men I think I am a better warrior than I was."

"And the wound?"

"Healed. I have shown it to a doctor and he asked me which surgeon had tended to the wound. He was surprised that it was an archer."

"My men often campaign far from the main camp. We know how to tend to wounds." It was almost my turn to enter and I said, "Be careful when we reach Scotland. If you thought Flanders was dangerous then Scotland is more so."

"I will, my lord."

The feast was not a grand affair for it was more of a council of war. The constable had not been idle and he had all the information to hand. "The Scots are still besieging Roxburgh and Berwick, King Edward. I have no doubt that the arrival of the men on foot will make them relive their siege." He nodded to me, "Sir Gerald there showed what archers could to Scots in siege camps."

"And where is Wallace, the Guardian of Scotland?"

"He is in the forests close to Selkirk where he is busy raising an army."

I saw the king give me a shrewd look, "Then he is using his past skills once more." He nodded. "It will take the men on foot some time to get to Roxburgh, Bishop Bek I would have you lead the cavalry to Roxburgh. I will stay here with my household knights. I will follow but at a more leisurely pace."

Only the Earl of Surrey was older than the king and me. I knew that campaigning was not as easy as when we had been younger.

He pointed to me, "Warbow, when you reach Roxburgh take some of your archers and find the Scottish army. You and your men know Wallace and work well in woods. I would know his numbers."

I gave a half bow, "Of course, King Edward."

"I know that we are a large army and I doubt that the land can keep us supplied. I have arranged for ships to come first to here and thence to Berwick and to wait close to Edinburgh at Leith. We shall be better supplied than the Scots and we shall have a victory."

They were confident words and when we rode north, to Alnwick, there was a cheerful air amongst the knights who headed up the road once trod by Roman legions. What my men were not happy about was serving alongside both the Welsh who were even more of an enemy to my men than the Scots and the crossbowmen who rode with the Earl of Surrey. Like us, fifty of them were mounted and, as we rode north there was banter between the two sets of missile-armed horsemen.

I rode next to Gwillim and Mordaf, "I know that there is banter and I am happy with that but warn the men that there will be no violence, no matter what the provocation and when we join the Welsh the same will still apply."

Mordaf shook his head, "It will be hard, my lord, for such enmity runs deep."

"I have spoken and you will make it so."

I knew that they would both obey me. It was not just my men who held such views of the Welsh. The recent bitter wars had left their mark and whilst we all respected their skills, especially with the bows there was still deep mistrust.

"We will be operating in Selkirk Forest. I want the best twenty archers to be part of our scouting party. We have to find the Scots. I will lead."

Mordaf was brave enough to beard me about my inclusion, "Is that wise, my lord? Your son could lead."

I growled, "Aye, he could but I will lead. I am not yet in my dotage and I am the one who fought Wallace. I know his mind better than my son and, Mordaf, I am still the most experienced archer in this whole army. Think about that."

"Yes, my lord, no offence intended."

"If there was, Mordaf, you would now be riding as a guard for the baggage train." I knew, even as the words came out of my mouth that I was treating him the way King Edward treated me. He was right to question me but I knew that once I allowed Hamo to do something that I normally did then I would never go to war again. While that had a certain appeal, I was not sure I could sit in Yarpole knowing that my son was taking the risks that were mine to endure.

Word reached us long before we arrived at Roxburgh that those besieging had fled west, confirming that the forest of Selkirk was the muster point for the Scots. We also learned that Wallace was being draconian in his recruitment. Men were not asked to join; they were commanded and that gave me hope that the resolve of the Scots might not be the same as it had been at Stirling Bridge. The rebels were safe in the forest. Knights would lose the battle if the king attempted to oust them. Wallace was clever. He threatened the king but he was safe from attack.

The land through which we passed was empty. The Scots had retreated before us, probably to Selkirk and they had taken every scrap

Wallace's War

of food that was left to them. We had to rely on paying for food at the religious houses along the way and the food was not cheap. It had cost the king almost two hundred pounds to buy from the prior of Coldstream for £50 of corn, 497 ewes with lambs and 100 sheep. We had eaten well that night but since then the army lived off beans that they found in the fields and unripe oats and barley. Until we reached the port of Leith, we would have to tighten our belts. My men were luckier than most. My archers foraged and hunted. We augmented our poor rations with rabbits, squirrels and one joyful night an old, lamed hind. We deprived the wolves of an easy meal.

It was when we reached Dalhousie that the king sent me off to find Wallace. My instructions were clear. I was to find out numbers and that was all. He knew that while he was in Selkirk Forest we could not attack but he needed to know what size of an army he was facing. Leaving Hamo in charge and with an unhappy Jack also left behind I went with Mordaf and nineteen others towards the vastness of Selkirk Forest. The king would be moving west of Edinburgh, the better to threaten Stirling. Dalhousie had been ravaged of both the grazing and any food that might be consumed.

King Edward was right and my men and I worked well in forests and woods. Even if we had never been to one before we knew how to look for the signs and the paths. It was second nature to us. Even so, we were careful. We used two men, one on each flank, some hundred paces from us, and they ensured that we were not surprised from the side. It was a dangerous commission and we had two men in the line constantly watching to make certain that they were still there. It took half a day to find the path that was trodden most frequently and when we did find it, we stopped and made our own camp. As before, at Carlisle, it would be a fireless camp but this was summer. The nights were long and the days, for this part of the world, were warm. We could endure a couple of nights of discomfort to find the information that the king needed. My fear was for the two boys, James and John. It would be harder to protect them in this environment. For the boys, it would be just one grand adventure. That was why I had left them with the rest of the archers. There would come a time when they would join us in the forest but that would be with the whole of the company.

The Ware brothers had proved to be good scouts and the next morning I set them off, on foot, to find the Scottish camp. The large amount of horse dung we had found on the main path suggested that their camp was close. While they were away my men hunted. There were two reasons for this. One was to feed our own men but the other was to deny the Scots food for their army. I was the one left to watch the horses and guard the camp. As I sat, alone, I remembered when I had been a young archer and given the same sort of task. It did me no harm to have to endure such a menial task.

The hunters brought a good harvest and the animals were skinned, gutted and hung from trees to keep them away from foxes and rats. William and Edward returned later than I expected, an hour before dusk.

"Was there trouble?"

"No, my lord. We found the camp quickly. More men marched into the camp and Edward and I simply followed them. We did not have our bows with us and they thought that we were volunteers. We were cheered."

My men had taken a risk but their safe return told me that it had been justified.

Edward took up the story, "We were fed. It was a hunter's stew, thickened with oats. While we ate, we were able to see the layout of the camp. It is huge, my lord. The lords have tents but there seemed to us that they were a tiny part of the army. The bulk seemed to be common folk like us. Most of the men we saw seemed to use a long spear and men armed as we, in different encampments."

Mordaf asked, "Did they not question your accents?"

William grinned, "We did not need to speak. None asked us anything and we kept apart. We played the part of miserable men."

"Tomorrow, I shall accompany you to the camp for I need more accurate numbers than simply that the camp is huge."

William looked concerned, "My lord, I do not think that we can repeat the trick. We slipped away when evening approached and men went into the woods to make water. Someone will notice when we do not return."

"I know, William, and we will not try to repeat anything. We will hide in the woods. You know how the camp is laid out. Can you find somewhere for me to observe and to count?"

William smiled, "Aye, my lord. We were told where to empty our bowels. Wallace, it seems, is organised. They move the place each day. It is like the spokes on a wheel. The men avoid the areas that they have already used. If you do not mind the smell, we can hide close to the camp and know that none will come close."

Edward added, with a wry smile, "You just need to watch where you step."

We were less than three miles from the Scottish camp but I took the decision to use our horses and bring all my men. Mordaf and the rest of the archers would wait half a mile from the camp. If things went awry,

Wallace's War

we would have just half a mile to run. Mordaf would have archers with strung bows and nocked arrows ready to cover us.

The brothers were right and we picked a precarious path through piles of human dung which William said was three days old. It stank. We reached a wall of brambles that were already beginning to ripen. They hid us but still afforded us a fine view of the camp. I began to count. I worked out, from William's words that the bulk of the men were armed with the long spear. They were easy to count. Many were already stacked while others were being used. I counted the spears. I guessed the number of swordsmen based on that number. William had been right, there were few lords. His horsemen numbered just over a thousand. I counted the horses and also the standards on the tents for like English lords, knights were precious about their colours. There were banners but not many; I guessed that less than half were knights. Wallace, the Guardian of Scotland, was using warriors rather than the fickle nobles. From what I knew of Scottish politics that was wise. The nobles, men such as Balliol and de Brus, had shown themselves to be self-serving and willing to change sides if they saw a rival advanced. We had to move to another dung heap and I was not able to guarantee that I had counted every warrior but I had a clearer number than before. We had seen enough and we went back to our horses. We were lucky and no one saw us.

As we mounted Mordaf said to the four men with strung bows, "You four keep the strings on your bows and ride ahead as scouts."

He rode next to me and, as we headed towards the east he said, "How many men, my lord?"

"A thousand horsemen and perhaps nine or ten thousand men on foot. The king outnumbers them."

Mordaf nodded and waved a hand at the trees, "But Wallace is safe in this natural fortress of trees is he not?"

"You are right but at least we know where he is to be found."

We were almost out of the forest when a Scottish lord and his retinue appeared ahead of us. There looked to be eight horsemen and twenty or so men armed with the long spears that they trailed over their shoulders. Mordaf's orders saved us for our men were able to react more quickly. The four archers at the front dismounted and took cover to the side of the path where they sent arrows at the Scots whilst shouting a warning for us. This was the time for decisive action. "Draw swords and charge them!"

While my four archers sent arrow after arrow at the Scottish warriors, we charged down the centre of the path. As soon as we passed them the archers mounted and, slinging their bows over their shoulders, they followed us. The twelve arrows they had released had two effects. They had emptied a couple of saddles and driven the others to take cover. Had the men with the spears had the wit then they could have formed a hedgehog of spears and made us go into the trees where there was a likelihood of us coming to grief but the lord had been one of those unhorsed and there was none to give a command. We used our swords to carve our way through them. The men with spears, seeing horses coming at them, took to the trees and we passed through them. I glanced over my shoulders and saw that we were all safe. None of my men had come to any harm. The harm was that the Scots would know English archers had been in the forest and probably knew their location. Wallace was not a fool and as I had discovered in the forests of Galloway, he knew his way around trees and he would simply shift his camp.

The king was pleased that he now knew the numbers of his enemy but disappointed that we had been seen. His rebuke to me was a baleful glare.

"If they are in the forest then we cannot hurt them, yet. We will need to prompt Wallace to leave his lair. I need him to be diverted." He rubbed his chin and then his eyes lit up with what I knew would be a plan. "As we cannot attack Wallace and his rag-tag army, I can use you and your men to go with Bishop Bek. He and the Sheriff of North Durham, Sir John Marmaduke will take the castles of Dirleton and Tantallon as well as any others that lie along the coast. If you wait here then you can go with the bishop and begin to plan what you will do."

The two men arrived and the king gave the same bald instructions he had given to me. Bishop Bek did not look happy. He shook his head, "King Edward, our men have eaten nothing but peas and beans for many days. They are starving and we have no siege engines."

I knew it was the wrong thing to say but I sympathised with the bishop. The taking of castles was not easy.

The king erupted, "Be off, use all your cruelty, and instead of rebuking you I shall praise you. Take care that you don't see me until the castles are burnt." We were summarily dismissed and our orders were confirmed. "I will make a camp at Linlithgow. Join me there when you have obeyed your orders."

The bishop, his facing burned red with embarrassment and anger stormed ahead of Sir John and me. "My men are attached to your battles, my lord."

Sir John smiled, "And that will please the bishop when he is calmer. We shall leave on the morrow and if we had the rations then the bishop would invite you to dine with him."

I smiled, "Then if you and the bishop will eat with us, we might have a more substantial fare."

The knight cocked an eye and then smiled, "I heard you are a resourceful fellow. We will come to your camp."

Mordaf had already begun the cooking of the animals we had hunted. It was an eclectic mix but that always made for a more interesting stew. I gave him our orders, "We are to go north to Dirleton and take some castles in East Lothian. The bishop and the sheriff will dine with us."

"I will have the men find somewhere for them to sit."

Hamo, Jack and Ralph joined me. I told them what we had discovered and then the king's new command. Hamo nodded, "This is not going well for King Edward, Father. The ships he expected have not yet reached Leith and the men are hungry. There is an angry mood in the camps, especially the Welsh one." I knew that the king and his earls would be well supplied, Normally King Edward was a master of supply and his men never went hungry. The failure this time might result in another defeat and if that happened then Wallace would rule Scotland and the unthinkable would happen. The king would be defeated.

Wallace's War

Chapter 12

The bishop was in a better mood when, the next day, we rode for the first of the castles, Dirleton. He had eaten better at our camp and I had promised that I would have my men hunt so that his men had more than peas and beans for food. Dirleton lay on the coast and the bishop chose it as the other castles he had been charged with taking lay further east. This would allow us to be close to Leith where we would be able to have news of our supply ships.

The defenders knew that we were coming. The de Vaux family were of Norman origin and they knew how to defend themselves. As we approached the fortress, I saw the problems we would face, especially without siege engines. The keep was circular with a good gatehouse protected by a bridge over a ditch which was the only way in. There were four towers on the walls and my heart sank for I had helped to defend Newcastle which was not as strong as this castle. We ringed the fortress and while the Durham warriors took off their mail to build camps and embed stakes to prevent a sortie I went with the bishop and the sheriff to view the defences. We were four hundred paces from the castle and beyond the range of both their crossbows and bows.

Bishop Bek shook his head, "Without siege engines, how do we take the castle? The walls of the donjon are too high for ladders and the ditch means we cannot mine it."

"How many archers did you bring, Bishop Bek?"

He looked at Sir John who said, "Four hundred."

"Then with my archers, we clear the walls and the gatehouse and steal an idea from the Scots themselves." I could see that they were intrigued, "When I was at Newcastle, they brought up a ram filled with kindling to burn the gate. We can do the same except we do not use a ram, which will take time to build. We use men protected with shields and we do not risk the men running with fire. We will use fire arrows to ignite the kindling and to keep the fire going. I fear that we may burn the bridge but that will be a small price to pay if we are able to gain entry to the castle."

The bishop nodded, "It is better than any plan I might have." He turned to Sir John Marmaduke, "Have twenty men make camp on the far side close to the postern gate. That should be enough to deter them from sending for help. We will camp on this side and make the main assault on the gate."

"My lord, if you would have your men collect kindling and make it into faggots then I can have my archers make fire arrows. Tomorrow,

Wallace's War

we will begin to thin their defenders and then we can attack the day after."

Sir John said, "You sound confident about this, Warbow."

I nodded, "When we were in Flanders, we had a town protected by a river to take as well as a stout donjon. Fire arrows worked there and my men know how to make them. Send your centenars to me and I will give them instruction."

The Durham archers seemed in awe of me and I suppose it was because I was one of them yet I had been knighted. They knew of my skill and of what I had done in Wales as well as, more recently, in Flanders. My exploits at Evesham and then latterly at Newcastle gave me more respect than even the bishop enjoyed. "Tomorrow we will send so many arrows at their walls that we will blot out the sun. We will send twenty flights and then stop. I plan on making our arrow showers, like the weather here, unpredictable. The aim is to make them fear to watch what we do. Tomorrow, we kill but the next day we both kill and set light to the castle." I explained what we had done in Flanders and how we would do the same at Dirleton. "Our attack will keep their men from the walls so that our men on foot can safely deposit their bundles and then our fire arrows will burn their gate."

John of Auckland asked, "Sir Gerald, what about the men who are behind the arrow slits? We cannot kill them."

"Firstly, I have counted the slits and there are less than a dozen. Secondly, I have been in a besieged castle and the arrow slits are not as easy to use as you might think. When you go back to your men tonight, have them construct pavise shields. There are enough alder, elder and saplings to do so. They do not have to be pretty, just something to give your archers cover while they nock an arrow. We will be sending our arrows into the sky to descend upon the fighting platform." I smiled, "We are all archers and know that once we have the range we need not even look for we know where our arrows will fall."

Their grins told me I had used the right combination of praise and caution. A knight could not have done what I had just done. I knew how an archer worked. A lord knew the effect of good archers but not how they achieved that.

When I returned to my men I had them begin to make both pavise shields and fire arrows. It would be my men who would send the fire arrows. It was a skill the Durham archers did not possess.

"Jack and Ralph, I have a task for you tomorrow. I would have you ride to Tantallon Castle. I want to know what we should expect there."

They were both pleased to be able to do something useful rather than just watching my archers work.

Wallace's War

The next morning the Durham archers were keen to impress. They were at the mark before my men and they had planted their arrows in the soil to make their releasing faster. Their pavise shields were in place and whilst, like ours, they looked crude, they would stop a bolt. My archers nodded and smiled as I passed. Archers were always competitive. I had never known a session at the mark on a Sunday morning when there was not a wager. That the priests might frown on such an act on a Sunday never seemed to bother them. As Dick once said, "God gave me this skill and he must be an archer. He would not mind a harmless wager on our skill." We placed our pavise shelters before us and then fitted our bow strings. My bow was powerful. Jack could not even begin to fasten a string to it and it would be some years before he could draw it. It was a relatively new bow, being just two years old and Oswald the Bowyer had spent three months making it. I would be sad when I had to have another made. I looked down the line. Bishop Bek rode up. His horse wore the red caparison with the two Maltese crosses and his nineteen knights and three mounted men at arms who accompanied him also looked splendid in the morning light. The defenders would know that it was Prince Bishop Bek who led the attack. God would be on our side. The archers all knelt as he blessed us. It was, of course, an act meant to show the defenders that with the Prince Bishop leading us we had God on our side. The bishop and his men would take no part in the attack this day but their colourful presence was a warning to the defenders of Dirleton.

The preliminaries over I drew a war arrow and shouted, "Nock!" The order was repeated by the centenars and vintenars. I had a target in mind.

There was a Scottish archer on the walls who was also drawing back his bow. The archers and crossbowmen were the more deadly targets and I had chosen mine.

"Draw!" The sound of the yew bows being drawn back made the hairs on the back of my neck prickle and the Scots would know what was about to be unleashed. Their archers would also be drawing but their bows were a pale shadow of ours. Their best archers, the only ones who could come close to us were with Wallace in Selkirk Forest. These were garrison archers and whilst stronger than the other warriors in the castle did not train as hard as we.

"Release!"

Even as our arrows soared, we all chose a second arrow. I knew that the others would all keep sending arrows at the same target but I was selecting mine. I watched the arrow aimed at me by the Scottish archer fall thirty paces short. Despite the elevation, his bow and lack of strength meant that we had the range. Only one or two bolts smacked into the pavise. I saw my target, the Scottish archer who had missed me, fall backwards as my war arrow pierced his skull. Shouts and cries from the walls told me that our first attack had worked. Two men fell from the walls into the ditch while others tumbled back into the castle. I let the second flight descend before I sent my arrow. This time it was at a place I had just seen a crossbow disappear behind the crenulations. I drew a third and watched the arrow as it fell. The crossbowman's head appeared and my arrow struck his shoulder. If he was not dead then he would not be able to send a crossbow bolt. As the crossbow fell into the ditch I smiled, for they had lost a valuable weapon.

I did not send twenty arrows but I stopped when the others did. Our archers put down their bows and stretched their arms. One or two of the older ones had their backs massaged by their fellows. Had I wished then Hamo would have done the same for me. I turned to him, "The first attack went well."

He nodded, "And I see that not one of your arrows missed."

I shrugged, "Call it a master's whim. I lead. I was pleased with the attack."

Mordaf shouted, "They are now braving the walls again, my lord."

"Count their weapons."

They sent arrows and bolts at our pavise. Some of the bolts hit but few of the arrows. We had chosen the perfect range.

"I count twelve crossbows and twenty bows, my lord."

I nodded and Hamo said, "So long as the crossbows are not harmed, they can use them again."

It was one of the reasons my archers hated what they called the infernal weapon. Little skill was needed to use one. They had drawing hooks attached to their belts and could easily pull back the string and releasing from the walls of a castle meant that they could rest their crossbows on the walls.

"There are but a handful, Hamo. By this afternoon we will have winnowed their numbers. We must have hit spearmen too."

What we would not have harmed would be the mailed men in the castle. That there were few of them was little consolation but it would not do to waste bodkin arrows. When we fought their main army, I knew that we would have a thousand mailed men to send the bodkins at. Castles meant war arrows.

Archers, even good ones using the best of bows cannot release arrows interminably and by mid-afternoon, I called a halt to the attack. Arms and backs burned from the effort and we had sent more than five thousand arrows at the walls. We still had plenty but we needed the king's ships to resupply us with missiles as well as food. The bishop and his men had dismounted to watch our attack. "Fine work, Warbow. I think we have broken their spirit."

I shook my head, "These are Scots, my lord. The fire will do that on the morrow."

Just then Jack and Ralph rode in. I smiled when it was Jack and not the pursuivant who gave the report on Tantallon Castle. "It is not as strong as this one, my lord. It has a wooden palisade and a good ditch but it has a wooden hall. We rode along the coast and all the castles to the east are made of wood. There are three more of them, including Tantallon."

I gestured to the bishop, "Then Bishop Bek, if this one falls the rest can easily be intimidated. I would choose your men for tomorrow carefully for if this attack fails then they will be prepared."

"I have the men in mind already."

We still had a little of the butchered animals we had hunted in Selkirk Forest and we used what there was in a stew that would otherwise have been beans, peas and the greens my men could forage. It had bubbled away all day while we had drawn arrows. If there had been bread it would have been a fine meal but, as it was it satisfied but my men still yearned for both bread and beer. The beer we drank was so watered down as to be little more than flavoured water.

The next day we gathered the fire arrows we had made and took them to the pavise. Twenty of the bishop's men at arms had stood to all night in case the Scots tried to sortie but they had not. I had been in a castle under siege and I knew that enduring a siege was not easy. They had men waiting night after night, all night and when we attacked, they would be on the walls and tired. A defender in a siege had to react to what others did. They knew not what to expect. As I stood with my archers, smoke from the braziers drifting before us, I saw fewer helmets on the walls. There were crossbows but they were spread out along the length of the walls. There also appeared to be fewer of them.

I was the one in command of the initial assault. Bishop Bek had chosen his men to carry both the shields and the kindling. They waited behind my archers. The men on the walls would have their eyes fixed on the archers and the menacing braziers. The smoke from the braziers told me that the wind was behind us. Every archer would adjust their flight with that knowledge in their heads. The eyes of all were on me. I had spoken to my officers before we had lit the braziers and they knew what to do. I took an arrow and after nocking it, sent it at the knight who was peering over the walls to ascertain our plan. My arrow was a bodkin and it struck him in the shoulder, knocking him to the fighting platform. Even as my arrow was in the air every archer had nocked and drawn. This time we had not made it easy for the defenders by shouting the commands which gave them a warning. The arrows struck stone, helmets and flesh. The heads disappeared from the walls.

Sir John waved his sword and the twenty men with the kindling ran across the bridge to the gate. Half of my retinue had been given the task of using fire arrows and whilst the rest kept up a steady shower of arrows at the fighting platform, the chosen ones picked up a fire arrow and waited for the kindling to be placed. I heard a couple of bolts, sent from arrow slits, smack into the shields and pavise but none of the Durham men fell. A head appeared over the gatehouse and managed to cry out a warning before an arrow knocked him from the wall. The shields afforded enough protection for the men with the kindling and faggots to make a neat stack of them and then they pulled back with their shields held above and before them. I lit my arrow and the others did the same. More than forty arrows, streaming smoke and sparks, flew in the air and then landed. Our experience in Flanders meant that we did not rely on one arrow and we each lit another. The art of using fire arrows was speed. You nocked drew and released in one motion. Any delay might burn your hand or your bow. The fire began to lick the top of the faggots and we each sent our next arrow into the gates. They would be harder to burn and many of the arrows would die. The wood from the arrows, however, would add to the fire from the faggots. After six fire arrows, we ceased and prepared to send war arrows at any who came out of the postern gate to extinguish the flames. Five brave men tried it but all five did not even manage to reach the fire. Thirty arrows struck them.

Hamo had not been in Flanders and he shook his head, as he said, "A powerful weapon, father."

Nodding I said, "Aye, but you need to know how to use them. They can be a waste of arrows if misused."

"But you have not." He pointed as the flames suddenly leapt up and engulfed not only the gate but the wooden supports for the gatehouse. The fire had taken hold and would not be extinguished. The flag on the keep was lowered but the gate burned on. King Edward had wanted the castle to be indefensible. With a burned gate it would be.

By the end of the day, the castle was ours and after disarming the garrison they were sent on their way.

As we ate that night Ralph asked me, "Sir Gerald, why did the bishop let those men go? Surely, they might fight us again."

I nodded, "Some may well do but they have tasted a bitter defeat and will not fight as well, but the main reason is that they will tell the other castles what we did here. You and Jack know that this was the strongest castle. Will the others hold out?"

He smiled and shook his head, "I am learning about war, Sir Gerald."

I was proved right and over the next three days, the nearest castles all surrendered at our approach. We disarmed their men and emptied the castle of their supplies. The wooden castles were all burned and we headed for Leith. As we marched down the coast road, we saw the fleet of supply ships as they edged up the estuary. They looked to have been battered by storms and it explained their late arrival.

I was riding with the bishop who said, "We can take the supplies directly to the king at the new camp at Kirkliston. He may actually be pleased with us."

I smiled, "Bishop Bek, you and I have served the king longer than any. When was he pleased with anything? Had Queen Eleanor still been alive then she might have prompted him to a grudging smile. He is King Edward and we cannot change his nature but he is the one to break the spirit of the Scots."

We reached the port at the same time as the ships. As with the rest of the land, the ones who opposed us had fled, taking all of value with them. The ones who remained were the practical people who would live with whoever controlled their destiny. It took a day to find enough wagons and draught animals to take the food back to the main camp. Ironically the first ships to land brought 200 tuns of wine and only eight wagon loads of food. The captain told us that the rest of the ships were a day behind. Leaving Sir John Marmaduke to await their arrival we headed back to Kirkliston.

The king nodded his approval when the bishop reported the fall of the castles. While the supplies were distributed equally amongst all our camps, he spoke to us of his plans. "Now that the food has begun to arrive and with the east secure, we will move forward to Stirling. I would have the defeat there expunged with the blood of the Scots." I saw the Earl of Surrey wince at the criticism. The question is, where is Wallace? Is he still in Selkirk Forest or is he moving to bring us to battle, Warbow? The day after tomorrow, find him for me."

I kept a straight face as I said, "Yes, my lord." My archers, it seemed, were the only ones capable of finding our enemy.

He then went through the order of march and the order of battle. "My aim, my lords, is to bring the Scots to battle. I want them where they cannot flee back to their rat holes. I would have both them and their spirit of resistance crushed. We have wasted enough time here, in this barbaric land."

Just then a dishevelled Geoffrey of Wendover rushed in, "King Edward, the Welsh have rebelled. They got into the wine and have become intoxicated. They say they will not fight!"

King Edward was ever decisive and he snapped, "Warbow, take men and contain them. I will have my household knights arm."

Bishop Bek came with me and shouted, "Sir Richard of Norham, fetch your men at arms, we have a task for them."

"Hamo, have my retinue join me." I drew my sword and turned to Geoffrey of Wendover. "You are not hurt?"

He shook his head, "No, but some priests tried to restrain them and half a dozen were killed." He shook his head, "Men of God!"

"Drunk warriors see neither cross nor man." I heard the sound of footsteps behind me and saw Mordaf leading my archers. They had already strung their bows. "Mordaf, I would have you behind Sir Richard and his men. Only release when I command and only take out those who threaten. We cannot afford to slaughter our own men."

"Aye, my lord."

Sir Richard had a drawn sword and was next to me, "You know these Welshmen, Sir Gerald?"

I gave him a thin smile, "No, Sir Richard, but they know me."

We heard the shouts and screams as we neared the wagons with the wine. Bodies lay on the ground and it was not only the priests who had been slain. Some of the carters had fallen foul of the drunken Welshmen. Sir Richard and his men at arms flanked us. Ralph and Geoffrey had their swords drawn. Jack, I saw, had fetched his bow and was behind us with Hamo, Mordaf and my archers. James and John had also come with spare sheaves of arrows. They were brave boys.

I bellowed, "In King Edward's name lay down your weapons. This is most unseemly." Some men stopped and stared but such was the noise that I had to shout even louder and this time in the Welsh of my childhood, "Lay down your weapons!"

A huge drunken Welsh archer with a chest like a beer barrel spat in my direction. He missed. He raised the jug of wine to his lips and emptied it. He hurled it to the ground and then shouted, in Welsh, "So Longshanks sends his pet dog, Warbow, to do his bidding." He drew his short sword, "I spit on you and tell you that we will not serve King Edward. We are going home." He launched himself at me. He was followed by more than three hundred others.

Mordaf and my archers could not send arrows at the leading warriors for fear of hitting us and so I drew my dagger as the drunken barrel hurled himself at me and tried to bring his sword down and split my skull. It was easy enough for me to block the blow for I too was an archer. I was going to punch him in the head with the pommel of my dagger when Jack sent an arrow over my shoulder. It pierced his eye and penetrated until only the goose feathers could be seen. I looked for my next attacker but Mordaf and my archers had begun to slay those just behind the first attackers and Sir Richard and his men at arms had easily dealt with drunken Welshmen armed with short swords.

A horn sounded and hooves galloped up. King Edward and his household knights, dressed in mail and with couched lances appeared on the flanks of the Welshmen. He roared, "Lay down your weapons or by God, I will hang you all!"

Such was the force and power of his words that, allied to the sight of the eighty dead Welshmen, they laid down their swords.

He pointed with his swords at the dead priests, "Was this well done?" The Welsh looked shamefaced. "You wish to desert me? Good. Then join the Scots and we shall defeat you all in one go and save the exchequer the trouble of payment. Now disperse and present yourselves on the morrow, ready to be soldiers once more."

Such was the power that they all obeyed but the king waited until they had returned to their camp before he dismounted. He turned to the Earl of Surrey, "Have the Welsh dead burned but bury the priests and carters in the churchyard." He waved over the bishop and me. I saw that he was disturbed by what had happened. Unusually for King Edward, his confidence had been shaken. He spoke quietly to the bishop and me, "Tomorrow, Warbow, I would have you find Wallace. I know I have given you little rest but this atrocity has shown me that I do not have a united army. Bishop, have the army move towards Leith and Edinburgh. I can see that my men need full bellies. Warbow, find Wallace and if he has headed, as I believe he might, to ravage the west while we wait here then return with all haste and tell me."

I nodded, "Yes, King Edward."

Leaving the king and the bishop to discuss the plans I returned to my men. They were collecting arrows which could be reused, "We have little rest ahead of us, I fear. We head back to the forest on the morrow. The king would have us find Wallace."

All around us the rest of the army was given the orders that they would be breaking camp the next day. Linlithgow would be freed from its English yoke although as we had eaten everything for many miles around, I doubted that the locals would have time to rejoice. They would be too busy seeking food themselves.

Chapter 13

This time I would be taking all my men and that included James and John. Selkirk Forest was huge and I expected Wallace to have moved his camp since the last time we had spied upon him. I sent William and Edward to find the trail into the forest and we followed. We had covered barely half a mile when Edward rode back.

He reined in, as did we, and I saw, from his face, that he was agitated, "Sir Gerald, two Welsh spearmen left the camp at the same time as we did. My brother thought it odd and sent me back to tell you."

Hamo asked, "Why odd?"

"Firstly, they were riding horses. Welsh spearmen walk afoot and secondly, they too, were heading for Selkirk Forest."

I think that I had fought in so many wars and become embroiled in so many plots that my mind worked differently from most men. I saw through the mist and found the heart of the plot. I turned to Hamo, "They are spies." I saw the incredulity on his face and that of Ralph. I sighed and explained, "I heard somewhere that Wallace was descended from Welshmen and perhaps that mischief with the wine was more than a drunken aberration. I believe that these men are Scottish spies. Hamo, you take command of the men. Do not enter the forest but camp outside. I do not wish to scare these spies. I will take Jack and go with William and Edward. If we need you, I shall send Jack back to you."

I saw my son's face frown, "Is this well done, father? There are others who could do this. William and Edward are more than capable of discovering if you are right."

"Aye, my lord, we have crept into the camp before and we can do so again."

"No, Edward, I shall be with you. Fate threw Wallace and me together in the forest north of Carlisle and I will not be the one who severs the thread that binds us together. All will be well. Now, do as I command."

I whipped the head of my horse, Brutus, around and urged him along the road. Edward and Jack soon flanked me. They wisely said nothing. It did not take us long to catch up with William who had stopped and was sheltering behind a pair of spindly rowan trees that had taken root by the side of the road. The two Welshmen were clearly not horsemen for we could see them in the distance. Their horses had stopped to graze the grass at the side of the road. Inexperienced riders allowed their animals to do that. William turned and smiled, "They must have stolen two horses. One has already been thrown. They are not very confident riders. When they are able, they ride fast but their horses appear wilful or perhaps they take advantage of poor riders. When they smell water, they wander off to drink and they devour any grass that they can find."

I nodded, "All the horses in the army are hungry." Our horses were also eating the grass beneath the tree. The difference was that when we wished we could stop them and they would move on. "How do you know that they are Welsh spearmen, William? I see no spears."

"They both have small round shields on their backs beneath their cloaks and they carry a short sword. If they are archers we would know. Their build is wrong."

I stared at the two men and saw he was right. While the two men were clearly strong warriors, they did not have the broad chests that marked Welsh archers. At the very least they were deserters and I believed we would learn much from following them.

As we watched we spied one Welshman reaching up to cut a switch from a tree and use it to begin to beat the rump of his horse. When the horse obeyed the second emulated him. The two galloped down the road towards Selkirk Forest. We followed. We left enough of a gap so that they would neither hear nor see us but they were so concerned with their animals that we could have ridden behind their tails and they would have been oblivious to our presence.

Selkirk Forest was enormous but it had once been bigger. Outside the forest proper were the remnants of trees that had once lain deep within its boundaries. Farmers had slashed and burned to make fields and the result was that long before we reached the road that passed through the forest, we found ourselves riding in the shade of ancient trees. We were able to risk riding a little closer to the two Welshmen. The road that cut through the forest was not Roman. It had been made as a crude way to pass through the forest. From our previous visit, I knew that the Scottish army would be somewhere far from the road. I wondered how the two Welshmen would find the camp. They halted precisely one thousand paces into the forest and I guessed that had been pre-arranged for they took the opportunity to dismount. They did, however, keep hold of the reins of their animals, which took advantage of the halt to eat. I saw one Welshman cup his hands and call something. I could not make out the words but we ensured that we were well hidden. William peered from beneath a branch that was heavy with leaves. We too had dismounted. The difference was that we did it because we cared for our horses not because we were uncomfortable.

We waited an hour passed and the two cupped their hands and called into the woods another six times. The Scots who came from the forest just appeared from both sides of the rough road. We were lucky that we had chosen a vantage point that was far enough away so that the Scottish scouts came nowhere near us. The Scots surrounded the two men and then, after a short conversation, they were led away. We saw the direction they took but we did not follow, not immediately anyway.

"We will follow on foot. Jack, lead William's mount. You can find their trail?"

William nodded, "I am guessing, my lord, that there will be few horses in the woods and as the two horses have eaten every time they have stopped and have still to drop dung, even Jack here could follow their trail."

Jack smiled, "I will get better, William of Ware, by watching you."

We headed down the road. William strung his bow and nocked an arrow. Once we reached the place they had been met he entered the trees and after he was satisfied that they had not left a sentry he waved us forward. William was right. The trail was clear. They were not walking in single file and there were branches that has been broken and fresh leaves on the ground. The hoofprints of the horses were the biggest giveaway. There had been rain and the ground was soft. Even without a rider, the prints stood out. The clear trail allowed William to keep a good watch ahead. We travelled further than I had expected us to. It was the middle of the afternoon when we smelled woodsmoke and heard the noise of a camp.

We stopped immediately. "William, you and I will get closer to the camp. Edward, you and Jack stay here. We will return as soon as we can."

Hamo, Mordaf or Gwillim might have objected but Jack and Edward just nodded. William hung his bow from the saddle and we both raised the cowls on our cloaks and hurried after the Welshmen and their Scottish guides. I had expected sentries but I deduced, later, that the men who had escorted the Welshmen were the sentries. We moved from tree to tree and the horses and Welshmen attracted all the attention. More men had joined the Scottish army since our last visit and that suited me. So long as we remained silent, we might be taken for two more recruits. I spied the livery of some lords who had lands in both England and Scotland. This was an army recruited from a wide area. They would all be strange to each other. Men crowded around the two men as they were led to a large tent that I took to be Wallace's. Once we spied the tent William and I hurried through the trees to get closer to the tent. We joined men who were watching Wallace as he and his lords emerged from the tent to greet the two Welshmen.

Wallace's War

A huge cheer greeted him when he came out. William and I joined in as did the men behind whom we stood. There was a line of eight men before us and they did not turn to see who we were.

Wallace held his hands up to silence the army and such was his presence that they all obeyed. "Welcome kinsmen! I take it that your arrival means that there is news and you are no longer needed as spies in King Edward's camp."

He spoke in English and that made sense for I doubted that the Welshmen would speak his language. One of them must have nodded and then he spoke, "Aye, Sir William, King Edward has learned that the other Welshmen he hired are less than happy with the lack of food. We managed to start a riot and some of King Edward's army died."

I thought that was far from the truth. The Welshman was implying that there had been both English and Welsh casualties. The priests and carters apart, all of the dead had been Welsh. He was telling the Guardian of Scotland what Wallace wanted to hear.

"King Edward has retired to Edinburgh. It will take his army a long time to reach it and it means he cannot attack Stirling as he planned."

We could only see the back of Wallace's head but the vigorous nodding told us that he was pleased, "Then we have our opportunity. Sir Andrew may be dead, God rest his soul, but his legacy lives on. He was the one with the vision to see that this English army could be defeated and I have taken on his mantle. We will break camp and tomorrow fall upon his baggage train. We will all be rich men from the treasure taken from this English king. Without a baggage train, he cannot fight and will slink back to England a broken and defeated man."

The legend of the loss of the crown jewels in the Wash during the time of King John made every enemy of the English assume that the King of England travelled with treasure and gold.

William and I turned as soon as Wallace's words were uttered. The cheers disguised our disappearance and men turned to each other to speak of what they would do with the gold they thought they would take. I might have aged but I was still an archer who was most at home in the woods. We disappeared within a few strides. Whilst ensuring that none had seen us leave, we hurried back to the horses. Edward and Jack had their bows strung when we reached them. "There will be no need for weapons. We have to get back to the camp as soon as we can."

The breaking of a camp is never quick. The vanguard had already left to set up a marching camp when we arrived but King Edward and the bulk of the army were still there. It was cold rations that they were eating and, after picking up Hamo and the rest of my archers, our galloping hooves ensured that we were greeted by drawn swords and a hedgehog of spears.

I dismounted, stiffly, for it had been a long day and I had not eaten since breakfast. Sitting in a saddle for so long had taken it out of me, "King Edward, Wallace is but twenty miles from here and Welsh spies have told him that we retire to Edinburgh. He intends to fall upon the baggage train."

"Praise God, who up to now has delivered me from all difficulties. They shan't have to follow me, for I shall go to meet them this very day." He waved over Geoffrey of Wendover. "Ride to the Earl of Surrey and ask him to meet us on the road to Selkirk. We shall bring him to battle and end this tribulation in the north. Bishop Bek, have the supplies that just arrived in Leith follow us."

We left the camp well before dawn and I ached all over. This time we were kept closer to the main army and King Edward. I used Mordaf and a dozen archers to keep us informed about any threat to us. The line of march was in battles with the Earl of Lincoln guarding the baggage train. It contained no jewels but something even more valuable, the first of the food from Leith. Bishop Bek's men had ensured that the king would not vent his rage on them. We would eat. It was Peter son of Walter who rode in and brought us the news that Mordaf had found the Scottish army. They were ahead of us and retreating towards Stirling by way of Falkirk. Wallace had his own scouts out and although we had not seen them they must have seen us and he had wisely decided to withdraw as he realised that we were no longer retreating.

I reported to the king who was not unhappy, "I did not relish a fight in the forest, Strongbow. It does not suit our heavy horse."

"Nor does it suit their schiltrons, King Edward. Wallace will choose somewhere that does give him an advantage. He might be reinforced but we still hold the upper hand in terms of numbers."

"Quite so. We will make a marching camp this night and keep our spears in his back. Perhaps we can harry him into a mistake."

It was late when we found a suitable place to camp at Burgh Muir. Mordaf reported that the Scots were within a few miles of us and so King Edward ordered men to sleep in their mail and use their shields and cloaks as coverlets. For my archers, this was no hardship as we were used to sleeping that way. None of the army used horse lines and our horses were tethered close to where we slept. The poor squires had the hardest task as they had to watch the war horses and their masters would be less than happy if aught happened to their very expensive steeds.

Wallace's War

We ate before we slept. My stomach had still to recover from the day without eating. Hamo said as he prepared his bed, "This campaign began badly, Father, but at least we now appear to have found luck."

I laughed as I drank from the ale skin, "You do not find luck, my son, it finds you and the thing about luck is that you never know if it is bad luck or good luck until well after the event. The riot by the Welsh might be considered bad luck but it resulted in our being able to gather intelligence at the Scottish camp. I find it is better not to invoke the spirits by speaking of luck."

Ralph made the sign of the cross, "That sounds blasphemous, Sir Gerald."

I shrugged as I laid my blanket on the ground, "Blasphemous or not, Ralph, you will find many strange things happen on the battlefield and not all are of God's doing. In my experience, God has too many other things to occupy him than what men do in his name on the field of battle. When we fight the Scots, it will not be for God, even though we invoke his name and the saints we hope support us but the reality is that we fight to control Scotland."

I found it easy to get to sleep for I was tired but, as I always did when on campaign, I slept with an ear open and my hand on my sword. So it was that when I was woken, by the shout in the night, I was armed and on my feet in a heartbeat. Alarmingly the noise came from where the king had been sleeping and leaving Hamo to organise the men, for there were shouts of, 'we are under attack' and 'the Scots', I ran to the king's side where I saw that he had been hurt. It was hard to see the cause although the shamefaced squire who led the king's charger appeared to be part of the cause.

The doctors were tending to the king who looked up at me and snapped, "Warbow, send the men back to bed. There was no attack. This squire decided to empty his bladder and my horse trod on me."

"And you are hurt, my lord?"

He gave a wry smile, "I would rather not have been stamped upon but broken ribs will not stop me from fighting in the battle and I shall take out my anger on the Scots we face. Now be off and silence this cacophony of noise."

It took me some time but my presence, added to my roaring voice soon restored order and men returned to their beds. When the camp was quieter, although still far from silent, I returned to Hamo and my men. I told them what had occurred. "So you see, Hamo, it is better not to mention luck at all. The king was hurt but not in battle and it could have been avoided. I suspect the squire will no longer be King Edward's squire and will have to live with the shame of his inattention for the rest of his life. But let us just say it was an avoidable accident and not mention the other word."

He nodded, "And will you sleep?"

I shook my head, "Once I am awake then I cannot get back to sleep. I never could. I will walk the camp in case there are men who still fear the Scots intend to attack this night."

Jack asked, "Will they?"

"If I were leading them then aye but Wallace will not wish to risk losing his best men in a night attack and he would have to use those men if he was going to succeed. You sleep, Jack, for tomorrow will be a long day."

There were, indeed, some who were fearful that the Scots would come while they lay asleep and despite my pleas, they stayed awake. When I returned to the king, I saw that he had his injuries tended to but was awake. There was a new squire with the horse. The other would have been relegated to the baggage train and I doubted that he would be given another chance to serve the king.

The king was standing and rubbing where he had been injured. The horse had stamped on his side and I guessed broken some ribs. It would make breathing difficult. I could see that he was in pain and each time he moved he winced, "You should not fight today, King Edward."

His eyes narrowed, "So, Warbow, you still try to instruct a king."

I shrugged, "You and I are old warriors, King Edward, and we both know that on a battlefield any weakness can be exploited."

He waved me closer, "Warbow, I can say this to you for I know you are close-mouthed and can be trusted. The fact is that you may have been right and I should have stayed in England and not gone to Flanders. I believe that had I been at Stirling Bridge then my army would not have been defeated. I have to lead tomorrow. I do not need to fight but I need to be both seen and I need to see."

I nodded, "I can see that. You will need my archers to end this."

"I know but I need the nobility of Scotland to feel my wrath. Besides, the bulk of the army will still be marching from the east. It will be these knights and your mounted archers that reach the battlefield first. Another reason why I have to lead." He gave me a rare smile, "What will I do when you are no longer able to draw a bow and lead my archers?"

"There is always my son, Hamo."

He lowered his voice, "I know your son is well thought of but is he Gerald Warbow? Can he do what you have done?"

"He may exceed me, my lord, we cannot know. All that a man can do is his best in the time the Good Lord allows him on this earth. I would rather that Hamo enjoyed a peaceful life and just draw his bow to hunt or at the mark rather than make his life through war."

"And there we differ. I hope that my son, Edward, exceeds his father's exploits. I would have him retake our French Empire once more. The days of the second King Henry saw us rule more of France than the French and that is my ambition."

"He did not conquer Wales and Scotland as you have."

He nodded, "France is the prize, Warbow." He waved a hand around him, "This is not the rich land that is France." The waving of the arm made him wince and he said, sharply, if I am to be awake then the rest of the army can suffer too. Have the army roused. We march for dawn cannot be far away."

I nodded. He was being unfair but he was the king and I said, "As you wish, King Edward." Cupping my hands I bellowed, "Stand to. We rise and go to war. This day we avenge Stirling Bridge and the brave men who fell that day."

The call was taken up and repeated. I headed back to my camp and by the time I reached it all were awake. My men were old campaigners. While most of the army had not eaten and had not thought to fetch food my men had. Mordaf handed me a slice of ham and a piece of cheese. "You need sustenance, Sir Gerald." I cocked an eye and he smiled, "I have more, my lord."

I ate. It would not keep me going all day but chewing and swallowing might make my stomach believe I had enjoyed a meal. I washed it down with ale from the skin Jack gave to me. I raised my voice so that my men could all hear me, "Today we ride with the knights. Until the other archers and spearmen reach us we shall be the only protection for the king."

If the knights nearby heard me and were insulted, I cared not. I knew the quality of my men. In my view, some knights regarded war as an opportunity for glory. I knew the reality.

Wallace's War

The Battle of Falkirk
Initial dispositions

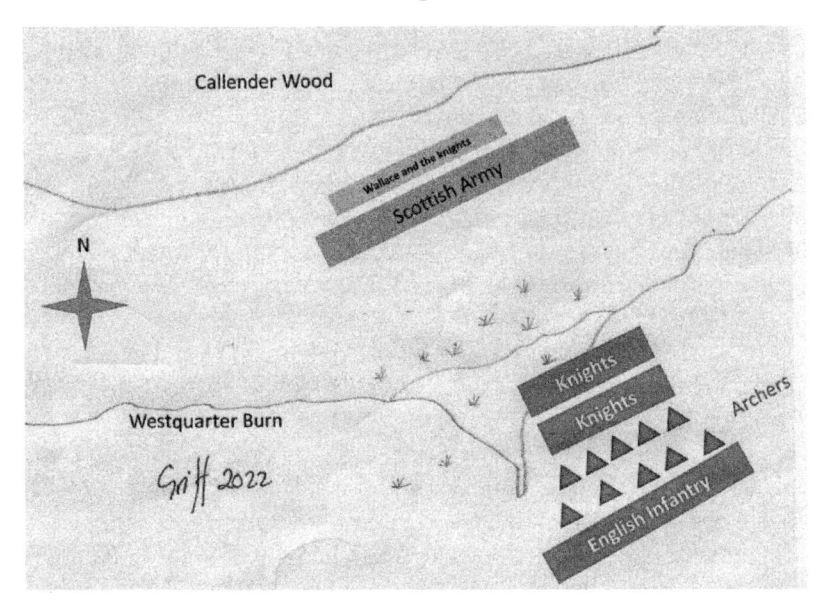

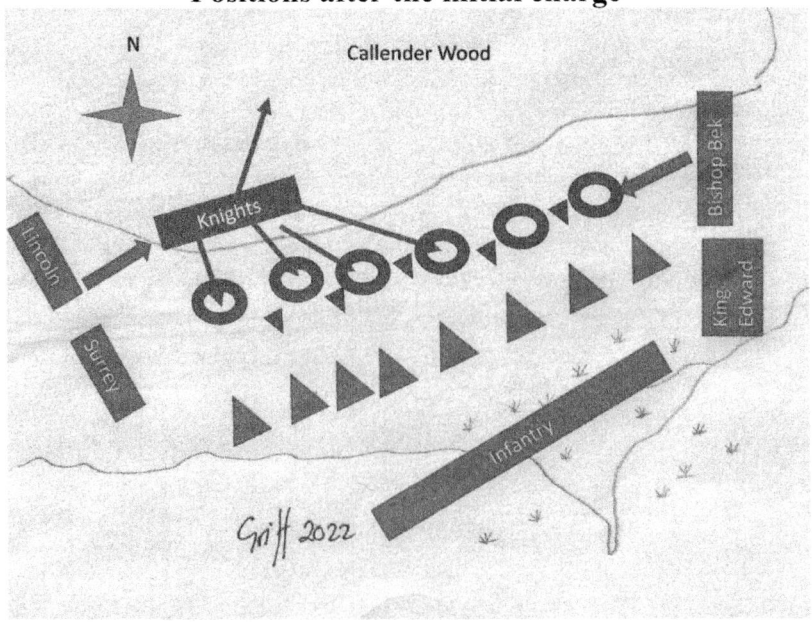

Positions after the initial charge

Chapter 14

It was William and Edward who rode as the scouts before the jingling knights and mounted men at arms. It was still dark when we left our camp but I knew that the noise of our approach would reach the Scots and they would be ready. Wallace had shown me that he did not make silly errors when it came to being prepared. The two archers rode back when we neared the crest of Redding Muir.

They spoke to the king but their eyes were on me, "King Edward, we have found the Scots. They have spearmen and they line the crest."

The king nodded, "Geoffrey of Wendover, give the orders to the commanders and have the army form a line of battle."

I approved the caution. In the half-light before dawn we were vulnerable to an attack from the darkness. "Dismount and string your bows." I remained mounted as my men slid from their horses and obeyed my orders. They needed no instructions to tell them to tether their horses. Only Ralph and I remained mounted. On this day Jack would stand with the other archers and he would use his bow in a battle for the first time. James and John would be ready to replenish any archers' supply of arrows and to tend to those who were wounded. Mordaf and Jack had trained them. As I had when Hamo had fought for the first time I would have to steel myself; he could be hurt or even killed but I was Gerald Warbow and I led archers. When I was in battle, I was not a father.

The four battles advanced up the slope towards the low crest of Redding Muir. My archers and I went before them. Archers move quickly and they did not slow up the horsemen for King Edward rode cautiously up the slope. When we reached the top, it was clear that the line of spearmen seen by William and Edward had been a guard to warn the main army of our approach and they were falling back towards Callender Wood. Wallace was cautious.

"We will halt here. Warbow, have your archers act as sentries. Geoffrey, have the mounted men dismount and erect a tent as a chapel. Bishop Bek, we would have your blessing before we go about God's work on this day."

I rode a little way up the slope. It was still too dark to see clearly but, in the distance, I could hear the sounds of men moving and shadows that suggested they were preparing to fight us. I saw that there was what looked like a forest at the top of the hill ahead, that would be Callender Wood, but before us was a line of vegetation. "Ralph, let us ride and see what awaits King Edward and his army."

Wallace's War

"Are you sure, my lord?"

I laughed, "We are mounted and we have our swords. Besides, we would smell Scotsmen if they lay in wait. Have courage."

He said, stiffly, "I am not afraid, Sir Gerald."

"Ralph, we are the eyes and ears of the army. Come."

As we neared the line of vegetation, I saw it was a line of trees and bushes. Even before we reached it, I knew what it was, it was a stream, what the Scots called a burn. I saw that it was both shallow and narrow. Horses could negotiate it but not at the gallop. Perhaps the two Scots who leapt from the darkness thought that they could take two horses and their riders or they may have just been surprised by our sudden arrival. Whatever the reason their rising made Ralph and his horse start. I saw then that he was a good horseman as he fought to control his mount. My hand had already been on my sword's hilt and I drew it and slashed at the spearman who thrust his weapon's head at me. I swashed it away and brought the sword back to hack into the side of his head. His companion hesitated and that slight delay cost him his life. I kicked Brutus in the side and he ran at the spearman; he was a warhorse and was now in his element. In the half-light before dawn, the Scottish warrior misjudged my position and I ducked my head beneath his spearhead to drive my sword into his chest.

Ralph, having got his horse under control, appeared at my side with his sword in his hand. I shook my head, "Perhaps these Scots bathed for I could not smell them. We have seen enough. Let us return to the king."

By the time we reached the main battle line I saw that the tent had been erected and Bishop Bek, the king and the other commanders all knelt in prayer, I remembered that this was the day of the Magdalene. I dismounted and handed my reins to Ralph. I, too, knelt as the priest's words intoned the mass.

At the last 'Amen', I stood and saw, a mile to the north, the Scots forming up. I had been right. There was a wood before which they arrayed themselves. It was another mark of Wallace's skill. He had chosen a battlefield that suited him. The woods would slow down horsemen and allow his army to escape. The boggy ground would slow the cavalry charge and his long spears would hold the slowed horses at bay. At Stirling Bridge, the men who had fallen had done so because there was no escape. The king approached me and I pointed ahead, "There is a stream yonder, King Edward. It will have to be approached slowly."

He nodded, "We now know where they are and they are fixed upon the hill. Fetch my horse."

Wallace's War

I waved to Ralph who brought my horse. The king and I mounted. The earls of Lincoln and Surrey along with Bishop Bek and the Earl of Hereford also mounted. I waved for Ralph to stay where he was. I led this august body of nobles towards the burn I had seen. The king stopped when he saw, in the distance, the two bodies.

"Your handiwork, Warbow?" The Earl of Hereford knew me from the Welsh wars.

"Aye, my lord."

"Then you have drawn first blood this day. Well done." The Earl of Hereford was known as a knight who enjoyed fighting and I think he envied me the accolade.

"Thank you, my lord."

The king pointed, "The stream will slow us. What are the Scots doing?"

We could see movement and I stood in my stirrups the better to see, "I think they are forming their circular schiltrons, King Edward, and unless I am mistaken, they are putting their archers between them."

The Earl of Hereford asked, "Circular schiltrons?"

The Earl of Surrey said, "They are rings of spearmen with long spears. It means you cannot get around their flanks or their rear. They are self-supporting and out range our lances and spears."

The king had been running through the choices open to him and he asked, "Have they anchored their flanks?"

The Earl of Lincoln shook his head, "No, King Edward, and their cavalry appears to be on their right flank."

The king was quiet. I saw him rub his injury, the broken ribs, "Let us make camp and eat. I know not about you gentleman but I have not eaten since yesterday and an army that is fed fights better. Besides we still have to wait for the men on foot to join us."

The Earl of Lincoln pointed behind us where we saw the shadowy snake of spearmen as they joined the horsemen, "King Edward, they have come already."

The Earl of Hereford said, "We have them at our mercy, my lord. If we camp and eat, we invite either an attack or, worse, flight. We want not this will o'the wisp that is William Wallace to disappear."

The Earl of Surrey shook his head, "He may be unknown to you, Sir Roger, but I have fought him and know that he is a cunning fighter."

The Earl of Hereford shook his head, "Wallace was at Stirling Bridge but the man behind that victory was Sir Andrew Murray and he is now dead. Wallace is not a noble, what does he know of war?"

Wallace's War

King Edward had been silent and he said, "Hereford, Warbow here was not noble born but he has a mind like Alexander or Caesar. Do not dismiss Wallace so lightly."

The Earl of Lincoln urged, "King Edward, we have men ready to support us. With Warbow's archers, we can attack. We can eat when we have won."

The king turned to Bishop Bek who had, as yet, said nothing, "Bishop?"

"I have been counting their horsemen, my lord, as the light improves, and as far as I can tell there are but five hundred horsemen. If we drive them from the field then the spearmen will be at our mercy. I fear that when he sees our superior numbers then Wallace will simply disappear into the forests. We cannot afford to chase him all over Scotland. The Welsh mutiny may presage a larger rising amongst the men. They need food or a victory."

It was Bishop Bek's argument that persuaded the king but it was the king's plan that was employed. "Lincoln, you and your battle will attack the horsemen on the enemy's left flank. Surrey will support you. I will lead my battle on the right and you, Bishop Bek will follow me. The infantry will follow us. Warbow, organise the archers; you need no instruction from me to tell you how to use them."

I hesitated but then put my neck on the block as I counselled, "Is that wise, King Edward, to attack without infantry support?"

He growled, "Warbow, just do as I command, eh? I am king and we will follow my battle plan."

I had done all that I could and I gave a half bow, "Just as you command, King Edward."

We wheeled our horses to ride back to the main army just as the sun began to shine. We would fight in daylight and that would suit my archers.

Bishop Bek rode next to me and said, quietly, "You take chances, Warbow."

I shrugged, "You and I, Bishop Bek, know the king better than the others. We were there in the Holy Land with him before he was king and we have a duty to be honest with him. Enduring his censure is better than collecting his body after the battle is lost."

"Will it come to that?"

I shook my head, "He will have heeded my words and I am content."

As we passed a knight and his retinue, I recognised neither, the knight shouted over, "Let us loose, King Edward, and we will drive these barbarians back to their holes in the hills."

Wallace's War

The king gave a dismissive nod, "We will, Sir Ralph, fear not."

I turned to Bishop Bek and said, "Who is that cockerel? I have not seen him before."

"He is a blowhard, "Sir Ralph Basset of Drayton. He talks a good talk but, so far as I know he has not warred before." He shrugged, "He has a horse worth fifty marks or so he tells everyone."

I smiled, "Take care today, Bishop Bek. Those spears can unhorse a man and a knight on foot is vulnerable."

"I know. And you take care Warbow. The king has few enough of us who have remained loyal his whole life. He needs his bishop and his archer."

I had been given my task and while the battles were organized, I sent Mordaf and Gwillim to gather the archer officers. I knew not who would take command of the spearmen but I would make certain that the five and a half thousand archers were well used. The twenty archers stood in a half circle around me. "Our orders are to support the horsemen. When they advance, we will advance in a long double line. I will lead the right flank." I pointed to each centenar as I gave them their instructions. "You will be on the left close to the Earl of Lincoln." I went along them so that they knew which band of archers flanked them. "Take spare sheaves of arrows. I do not think that this will be over quickly."

John of Nottingham asked, "Do we loose when the knights attack, Sir Gerald?"

I shook my head, "There is too much risk in that but we can attack their archers. As far as I can tell there are about fifteen hundred archers and, like you, John of Nottingham, they come from a forest, Selkirk Forest. Do not underestimate them but if we can defeat them then if the king has destroyed their horsemen, we have nothing to fear." I heard the horns summoning the knights and men at arms into their lines. "Now go and God be with you."

I went to my men, I saw that Mordaf had my unstrung bow ready for me. Each of my men had two sheaves of arrows and I was handed two. Mordaf said, "Would you like one of us to carry your second sheaf, Sir Gerald?"

I growled, "When I need help, Mordaf, I will cease going to war and warm my backside by the fire. Now come. We will move before the horsemen."

I knew that they would move in a solid body. There was plenty of room for my archers to scamper across the rough ground and keep pace with them. I turned to Ralph, "You stay here with the horses." I nodded towards John and James, "And you two, also. We shan't need arrows for a while." The boys looked crestfallen.

"But Sir Gerald, you may need me."

I smiled, "Ralph, my daughter needs a live man to be her husband. You cannot draw a bow and your bright livery will attract the attention of the Scots. My men can hide easier without you. Stay with Geoffrey of Wendover." I pointed to the other pursuivants. "You are new to this but they are not. Now go."

He nodded, "Take care."

"I always do and that is why I am one of the few greybeards on this field of battle."

We headed down the slight slope towards the Westquarter Burn. I saw the King form up his knights. He had the largest battle and there were more than eight hundred and fifty mounted and mailed men with him. He also had with him, much to my men's disgust, one hundred mounted crossbowmen, mercenaries. I was not sure how much use they would be but they would certainly slow him down as they moved towards the Scots. Bishop Bek had taken his battle and placed it, as ordered, behind, the king's. We ran across the gaps between the four battles. Already the Earl of Lincoln was forming his battle to charge the horsemen and the Earl of Surrey had left a sufficient gap so that he could make a second attack if it was necessary.

The burn was shallow and narrow but I did not make the mistake of trying to leap it. Instead, I waded it. Better to have wet feet than a broken ankle. I saw that the ground between us and the Scots was a wet and muddy morass. The horses would not be able to cross it quickly. I put that thought from my head as the king's plan depended upon the Earl of Lincoln driving the horsemen from the field and that would allow our knights to use the more solid ground on the upper slopes. None of us had strung our bows and as we headed up the slope, I tried to work out the best place to do so. As the Scottish archers had the advantage of the elevation the ridge afforded, I decided to be cautious and we halted three hundred paces from the Scots. I was confident that they would not waste arrows on a few archers especially as we were spread out. Archers never had enough arrows and they wanted the ones they have to reap a harvest. The knights would be their target. After taking off my cloak, as did the rest of the archers, I strung my bow. I looked behind us at the rest of the archers and the spearmen. We were the only archers to have crossed the burn but the rest would soon manage that. It was the spearmen who would take longer for they could not run. In addition, the Welsh looked to be lagging behind. I wondered at both their loyalty and their commitment. I put the thought from my head as I knew that this day would be decided by two things, the bow, and the horse.

Just then I saw Wallace appear. He was mounted and he rode his horse across the ground between us. He was brave for we could have felled him. There are unwritten rules about such things and he led a charmed life. He halted in the middle of the line and, after dramatically rearing his horse shouted to his men, loud enough for us to hear, "I have brought you to the revels, now let us see if you can dance!" His men all cheered and the Scottish leader wheeled his horse and rode along the line with his long two-handed sword held in one hand.

Hamo nodded, "He is strong and he has courage."

"He has, my son, but if everyone heeds their orders then it will avail him nothing."

It was then I saw an altercation as Bishop Bek's men caught up with the rear of the King's Brigade. I recognised the livery of Sir Ralph Basset who appeared to point for the bishop to move back. I shook my head, the bishop was right, this was a blow hard and the bishop appeared to ignore the knight from Drayton. I turned my attention back to my men, "Nock a war arrow and await my command to move up the slope." They nodded and I saw that the other archers had joined us to make a loose double line. The spearmen had yet to cross the burn. By the time they were in position then the battle might well be over.

It was then I heard the horns and the Earl of Lincoln's Brigade, his battle of four hundred and fifty men charged the Scottish cavalry. In theory, the Scots should have had the upper hand for there were fifty more of them and they had the high ground. In addition, they had not had to ascend the slope and their horses should have been fresher. The Earl of Lincoln, however, led better men who had the superior mounts and the finest of armour. I heard the clash from where we stood. I was about to order the draw when, to my horror, a contingent of about one hundred Durham knights suddenly launched an attack at a schiltron. It was not what either the king or the bishop wished but once started, it could not be halted. I heard the horn sounding the retreat but the blood was in their heads and they heeded it not.

"Draw!" I had to ignore the reckless attack. We archers had to duel with the Scottish archers.

"Loose!"

More than five and half thousand arrows were sent at the Scottish archers. They were distracted by the two attacks of knights and barely a handful of arrows were sent at my archers. They loosed, instead, at the two bodies of knights. Horses were felled in that initial onslaught and then our arrows struck the archers. Not every arrow found flesh but they

Wallace's War

did not need to. If only one in four hit a man, then we would destroy them as a force. We kept drawing and releasing steadily. I saw one Cheshire archer hit by a Scottish arrow but, on our side of the conflict, he was the only one I saw felled. The archers broke and ran into the schiltrons.

"Hold!" I gave the command for two reasons. One, my archers needed to rest their arms and secondly, I wanted to see how the untimely attack had affected the king's plan.

The clash of steel on steel and the cries of both horses and men rolled down the slope. The Earl of Lincoln was winning and already the Scottish horsemen who had lost their mounts were joining the archers and filling the hollows of the schiltrons. The bishop's men had been hurt and I saw dismounted knights trying to fend off the jabbing spears of the Scots. The king ordered an attack on the schiltrons. It was a mistake and I saw it clearly. In the king's defence, his wound could not be helping and as the last of the Scottish horsemen retreated into the circles of spears, I suppose he saw his chance to end the battle. It did not. Worse, it meant we could not loose our arrows and so I took a decision.

Cupping my hands I shouted, "Archers, move closer to the Scots!" Picking up my bow I began to walk towards the nearest schiltron. It was the one that the king had chosen to attack and I was honour bound to defend him.

I watched the mounted crossbowmen dismount and send their bolts at the spearmen. It seemed to irritate them more than anything and the archers within the circle soon put the handful of mercenaries to flight. The battle was not going King Edward's way. The spears kept horses at bay and the lances and spears of the knights were ineffective. The archers within the schiltrons appeared to have few bodkins for the arrows they sent at the knights hurt only horses. Knights were calling to their squires to bring up a spare. The mail of the horsemen made them impervious to hunting and war arrows.

"Hamo, take command here. When the king tires of this stalemate he will ask us to end this for him. I go to speak to the other archers."

I walked down the line of archers and passed my instructions to each of them. To be truthful I could have stayed with my men for my instructions were just confirmation of what they would have done in any case but I wanted to be occupied. It galled me to stand and to do nothing. As I walked, I saw that the spearmen had crossed the burn and were forming up into lines. The king would have the steel of spearmen in the unlikely event that we failed to break the Scottish hearts. As I headed back, I saw that all the schiltrons were surrounded and every mounted man was engaged. It was as I headed back to Hamo that I saw not only Geoffrey of Wendover but also Ralph, my daughter's intended in conference with the king. I had tried to keep Ralph safe and now he was in even greater danger than Hamo and the rest of my men.

Hamo saw my face and said, as I neared him, "He is a pursuivant, father. He serves the king and not us." He was right but it did not help.

I heard a horn sound and Geoffrey of Wendover gallantly galloped across our front to ride to the earls of Surrey and Lincoln. Ralph rode towards us, "Sir Gerald, the king has ordered the heavy horse to retire and he asks you to slaughter the Scots. He wishes you to send every arrow that you have."

I nodded, "And you get back to safety now."

He shook his head, "I am commanded to pass instructions to the spearmen." He grinned, "Fear not, Sir Gerald, Geoffrey has given me advice on how to stay safe."

I picked up my cloak and threw it to him, "Wear this and you will look less like a target." He hesitated and I snapped, "It is not a request but a command. Now do it!" He did so and galloped off. I nocked an arrow. Looking down the line I saw a sea of expectant faces, each archer holding a nocked arrow. There was no rush. The Scottish spearmen could not move while the horsemen menaced them and I wanted every archer to be as rested as possible before we began what I knew would be a slaughter. The mercenary crossbows who had survived took their place to the right of us. I took comfort in the fact that their presence might draw more Scottish arrows to them rather than to us. I knew I was being selfish but archers have a deep-seated antipathy to crossbows. As soon as the horsemen were far enough away the Scottish archers who remained began to loose.

"Draw!" I pulled back and five and a half thousand yew bows creaked. "Loose!" It sounded like a flock of birds had taken flight but even as I saw the goose feathered cloud rise in the air, I nocked a second arrow and loosed. There is a rhythm to archery. All the training at the mark meant that a good archer could draw and release for far longer than someone who was not an archer could imagine. The secret was to keep the rhythm. The fact that my men and I had all trained together made the sound of our drawing and releasing almost melodious. When my shoulders and arms began to ache, I stopped and looked at the schiltrons. There were gaps appearing.

The horn that sounded came from the King's Brigade and I knew what it presaged, the end of the Scots. The four battles did not all charge at once nor did they charge at the gallop, for the horses were tired but the two thousand horsemen moved purposefully towards the broken schiltrons. The Scots were not yet beaten and outnumbered the knights. I shouted, "Archers, close with the enemy!" As we moved closer I heard the horn sound and the spearmen began their attack. At first, the lines would be clear, horsemen, archers and spearmen but I knew that soon it would be a melee. And I might find myself fighting alongside a horseman and a man with a spear.

We advanced in a loose line with arrows nocked but not drawn. As we neared them, we sent arrows on a flat trajectory to slam into Scotsmen who had no defence against the arrows. Even those who wore leather brigandines fell as the war arrows, sent at a range of less than a hundred paces, drove through leather as though it was cloth and into flesh. A schiltron functions because it is a continuous wall of spears. As the long spears fell so gaps appeared and horsemen were able to drive their mounts between the spears. The result was that the holes became bigger and the Scots began to fall. I began to use my arrows to strike at the back of the far end side of the schiltron who had no defence against the arrows for they could not see them coming. The Bishop's Brigade was driving into them and as our arrows struck them so the far side crumbled too. When the spearmen arrived and, using their shields, drove through the longer Scottish spears it was clear to me that it was over but Wallace did not command surrender and the Scots fought on. The men with billhooks chopped and slashed at the longer spears rendering them little more than firewood. I felt sick as man after man was killed; they were the enemy and Scotsmen but they were men. We suffered, seemingly, no losses and the Scots, without mail and archers, had no defence against a combination of arrows, spears and horses. When I had used the last of my arrows, I slung my bow and drew my sword. I might have been sickened by the slaughter but I knew that it was necessary. The more men we killed this day, the fewer the

0re would be to face us in the future and that meant we would be able to go home.

Hamo and Jack had also emptied their sheaves of arrows and drawing their swords they flanked me. Despite my age, even Hamo knew that I was the superior swordsman, I had been born with the skill. The Scots were now disorganised and falling back to the woods that afforded them their only chance to escape. I was not wearing gauntlets and that helped me. The Scottish spearman who jabbed his long spear at me aimed it at my chest. Using my left hand I grabbed the wooden spear and moved it to the side. I hacked down at the spear and it cracked. He dropped it and drew his own short sword. By the time he had done so, I was on him and driving my sword up under his ribs said, "Go with God."

Wallace's War

Knowing that Hamo and Jack would be able to defend me from any attack at my side enabled me to drive towards the woods. Already Scots were dropping their spears to run the last few paces to the safety of the trees. It was as I killed my third spearman that I spied Wallace and his bodyguards. I recognised the two Welshmen we had followed. A Knight Templar galloped at him. It was brave but foolish as the footing was treacherous, the trees afforded Wallace protection and Wallace had his two-handed sword. The blade hacked through the horse's legs. The beast tumbled to the ground and the Templar lay helplessly beside it on the ground. Wallace looked at me before he brought the sword down to split open the back of the helpless knight.

He shouted, "Kill Warbow!"

The two Welshmen and three other of his bodyguards ran at me as men waiting with horses gave an escape to William Wallace. My son and stepson and I had no opportunity to see whither they went for we had five men to fight. Luckily, they did not arrive all at once. Had they done so we would have died. The Welsh spearmen made the mistake of using their spears and Hamo had watched my technique. We both deflected the spears and thrust at the Welshmen. They had better protection than the Scottish spearmen and their metal studded leather jacks stopped our swords. I knew many tricks and I placed my left leg behind the Welshman's as I pushed his spear back towards him. He began to tumble backwards and this time I aimed at his bare neck, "Die, traitor." As he died the other Welshman was distracted enough to allow Hamo to end his life.

Jack was facing a Scottish swordsman as the other bodyguards ran at Hamo and me. My stepson would have to fend for himself. The swordsmen we faced were more skilled than the Welshmen had been and I drew my dagger to make a cross and block the strike at my head. I had no compunction in bringing up my right knee between his legs. No man can resist such a blow and he doubled up. I drove my dagger through his ear and into his skull. As Hamo dispatched his enemy I looked around and saw, to my horror, that Jack was losing and the Scotsman was about to drive his blade through my stepson's chest. I was too far away to help. Suddenly the Scotsman fell backwards. I saw the white goose-feathered arrow buried in his chest and saw a grim-faced Mordaf.

"I saved one arrow in case you needed help, Sir Gerald. I am glad that I did."

"As am I." I walked over to him and hugged him. "Now we have done enough. This pursuit is for the king and the knights." After the others stripped the dead of anything of value we walked backwards from the trees. Already the Scottish dead, poor though they were, had been ransacked of their few treasures. No prisoners were taken and we walked through a field filled with dead horses and men. Few knights had fallen but their horses had paid a heavy price.

I saw Bishop Bek who was leading his horse, which had survived through the carnage. There was blood spattered both on the horse and the bishop.

"A hard fight, Bishop."

"Aye it was and I lost men and horses I should not have, thanks to Ralph Basset."

"How so?"

"He taunted me and my men. He said, "Go and celebrate mass if you will for this day we will do the fighting. The man was a blowhard and I ignored him. My young knights were stung by his words and recklessly rode to attack the schiltrons."

As we headed back to the burn, I understood what had prompted the attack which had almost ended in disaster. I wondered if the king would chastise any for this breach.

As we moved through the battlefield my archers picked up as many undamaged arrows as they could. By the time we reached the burn most had filled one quiver. To archers, arrows were almost as valuable as food.

Chapter 15

Barely a dozen archers had been hurt and only three killed. That pleased me for Stirling Bridge had seen many slaughtered. I knew that the king would wish to pursue Wallace but the food he had wanted before the battle and the exhaustion of the horses meant that we would need a night of rest. As we neared the camp, I saw the yellow and gold livery of Sir Ralph Basset, his two knights and his nine men at arms. None had lost a horse and, so far as I could tell there was no blood on the caparisons of the horses or the surcoats. The twelve of them were in high spirits and laughing. I liked Bishop Bek and, on the road north, I had come to know many of the knights who had felt their honour was impugned. Some of them had been wounded by their reckless charge and others had lost horses. I stopped and said, "It is a shame, Sir Ralph, that you did not heed your own words and prosecute the battle in the same manner as the knights of Durham."

He coloured and his eyes narrows. I was dressed as an archer. I did not even have my cloak for I had given it to Ralph. "Who are you to question me? I am Sir Ralph Basset of Drayton and I will have you flogged, you pathetic archer."

Behind me, I heard bows being drawn. I looked around and saw that Hamo, Jack, Mordaf and another dozen of my men had arrows aimed at the knights and men at arms. I held up my hand and heard the bows relax. I drew my sword and showed him the nocked edge, "I am Sir Gerald Warbow, Lord Edward's archer and I know that I fought this day and emptied two quivers and then slew men with my sword. I see you and your men without a mark of battle and I would guess that if I were to examine your swords then they would be sharp enough to shave with." I saw some of his men look down and it confirmed that they had done little in the battle.

Behind me, I heard Jack say, quietly, "The king approaches."

I ignored Jack and said, "But if my words cause offence or I am wrong then allow me to sharpen my own weapon and we will let God decide who speaks the truth."

I am not sure if it was the arrival of the king or if Basset was afraid of me but he nodded his head, "I am sorry that I did not recognise you, Sir Gerald, let us call it a misunderstanding."

The king and Bishop Bek dismounted and the king snapped, "Let us hope it is, Sir Ralph. I have spoken to the bishop and I am less than happy with your words before the battle. From now on, until Wallace is taken, you will ride at the fore of my battle and I will see your mettle."

Wallace's War

He bowed and began to back off, "Of course, King Edward." The glare he gave me told me that I had made yet another enemy but I cared not."

The king shook his head, "Warbow, I know we lost fewer men today than we might but try not to kindle fights with my knights. One of them might get lucky and I could not replace my archer, could I?" He turned to the bishop, "Is there any sign of Wallace or his body?"

Before he could answer I said, "Wallace escaped, King Edward. He had horses waiting. He will be heading for Stirling Castle."

I saw the disappointment on the king's face, "Then we still have work to do." He winced as his ribs caused him pain. "We camp here tonight and on the morrow chase and harry him until he is in chains."

When we reached our camp John and James could not shut up about the battle that they had viewed. My decision to keep them from the battle meant that they had enjoyed a good view of it and had seen the effect of our arrows. As they spoke it became clear that it had confirmed their desire to become archers.

Our progress north to Stirling Castle was slow. The Scots had burned everything that could be used by our army. There was neither food nor shelter and when we finally reached Stirling Castle, four days after the battle we found just the castle and the Dominican Friary of Cambuskenneth standing. Not only the king, but the earls themselves were despondent.

After the castle was taken, it was a matter of days only, Geoffrey of Wendover fetched me to meet with the king. Ralph came with me and I asked Hamo to prepare the men to leave. I knew not whence we might be ordered but I knew King Edward well enough to know that whatever his plans were my men would be at the forefront.

He was smiling when I arrived and that surprised me for I knew that he was not happy with the way the campaign had gone. The Earl Marshal and the Earl of Lincoln, in particular, were asking to leave and return to England.

"Warbow, despite the fact that we have not enjoyed the victory I had hoped, you did not let me down and I will honour my promises. Ralph Fitzalan, I promised you spurs and you shall have them." Geoffrey of Wendover brought a pair of spurs on a cushion. They did not look new and I guessed they were the spoils of war. It did not matter for spurs were spurs. "Take a knee." As Ralph did so the king said, "I dub thee, Sir Ralph of Dunglass. Rise Sir Ralph and don your spurs." As he did so the king turned to me, "And I have not forgotten you. To you, I give the manor of Coldingham. It is not far from Dunglass and you shall be neighbours."

I did not gush as many might have expected but bowed and said, "You are too kind, King Edward." I knew that it was a poisoned chalice.

"Now, to the meat of the matter. Wallace escaped us and he could be anywhere but you are like a good hound, Warbow, and have sought him before. You have until All Saints Day to find him. I would have him brought to me bound and in chains but if you cannot then his head will do."

My heart sank. I would not be going home as I had expected. Instead, I would be looking for a needle in a field, nay fields of haystacks. I knew there was little point in arguing and I was already planning how to minimise the problems I foresaw. "His home is in Galloway and I will seek him in the forests there or just north in Carrick. He may well flee Scotland, my lord. He has neither earldom nor lands."

The king nodded, "I have heard by some who surrendered to me yesterday that he has resigned the Guardianship of Scotland. I believe that John Comyn and that snake, Robert de Brus are likely to be named as joint guardians. I will deal with them when time allows but first, we will punish Fife. Their lord, Macduff may be dead but I want the people there to suffer for their lord's support of the rebellion."

I was relieved that I would not have to endure that campaign. Ravaging poor people and their land was never my idea of war.

"And where will you be, King Edward?"

"In Scotland until the end of October. When I have punished Fife, I will head west to Ayr. De Brus has shown his colours and I would punish him too. I have supply ships coming from Ireland and I should be in the west by the end of August. Perhaps you will have news for me by then. If you cannot find me then go to Durham and speak to Bishop Bek."

The command had already reached the camp by the time I returned from the abbey to give my men the news. "We have heard the news, father. We march to Fife."

Shaking my head I said, "No, we do not. I have been given orders to find Wallace."

I saw the look in my son's eyes and knew that it reflected my own reaction. "Then we have a cold winter ahead in the vastness of the Scottish forests."

I shook my head and waved over Ralph, Mordaf and Gwillim, "I am sending most of the men home, Hamo. You will take Ralph, as well as John and James with the married men. Mordaf, Gwillim, I need just forty archers and they should be young and without ties. Let young Paul

Wallace's War

go home for his mother is old and I would not have her die while he was away with me."

Mordaf, nodded, "Leave it with me, my lord. John and James will think they are being punished."

I said, to Ralph, "Then you, Ralph, will have to make them think that you need them with you, now that you are a lord of the manor. When you marry, they will be your family too."

He smiled, "And I will do all that I can to make my new family proud of me. It will be an honour, Sir Gerald." He paused and then said, "Sir Gerald, you did not seem happy about our new manors, why?"

"They are in Scotland. I am too old to move my family, even if they wished, to come to travel beyond the protection of Berwick and Bamburgh. The Scots are a belligerent people and they will grow weary of King Edward's foot upon their neck. They will rise again and if King Edward does as he did after Dunbar, then the manors we have been given will revert to the Scots. When we have done with Wallace then I will visit the manor and ensure that it is well managed. I will take the income for as long as I can and when the Scots reclaim it, I shall forget it."

"But it was a gift from the king."

"And were there not manors belonging to Scottish lords in England? They will go to the friends of his son, or the Earl of Lincoln or some other great magnate. Coldingham and Dunglass are the crumbs from the table. The best cuts go to nobler lords than we two."

I saw the disappointment on Ralph's face. Hamo put his arm around his shoulder, "I know my sister, Ralph and she would rather stay close to Yarpole. My father will find a manor for you and he is right, Dunglass will bring in an income that will give you a good start in life."

Ralph said, "I have one given by the king when I was dubbed but I was excited to be given another."

Hamo laughed, "If I know my mother she will try to keep you and Joan as close to home as she can."

The rest of the army headed east as I led my men south. All of them would accompany the hunters until the River Nith after which Hamo would lead them south to Carlisle and then home. It would be familiar territory for it was where we had hunted Wallace before. I intended to begin my search south and west of Lanark.

As we rode, I used Hamo to listen to me while I gave him my plan. My son had a sharp mind and while he rode with us, I would use that mind. "I think that Wallace is too clever to stay so close to King Edward. He has been humiliated and he will seek to return to the place he knows the best. Galloway is his land. It is heavily forested and the people there will be loyal to him."

"He is a giant, father, he will be noticed."

"He is a hero, Hamo, for he thrashed the Earl of Surrey."

"That was Murray."

"Who is now dead. Wallace is the one that the ordinary folk will cheer. Did you not notice how few Scottish nobles were at Falkirk?" I answered my own question. "There were just five hundred Scottish horsemen at the battle and less than three in five were nobles. Falkirk saw Wallace leading a people's army."

"Then you seek his trail in the forests?"

Nodding I said, "Many of his loyal bodyguards died at Falkirk. He has a handful of men with him and King Edward heading to Fife plays into his hands. He can build up a personal army that will protect him. I will be surprised if any Scotsman tells us his whereabouts. We will have to use our noses."

We parted at Lanark where there was a small English garrison in the wooden castle. It was necessary as it guarded the road to Ayr. The men were glad of the arrival of my archers as our presence was an indication that they were not forgotten.

The young knight who commanded, Sir Humphrey Fitzwalter, had less than thirty men to guard the outpost. Sensing his worries Hamo, Ralph and I walked his wooden walls to offer suggestions for its defence. "Keep your ditches clear of rubbish and make sure you have good sight lines for your archers. The Scots do not make good siege engines."

Hamo nodded his agreement, "Even with Wallace leading them they could not break into Carlisle."

"And Wallace is defeated?"

I could not be dishonest with the young knight. He deserved the truth. I shook my head, "He escaped with followers. It is him that we seek." The young knight's eyes involuntarily went west. "Aye, he may well be there. My men and I will look for his trail."

"He is popular, my lord."

"I know and I have hunted him before. You and your men will be safe for a while. The king will come by October but this war means that there will be tighter belts this winter. Ensure that you have enough food. Where steel and wood might not capture this castle, hunger is a wicked enemy."

We rode with Hamo, Ralph and the others for a mile or so before we parted. During that time Ralph spoke to me about the knight and his parlous position. "It is not a duty that I would relish."

"He is a bachelor knight and must be without money. Normally they give such posts to gentlemen, even men at arms. He will hope to draw the eye of the king or his son, the Prince of Wales. He must be without benefactors or else he would have fought with us at Falkirk." I smiled, "Now do you see that the gift of Dunglass, whilst not the prize you first thought, will give you an income and if you do as I did and use it to buy men then you will be secure. My archers are the first that King Edward seeks. If I were you, I would do the same with spearmen, billmen and men at arms. Even a retinue of four or five would be almost the same number as a blowhard like Sir Ralph Basset."

They left us and headed down the wide, well-made road. We turned at the crossroads and went down a hardened road studded with stones. As autumn and then winter came closer so the path would become muddy until it was eventually impassable. The king was right. We had until All Saints Day to find him.

Jack said, "Where do we start, Sir Gerald?" He was looking ahead to where the track entered one of the many forested parts of Galloway; Wallace's fiefdom.

"We visit as many places as we can and what we are looking for are the villagers who greet us with smiles and tell us nothing. We look for those who tell us that Wallace was seen in a far distant part of this land." He looked confused. "That will tell us that Wallace is close and has told his loyal followers to deceive us. It is then we enter the forests and seek his trail."

We ranged across the land for a week and we were met with sullen faces and shakes of heads when we asked about Wallace. The people were not fools and whilst they hated us, they would not risk our ire and anger by actively opposing us. It kept us moving across the land, getting closer and closer to the mountains and high forests that I believed were the hiding places of William Wallace. The obvious signs of horsemen riding across the land, horse dung, were missing. That told me that we had not crossed his trail yet. I knew we had to be patient. As we neared the middle of August, we had a stroke of luck. There were fewer settlements in this wild land and we had begun to camp in the forest more than we stayed in villages. It allowed us to hunt. This was not a wild chase. We husbanded our animals and ensured that they had both grazing and water. The result was that, on some days, we were in the saddle for less than six hours. It was on one such day that Gwillim, who had been hunting, rode in and reported a horseman heading down the road that led from Ayr. "He took the track that goes to the hamlet of An Còrsa Feàrna." I waited for I knew that there would be more. "He was, by his garb, a warrior. He had a good horse, a sword and a coif hung around his neck."

I became immediately interested as this was the first sign we had seen of any Scottish warriors. "A messenger?"

Gwillim nodded, "That was my thought. I had William of Luston follow him. He took the road to An Còrsa Feàrna."

I made an immediate decision, "Break camp. We will head to An Còrsa Feàrna."

The body of William of Luston, along with his broken bow lay just half a mile from An Còrsa Feàrna. He had been slain by a sword. Gwillim's face darkened. William had been popular and, as a young archer had a future as a vintenar. Mordaf searched the ground around and after rising, nodded, "I can see what happened here. The man on the horse stopped. You can see where his horse relieved itself. William must have approached." He shook his head, "A mistake. The blood over there shows me where the Scottish sword was rammed up into William's body." He looked at his friend, Gwillim, and said, "It would have been a quick death."

"That gives me no comfort, Mordaf."

I waved an irritated hand for we had no time for remorse, that would come when we had time to mourn, "And now the messenger knows that we are on his trail. We will have to bury William here. If this is the land of Wallace then if any locals know where we buried him, they will despoil him and I would not have that. William deserved more."

The long days of August allowed us the time to bury him in daylight. We covered and disguised his body so that neither man nor animals might find it and stood in a circle around his body as Gwillim said prayers for the young archer. We mounted our horses and rode the short distance, through the forest road to An Còrsa Feàrna. Although we did not mention his name, every man was thinking of the affable young man who had made a mistake and had paid for it with his life.

I turned to Jack and said, quietly, "When you are at war then you cannot relax for a moment. If that had been Gwillim then he might have approached the Scot but his hand would have been on his sword."

"What do mean, Sir Gerald?"

I think Mordaf had the right of it. The Scot must have known he was being followed and feigned some injury to his horse. If you remember the blood was at a bend in the road. Inexperienced riders hurry at such places so that they do not lose sight of their prey. I am guessing that the man smiled and held out his left hand to invite

Wallace's War

William closer. The rest would be as Gwillim said. Beware an enemy who smiles and you must always watch the right hand and not the left."

We found more signs of the two horses as we rode into the village. The rider had stopped and one horse had left two small parcels which still steamed in the cooling air. Dismounting, Gwillim knelt and put his hand to the piles, "An hour or more, my lord."

I dismounted too, "Secure the village." Mordaf said not a word but he pointed and men rode their horses to ensure that none could leave. "Look for signs of the horses but I am guessing they are gone."

Gwillim said, "Aye, my lord."

The anger over William's death would ensure that all was done thoroughly. I shouted, "Come forth, I would speak with the head man."

Heads appeared from the houses. The fact that none had emerged when we had arrived told me that the villagers were Wallace's folk. The smile on the face of the bearded headman confirmed it, "My lord, how can we help you?" He did not speak in Gaelic but in English and that also confirmed my opinion. Thus far our questions had been greeted with a torrent of Gaelic.

"A man rode through here an hour since with two horses. Which road did he take?"

The man spread his arms and adopted an innocent look, "No one had ridden through here for a week or more."

I walked back to the dung and picked one of the lumps up. I was wearing gauntlets and I walked back to the man and pushed it into his hands, "This is fresh and you lie." I held up my hand and ten bows with nocked arrows were aimed at the handful of men who had joined the headman. "I have lost a fine archer and I will lose no sleep over your deaths. Speak the truth or every man in this village will die and that means, my friend, that the women and children will starve. Is this man so important to you that you would see this village die?"

King Edward's harsh reputation helped me. His slaughter at Dunbar of those who had opposed him was like a legend in Scotland. The man believed that I would do as I said. I would not but my steely stare convinced him.

He pointed down the road, "He headed towards Dairy. I swear I am telling the truth, my lord."

He was lying for I had been watching his eyes. Before he had pointed, they had flickered towards the hills that rose to the west. He was afraid of us but he was still trying to deceive us. I, too, could be mendacious. I smiled, "Good. We will stay this night and you will feed us." His eyes widened, "This is now King Edward's land and my men know how to harvest Scotsmen. We fought at Falkirk."

His face showed that he had heard of the battle and he nodded, "Of course, my lord. We have small homes but Angus has a barn."

"Then that will have to do. A word of advice, headman, warn your people that if any try to leave this village before we do then they will be killed."

He looked into my eyes and knew I meant what I said. He nodded.

The food was hot and we ensured it was not spoiled in any way by asking the wife of the headman to take a spoonful before we ate. We also had her daughter eat some of the bread they brought. There was hatred in the woman's eyes but she obeyed.

With sentries set I sat with Mordaf, Gwillim and Jack, "The rider headed west. We have no chance of finding his trail in the dark but daylight is another matter. We find his trail tomorrow and the leisurely pace we have set thus far will become a hard ride. Wallace must be close and I want him before he finds another rat hole."

Gwillim found the trail of Wallace and his men and we headed along a hunter's path which wound through the trees towards the piece of Water we later learned was called Loch Doon. Wallace now knew who followed him. This was a land of trees and water. We passed neither farm nor animal as we climbed. When we reached the loch, we found the camp of Wallace. It was, of course, deserted but they had left recently for the ashes were still warm. The trail we found went along the lochside. It no longer headed west but south and west. That may have been determined by the water but I suspected that there was another reason. By the time we reached the end of the loch, it was getting dark and our horses were wearying.

We did not light a fire. Wallace knew that men were following him but there was no point in giving him a beacon to attack us in the night. Mordaf pointed at the hills that rose to the west, "He will not try to climb that. For one thing, it would weary his horses beyond words and secondly, we would see him."

I nodded, "It explains his direction. That means he will either head west, to the coast or south and east."

Jack said, eagerly, "That is where he hid with the captives."

Mordaf nodded, "And that is why I do not think he will take that road."

I sighed, "But we cannot take chances. We have to follow the trail. Wallace is clever and if we try to outwit him, we may undo ourselves. This path we follow is the one we have to take."

Gwillim nodded, "Yes, my lord, but we need caution. No one wants to avenge William more than I but the Scots now know that it is archers who follow. Wallace will remember the hunt for the captives."

Mordaf said, "Aye, and he saw us at Falkirk. He will be ready for us."

With those sobering words in my ears, we retired but my mind was filled with images of dead archers and ambushes. I did not sleep for an hour or so. When I did fall asleep it was a fitful slumber and I woke early. As we saddled our horses, I said, "Mordaf, let us adopt the plan we used in Wales. I want two archers on the flanks. They should be a hundred paces ahead of us and fifty paces to the side. Pick men with good ears."

Jack asked as Mordaf waved over William and Edward of Ware, "But how will they be able to keep on the same trail as us and what if it crosses exposed ground?"

I smiled for his questions showed that he was thinking, "They will keep to the forest and use the natural trail. If they headed for the places where there are no trees then they would be spotted." I saw him nod as he took that in. "One thing more, string your bows and carry them slung on your saddles. Better to waste a string than lose a life in an ambush." Bow strings were precious. I took out my oldest string. If we were ambushed, we would not need to send our arrows a long distance and the old string would do. I strung my bow and then hung my quiver from my saddle. I mounted and then draped the bow around the quiver. It was ungainly but I could reach both quickly if I had to.

The trail we followed, whilst still heading largely south, occasionally took a turn to the west. The horse prints, dung and urine, not to mention the broken branches told us that we were not only on the right trail but they were heading for either the south or the west coast of Galloway and I knew what that meant. Wallace was taking ship. It also told me that they did not care that we were following for they were making no attempt to disguise their passing. Each time we came to a clearing we left the cover of the trees, gingerly and my archers nocked an arrow.

It was as we descended a steep part of the trail and approached another clearing that we heard a cry from the trees to the north and west of us. We threw ourselves from our saddles and each nocked an arrow. Our horses were well-trained and tired. They did not need tethering and they began to graze on the grass in the clearing. It afforded us some cover and, as I nocked an arrow, I spied a white face on the far side of the clearing. I think that it was the angle that enabled me to do so. The man was less than fifty paces from me and even with an old string, he was an easy target. My arrow slammed into his head and spun him around. It acted as a signal for the Scots who suddenly galloped at us from their places of concealment. There were twenty of them and they had swords and shields. Many had mail. I grabbed a bodkin and aimed at the nearest mailed man, who was less than thirty paces from me when my arrow struck him squarely in the chest. A bodkin can penetrate mail at two hundred paces and at the range I sent my arrow the only thing that stopped it passing completely through his body was the fletch. He was thrown from his saddle. Even before I could nock another arrow it was all over. The Scottish warriors lay dead or dying. Some of my archers had used war arrows to hit horses. William and Edward rode in from the flanks.

Mordaf shouted, "See if any remain in the trees."

I looked over to Gwillim, "Wallace?"

He shook his head, "I could not see him. All of these are too short to be that giant."

Jack shouted, "Sir Gerald, here is one left alive."

I went over to a man at arms who was lying at an unnatural angle. His horse had been hit and in the falling, he had broken his neck. He could speak and as I approached, he said, "Sir Gerald, Sir William thought it was you who followed us. You are like a hunting hound."

"And you, my friend, have a wound that will kill you." I waved a hand at the forest. Already it was becoming gloomier. Dusk was just a couple of hours away. "Do you wish a warrior's death or would you slowly die here with animals gnawing at you."

He attempted a smile, "If you would shrive me, Sir Gerald, then I will take the blade and go to God for I have done my duty by my master and my country." I saw the terrified pain in his eyes.

I nodded and took out the dagger, "There is a price."

He blinked his eyes, "I know. You have lost Sir William. He will have taken ship by now for he left some time ago. I cannot tell you more for he would not tell any of us whither we were bound."

The man was telling the truth and I nodded, "Then confess."

"I have done what I have done for Scotland. I have never stolen nor have I abused any maiden. I go to God with a clear conscience."

"Amen." The dagger ended his life and he had no more pain.

William rode in, "There are no others close by and eight riders headed west."

"Then mount. We now know they seek somewhere to take ship. We ride like the wind."

I saw Gwillim. He was wiping his blade on a body. He had taken the head from the body and was ramming it onto a spear. I looked at him for this was not like Gwillim. He said, grimly, "This is the man who slew William."

I nodded my understanding. Leading the horses we had taken we rode along the trail which soon joined a better road. It was dark when we reached Stranraer. It was a small port but it had a jetty. The lack of ships told me that we had missed Wallace and the eight horses we found in a field close by confirmed that Wallace had fled. We had missed him.

Wallace's War

Chapter 16

The villagers in the small port were terrified of us. Perhaps Wallace had painted a picture of us as savages and it took some time and some dire threats before they confirmed that Wallace had been taken away by a ship that had been waiting for some days. He had fled to France. The old allies of the Scots would welcome him. The next day we rode north to Ayr, leading a string of horses. I knew that the king was heading to Ayr to meet his supply ships. He would not be happy if I just went home without telling him to his face that we had lost his enemy. Ayr had a castle but Robert de Brus had slighted it and there was no opposition to us. We stayed in the castle while we awaited the king for it was a shelter, at least.

I spoke with my men about the ambush for I thought we had been lucky. Edward shook his head, "I made a mistake, my lord. I spied the waiting men and my arrow at the sentry was too hurried and he made a cry."

I shook my head, "Had the man not cried out then we would have kept moving. If they charged us before we had dismounted then some of us might be dead."

"But I made a mistake."

Mordaf shrugged, "Perhaps, Edward, your hand was guided." He gave a shrewd look at William, "Your arrow silenced your target." He nodded. Mordaf smiled, "I have seen you two at the mark and there is not an inch between you. You made no mistake, Edward and that cry, as Sir Gerald says, saved lives."

Mordaf was wise and I knew that with him leading my archers we were still a potent force."

King Edward arrived on the 27th of August. He had a fraction of the army that had been at Falkirk. Many lords had taken their men back home and the Welsh had followed them. After I told him my news, he became angry and his mood was not improved when, after a few more days his supplies had still not arrived. He sat alone with me in the slighted castle. He had his men repairing it for he intended to garrison it.

"Warbow, you have done well and I release you from your commission. I would have you ride to Carlisle. I will wait here for a few more days but if the ships do not come then we will head for Carlisle. Have the castellan gather food. My army is starving. I still have work to do but yours is over." He smiled, "Until next year. I will go to parliament and ask for more funds so that I can end this war and claim the whole of Scotland. Wallace's head would have been a good way to end this year but it was not meant to be. I will send for you again, next year. Your new manors mean that you can afford more archers. I will expect two hundred and fifty when we next come to this land."

"Yes, King Edward."

As we headed to Carlisle, I reflected that I would have at least six months at home. I would see my family and especially my two grandsons, Gerald and James. A wise soldier was philosophical about such things.

When we reached Carlisle, we were greeted not only by Robert, the castellan, but his wife who had been Eleanor Hall. She was especially delighted to see us and, as we dined that night in the castle, she asked me about Alice and her brothers. They had endured captivity and that bonded them as close as any family. After I told her all I said, "I should warn you that the king and his army comes south and they are starving. You will need to gather as much food as you can."

Robert nodded, "We have suffered less here than in the rest of the borders. Before you relieved our siege, Sir Gerald, we thought we might fall. Lord Percy was a good commander but we were just days away from surrender when Wallace pulled his army east. We are grateful to you and we will feed the king in your honour. You are that rarity, my lord, you do what you say you will." The next day, as we mounted our horses for the long ride to Yarpole he clasped my arm, "You should know, Sir Gerald, that this castle will always be a haven for you so long as my wife and I live."

I nodded, "And that gives me great satisfaction, Robert, for you are a true Englishman and as long as there are men such as you then Carlisle will never fall and that means England, this England, is safe."

We did not reach Yarpole until the middle of September. Most of the crops had been gathered in and already my farmers were planting winter barley. The animals were penned at night so that the old and the weak could be slaughtered at the end of October when we would begin preparations for the winter. As we rode through fields filled with sheep and pigs grazing on the stubble, I knew that the fecundity of the land and the diligence of my farmers were the reason we would not starve this winter. My men, after a hard summer's campaign with less food than we needed, were leaner than archers ought to be. The fattening animals boded well for us.

We had not sent riders ahead and the first my family knew of our return was the shouts from the village as we passed through. My wife and I shared out largesse with the manor and the warm greetings were genuine. Hamo was stripped to the waist. He and some of the archers had been winnowing the wheat. They were covered in a patina of dust. He grinned and shouted, "Back sooner than thought!" He seemed to realise that while we had more horses there was a rider missing. "Who fell?"

Gwillim dismounted and said, "William of Luston but he was avenged."

Ralph, my wife and daughter came from the house. Ralph had caught the end of the conversation, "And Wallace?"

"Fled to France. He will return and we are called to war again next year but for now we are home and I would see my grandson."

Mary hugged me warmly and said, "He is inside. He has the appetite of an archer already."

"Good."

Joan grabbed my spare arm and kissed me, "And I am pleased to see you home, father, for now, we can plan the wedding."

Ralph shook his head, "Joan!"

Mary laughed and said, "It is natural and it is right. You have permission from the king?" Ralph and I nodded, "Then we go to the church and have the banns read. This year the harvest festival will also be a celebration of marriage and that bodes well for a happy and fruitful marriage."

James had grown in the time I was away but he was still too young to recognise faces. I contented myself with bouncing him on my knee although Mary assured me that as he had just been fed and brought back a little milk, it was wind. I chose to believe that I induced the smile. I could see that Ralph and Hamo were desperate to hear of our chase and so, to spare the women, I walked with them and Jack to the stables where William was working out where to accommodate the new horses.

"Sir Gerald, we do not have enough stalls for them. We could leave them in fields but the winters here are harsh."

"I know. We have money to build a new one. Where would you suggest?" The Falkirk pickings had been poor but I had a purse that was bulging thanks to the taking of Dirleton Castle and the other surrendered fortifications.

He rubbed his chin, "The best place would be next to the other. That way we would only need to add three walls." He hesitated as he looked at me, "But that would mean demolishing the bread oven and moving the dovecot."

I had already worked that out. "The dovecot is easy and we have more people now to be fed. We can demolish the old oven and small outbuilding we used to store tools. The new oven can go there and the tools would be better stored closer to the fields and the stable anyway."

Wallace's War

It was good to be doing something that did not involve the killing of men. Ralph and Jack knew that they would have manors to run soon and they threw themselves into the work. I had to work out who would run Ashton for me. When time allowed I would choose a steward. I needed to speak to Ralph about Woofferton but now was not the time. We laboured for two weeks, aided, sometimes, when we needed the numbers, by my archers but it was largely me and my sons and William who did the work. It made us all closer. We finished it a week before the wedding. My wife had sent invitations to the Mortimers as well as Ralph's brothers but I was not surprised when none attended. My family was not important. Ralph as the younger, landless son was even less of a reason to attend. Riding to the Welsh Marches in autumn was not something to be undertaken lightly. Although we had the king's permission to marry I still wrote to him to give him the date and to invite him. He did not come but sent a pair of oxen for Ralph's manor. The fact that Dunglass was in Scotland meant he would have to use them at Woofferton and that accelerated the need for a steward. It was a kind and expensive gesture. I knew that he had done so out of memory of Queen Eleanor. Until Ralph appointed a steward, we would benefit from the two beasts.

William of Ware had a handfasted marriage with May, daughter of Ralph the Fletcher. My wife insisted that it become a proper marriage and they were married the same day at the same ceremony as Ralph and my daughter. My little parish church bulged with archers and their families. As we now had two new oxen I had an old one, Samson, slaughtered. Although the archers and their families ate in what was my warrior hall we all enjoyed the same food. The lack of guests from outside my family made the feast in my hall a wonderfully cosy affair. My grandsons behaved well and no one became too drunk. Margaret, her husband and my eldest grandson stayed for a week and we feasted often. The ox fed us all for more than a week. The bones were roasted and we enjoyed the marrow from the bones before they were made into a soup. The vegetables and fruits that would not last much longer were also cooked so that the leanness of my archers was replaced, once more by muscle and they looked like warriors again.

As we bade farewell to Margaret and her family Mary squeezed my arm, "When I met you at the Mongol camp, I never dreamed that I would have such joy in my life."

"You had fine clothes, other slaves to wait upon you and men were there to guard you."

"But I was a slave and I could only pray that one day I would find a husband who would give me a home. I assumed it would be a Mongol warrior and I would spend my life in a yurt." She waved an arm at my manor, "This is a palace compared with what I had and I have you to thank for that."

I shook my head, "There you are wrong, it was not me, it was fate and I dread to think what my life would have been like had you not come into it. We have a good life and I intend to make the most of it. Soon there will be more grandchildren and that is good news for a grandfather who cannot have too many grandchildren."

She punched me playfully in the arm, "Joan and Ralph are barely married."

I shrugged, "I was thinking of Margaret and Hamo. I cannot see either being satisfied with just one and when Jack is old enough and weds there will be more."

She laughed and then, as we turned to enter the hall, she heard the clash of steel as Ralph and Hamo practised, "And you will go to war, once more. We women will sit at home and sew and worry."

"And that is the life I chose when I became Lord Edward's archer. Do not spoil the moment with such talk. We have months before I need to go."

She smiled, "You are right."

The winter was harsh as they sometimes can be so close to the Welsh border but my wife and her women had husbanded food well. We spent the time preparing for Christmas. This would be a special one for there would be more grandchildren this time. The spirit I had brought back from Flanders helped to preserve both the meat and dried fruit so that the pudding we had was delicious. She knew, from her time in the east, how to use spices to their best effect. Whenever I was abroad and we raided I took the small pots containing the valuable spices. Most others just discarded them. The old boar we ate on Christmas Day should have been tough but we had cooked it slowly for a day, in a pit we built. The result was meat which fell off the bone and with a sauce made of the windfall apples we feasted better than King Edward.

I was invited to the feast of my archers in the warrior hall. I slipped from my own feast when my wife nodded that it was acceptable to do so. The food was different in the warrior hall. The archers had hunted and the roast meats they enjoyed filled the table. They liked wine but preferred mead and ale. I partook of both although I drank small beakers. I was there to show my men and their families that I was still one of them. Indeed on the next day, St Stephen's day we would all eat, every family, in the warrior hall and the food we ate would be the food that was left over from Christmas Day.

I sat with Mordaf and Gwillim. "You two should marry. Look how happy those with families are."

Mordaf smiled and nodded, the reddened cheeks telling me that he had drunk well, "You may be right, my lord but where would we find a wife? All the best women in Luston and Yarpole are taken and we have few unmarried women." I knew what he meant. There were few widows of archers. "For my part I am content. Jack is like a son to me. I know he is your stepson, my lord, but I like to think that I have given him skills and it is good to watch him grow."

"And you, Gwillim, what of you?"

He gave me a shy smile, "I had been meaning to ask you about that, my lord. Before we left for Scotland I heard that Iago ap Owen died." I had not heard the name before and my quizzical face made him explain. "We were best friends when we were growing up. He married Myfanwy whom I had courted. Her father was the head man and he chose Iago over me. He thought him the better man." He shrugged, "That might have been true then for I was wilder. That was when I left to hire out my bow. The village nestles in the shadow of Wyddfa, the mountain the English call Snowdon. A passing carter carrying sheepskins told me. She is no longer young but I believe she still carries love for me in her heart. With your permission I would travel home and court her."

I beamed, "Of course but you could have gone before."

"We had the stables to build and I wanted to have Christmas with my brothers in arms. Besides, she may say no and if she says aye, then we have the rest of our lives together. If it is meant to be then it will."

I was happy for my archer. He was young enough to sire children and his loyalty, staying to help build the new stable touched me. "And when you return there shall be a farm for you. You could run Ashton for me."

He shook his head, "I am no farmer, my lord. I think that was why Myfanwy's father chose Iago over me. Iago was a good farmer. No, my lord, a roof and a yard will do for I have been careful with my money. I have enough to augment that which you pay and Myfanwy will be treated like a lady if she chooses to come."

"Then take one of the cottages by the main road. Three are empty. Choose the best and it is yours."

Mordaf put an arm around his friend, "Choose before you go and we shall make it a place for you and your bride."

"She may say no."

It was curious that my lieutenant of archers who was so confident in battle should be so diffident when it came to women. Perhaps Myfanwy's father had seen that lack of confidence and misread it.

"It does not matter for you can still live in the house when you return but I believe that the news was meant to reach you and it has come at a time when you can do something about it. Seize the moment Gwillim."

"Yes, my lord."

When I returned to the hall and told Mary she was delighted beyond words. "I hope this widow says yes for the romantic in me would like such an ending to the story. It is a shame that Mordaf will live a lonely life."

"I do not think that he is lonely. He is amongst brother archers. Just as he views Jack as his son so he regards the archers in the same way. He is hard with them but that is because he wishes them to be perfect. He makes them the best of archers."

She patted my hand, "And that, my love, is down to you. You have high standards and Mordaf does not wish to let you down."

Gwillim showed his intent when he left, with a spare horse and gifts on the morning following St Stephen's Day. The snow had stopped but a hard frost made the roads all like stone. Wrapped in a cloak and with a beaver hat upon his head he bade farewell and Mordaf wasted no time in having the archers clean and repair the best of the cottages. Gwillim had chosen one with three bedchambers for he knew not if Myfanwy had children. Two of the bedchambers were small but the house had a good kitchen and a large room for the family. It also had a small hogbog. Gwillim might not be a farmer but fresh eggs every day and an occasional fowl for the Sunday feast were not considered farming. We knew not how long he would be away but the men still worked hard for Gwillim, like Mordaf, was popular.

In my hall we also had news. Joan had discovered that she was with child on Christmas Eve. The midwives in the village had more skill than any doctor and Alice found out on Twelfth Night that she too was with child. My wife smiled and said, "And somehow I know that Margaret will be carrying a baby too."

"How can you know this?" Margaret had left for her home on the same day that Gwillim had left for Wales.

She smiled, enigmatically, "A woman knows these things."

She was proved right and a messenger came from Launceston, in the middle of February, with a letter that confirmed she was pregnant. Mary beamed, "Three children all to be born in the same year. This bodes well. What is this year, husband?"

"It is the year of our lord twelve hundred and ninety-nine."

"Then they will all start the new century together. That is good."

Wallace's War

I could not argue with her logic for it did seem as though it was meant to be. The pregnancy meant that Ralph and Joan would stay with us for a while longer and I went with Ralph to appoint a steward for Woofferton. Egbert was a good farmer and he impressed us both. We then went to Ashton where I discovered that there was a bailiff there, Roger, and he was running the manor well. We told both stewards that their archers would now train with mine. I worked out that we would now have a one hundred and fifty archers. We just needed to find another fifty. The king had asked for two hundred and fifty but that number was impossible. He would be happy with two hundred Warbow trained archers.

Gwillim arrived at Yarpole on the 1st of March. The spare horse he had taken with him was now augmented by a pony. The spare horse and pony bore a woman and a boy. Myfanwy, it seemed, had taken up the offer made by Gwillim. It was a cold Spring day and Mary ushered the family into the hall while Mordaf and some of his archers went to the cottage to light fires and warm the chilly dwelling.

Myfanwy was of an age with Gwillim and the boy, we learned he was called Iago ap Iago, looked to be ten summers old. Neither Myfanwy nor Iago spoke English and so Gwillim had to translate. Sometimes language is unnecessary and Jack and Ralph, as well as Hamo, fussed over the boy while Alice, my wife and Joan made certain that Myfanwy was comfortable. The relief on both the faces of the two Welsh was clear.

"Iago ap Owen had been ill for some time and the farm allowed to fall into disrepair." He shook his head sadly, "Myfanwy nursed her dying husband and Iago here had to try to run the farm. They were in dire straits when I found them. I do not think the village looked kindly on them and they were glad to leave. We sold the farm but she was paid just silver. I bought the pony and we headed here. It was a hard journey." I saw hesitation, "My lord, we handfasted but before we lie together I would have us married."

"Of course. Until you are wed then Myfanwy and her son shall be our guests." He beamed. "As you have handfasted then Father Michael can marry you within a couple of days."

Our joy at the arrival of a new family and a wedding was tempered by the knowledge that King Edward would call upon us soon and Gwillim would have to leave his wife and stepson. The difference was that my family and my people would not neglect the newcomers. They would be cared for. That was our way.

Ralph and Joan still lived with us and whilst all was harmonious, I knew that Ralph needed to move into Woofferton sooner rather than later. The two young families were growing and I wanted no conflict in my home because of overcrowding. I spoke first to Hamo, "The manor at Luston is Jack's but if you wished it then you could live there and be lord of the manor."

He grinned, "Yarpole is my home and God willing, many years hence, when you are gone it will be my home." He gave me a shrewd look. "You were thinking of Ralph, were you not?"

I nodded, "I know that you have the skills to be the lord of the manor but Ralph…."

"Then speak with Ralph and Jack. Jack is still young and I know, from our times on the road, that he is happy to stay here and live in the warrior hall with the other archers."

My son was right and the next day the four of us rode in my woods to hunt. Three of us took bows and Ralph a spear. After we had taken a dozen rabbits who had foolishly left their burrows to forage, we sat and gutted them. "Jack, your manor at Luston…"

He looked worried, "Sir Gerald, I am not yet ready to be master there. I am still learning to be an archer."

"Jack, you are. You know it not yet but I do. Luston is a good manor with good people. It is less than two miles away and we are almost in earshot should there be a problem."

"I am still unsure."

"I could ask Ralph but that would mean uprooting Joan twice. Once to go to Luston and then, when you decide you can run the manor when they move to Woofferton."

That convinced him, "I will do as you wish, my lord, but I think that your confidence is misplaced."

"Good. Then it is settled."

"But, my lord, I feel that I should do something about Dunglass." Ralph was like a dog with a bone.

"You have Woofferton to manage, first." I had put Coldingham from my mind but I knew that he was right. We had not even visited the new manors. "But you may be right and we should visit."

Hamo laughed, "Yet neither of you wish to make the journey."

I glared at my son. He had an insight into my character. "We need do nothing for when King Edward travels north then we can visit our manors."

Hamo said, gently, "So you would first visit your home as an invader?"

He was right. "I do not wish to leave Yarpole and Ralph cannot for Joan will need him."

It was Jack who found the solution, "I can come with you, Sir Gerald. That means the hall will be emptier and when the babies come I shall be back and I can move into Luston when Ralph and Joan move to Woofferton."

I laughed, "This is a conspiracy." I shook my head. "If we are to go it should be now. You are right, Hamo, I need to speak to my people while there is peace. We will leave in two days. It will take me until then to calm down Lady Mary for she will not be happy."

In the event I was wrong. She understood why I had to travel north and she approved. Mordaf insisted on coming with us. I think one reason was that he was slightly jealous of the joy in Gwillim's life. His old friend no longer shared the warrior hall with him and that had to have an effect. Travelling north would give him occupation and he would be with Jack whom he was still training. Taking a spare sumpter and with neither livery nor mail, we left for the long journey back to Scotland.

Wallace's War

Chapter 17

The journey was neither as arduous nor as long as I had expected. Three men travelling together moved faster than a column of archers. We paid for inns and slept well with stabled horses. It took just over seven days to make the long journey north. We travelled forty or more miles each day and my back ached but it was a good journey. None saw us as warriors and we paid for all that we needed.

Our last stop was in Newcastle. That was for a number of reasons. I wished the castellan to know that we were in the area and I wanted to know more about the two manors. Although they were more than fifty miles from Newcastle, he might have information that would help us. It was a good decision for he knew of Coldingham, "The lord there was not a follower of Balliol and he was pleased that he was deposed but he was a friend of Sir Andrew Murray. He was with him at Stirling Bridge and when he died, he swore vengeance on the English. Falkirk saw the end of the that quest."

"But what about the people? Did they share his beliefs?"

Geoffrey of Blaydon stroked his beard, "Sir Gerald, they are like all people but especially in this part of the world. They wish for a quiet and peaceful life. It is hard enough raising animals and children, let alone planting crops without war being a constant threat."

"I cannot bring peace."

"But you can. When the king comes north next year, he can end the discord in this land. Wallace has fled to France and the others who might lead a rebellion still vie with each other for power. King Edward's strong hand will keep this land safe."

With those optimistic words, we left before dawn for a back-breaking fifty-mile ride. We reached Coldingham after dark and the manor was locked up. There was a wall and a courtyard but the gate was not barred. I strode up to the door of the hall and banged upon it. A light appeared above me and a shutter was opened. "Who is it that calls at this ungodly hour?"

The voice spoke English but was heavily accented. I guessed that locals would not call at such a time and this part of the work had, at one time, been part of Gospatric's Northumbrian earldom.

"I am Sir Gerald Warbow, the lord of this manor, and I thought it time that I called upon you to see my new land."

There was a pause and then the voice said, "I will descend, my lord." The door was unbarred and we entered a dimly lit hall. The young man had just lit a brand which gradually brightened the hall, "I am Colin of Coldingham, my lord, and I am the steward. If you had warned us of your intentions then we could have had rooms prepared."

He was young, no more than twenty odd summers and his relative youth surprised me for he did not look like a steward. The light from the brand illuminated his hands and they were smooth. Stewards usually have rough hands. As we stepped in I saw that this was a true border hall. There was a rack along the wall with spears and swords. None of the swords looked to be particularly well made but they were weapons. The spears looked to be hunting spears.

I smiled for I knew what he meant. He was using the master's bedchamber. "Do not fret, Colin of Coldingham. Keep your bed and we will sleep in the main room. The embers of the fire will keep us warm."

"I will fetch you food and drink, my lord."

I shook my head, "We have disturbed your slumber and tomorrow will be time enough for you to start to serve me. We will forage for ourselves. All three of us are old campaigners and the warmth of this hall has already refreshed me."

"No, my lord, that is not right. If you would stay in the hall I will attend to your needs. It is not necessary for you to have to find your own food. I command you to return to your bed."

He seemed too eager to please and there was something about Colin of Coldingham I did not like. For one thing, he was not subservient enough to be a steward. In addition, they were normally greybeards who had risen through the ranks of the servants.

As he reluctantly ascended the stairs, Mordaf chuckled, "Clever, my lord. We get to see the house as it is and not as Colin of Coldingham intends us to."

We lit a candle from the sconce burning in the hall and headed down a narrow corridor to the kitchen. My hall excepted, most halls had narrow corridors for they were only intended for servants. The kitchen was large and there were doors leading off. I guessed they were the larders for wine, butter, beer and other food needed for the kitchen. "Search all the chambers for food and ale." Just then there was a flicker from the brand as though a door or wind hole had been opened. I put it from my mind.

The first door I opened had a couple of hams hanging from hooks and there were rounds of cheese as well as some butter beneath a pot cover. I took a ham, cut a piece of cheese and a pat of butter.

Jack came from another room with a jug of ale, "I will find some beakers."

Mordaf looked around and spied the bread. He gestured to it and Jack went over to begin to cut it into hunks. It left just two doors to open. As I placed my finds on the kitchen table Mordaf said, "Strange, my lord, this door is barred from the outside." He unbarred and opened the door and there, cowering in the corner was a meanly dressed woman of about thirty summers although beneath the dirt and the low light from the sputtering brand it was hard to tell.

It was at that moment that we heard a horse neigh. Sometimes you know when something is amiss. "Jack, stay with the woman and tend to her. Be gentle."

"Yes, my lord."

Mordaf was already racing down the corridor. I followed closely and saw him grab a spear as we left the hall. As I grabbed a second spear, we both saw Colin of Coldingham on the back of my horse, Brutus, with a chest in his hands. "Stop, I command you."

He dug his heels into the side of my horse and the powerful beast leapt towards the open gate. Mordaf did not hesitate. He was an archer but he had a powerful arm and a good eye. He hurled the spear which transfixed Colin of Coldingham. His arms spread and the chest crashed to the ground as the dying steward followed. I ran after my horse and called to him. Recognising my voice, he stopped and I led him back.

By the time I reached Mordaf my captain of archers had checked the body and shook his head, "He is dead, my lord, I am sorry. He was stealing your horse."

I went to the chest and opened it. "Do not be sorry, Mordaf for the man was stealing the valuables and the gold from the hall. I thought he was behaving strangely. Close the gate and I will stable my horse."

We left the body where it was and took the chest into the hall. This time we barred it.

"I will search the upper floor and you search this one. I want no more surprises."

There were three bedchambers but only one had any bedding upon it and it was still warm. It was the one vacated by the dead steward. There were only men's clothes. The steward was unmarried. I descended the stairs having found that there was no one else there. Mordaf shook his head when I met him, "Empty, my lord, and not a sign of a woman."

"Except for the one you found. Here is a tale."

We entered the kitchen and saw that Jack had put his cloak around the woman's shoulders and she was drinking a beaker of ale. He shook his head, "I heated a poker and warmed the ale, my lord, for she was shivering."

"Who is she?"

"I have yet to speak to her."

"Get Mordaf and me some food." I hoped that she spoke some English for I could not speak Gaelic, "I am Sir Gerald Warbow of Yarpole and I am the new lord of the manor. Who are you and what is your story?"

I saw that the warmed ale had stopped the shivering that Jack had described, "Is he still here?" Her voice sounded fearful and I knew whom she meant. More important her words were in English.

"Colin of Coldingham?" She nodded. "He is dead. He tried to steal my horse and the treasure that was within this hall."

She beamed and made the sign of the cross, "Then God has answered my prayers and delivered me from this monster."

Mordaf and I exchanged a look and we both sat. This would take time and was a knot that needed to be untangled.

She saw our look and smiled, "I am Betty, the wife of Rafe of Beadnell." Beadnell was south of Bamburgh and we had passed it on our way north. "The Scots came after Berwick was sacked and before the Battle of Dunbar. They came on a vengeance raid. Every man was slain and the women and children were taken as prisoners. My two sons were but bairns. I have not seen them since that day." She began to weep and Mordaf slipped his arm around her shoulder.

I spread some butter on the bread Jack had laid before me and sliced some ham. Jack was staring at the woman, "Come, Jack, eat. Betty, drink more ale and take your time. Do not distress yourself."

She smiled. Mordaf did not take his arm from her shoulder and she smiled at him, "You are both kind. I have not enjoyed such kindness since Rafe was killed. I have forgotten that men can be so. I must go on for others should know of the depravity of this family."

"This family? You mean Colin of Coldingham?"

"Yes, the son of the lord who was killed at Falkirk."

Suddenly it all made sense.

"There were three of us from the village who were taken and brought to this hall of horrors. One died in childbirth while another, Mary, was so abused that she took her own life. I thought to do so but I wanted to tell my story to someone. After the lord was killed I was kept as a slave. I was locked away each night when he had finished with me and during the day, I was forced to work for him. The days were bearable but the nights…" she shuddered, "suffered abuse that a man should not inflict upon an animal."

"Were there other servants?"

"Aye, but they live in Coldingham. They know nothing of my life."

Mordaf pulled Betty closer to him, "I am just sorry that he did not suffer more. I killed him too quickly."

She looked up at Mordaf, "You were the one who killed the beast?" He nodded, "Then I am indebted to you."

I had finished my food and I drained my beaker, "Here we have a taxing problem. What if Dunglass is the same? How can we return to Yarpole when there is no steward here?" I needed sleep. "Mistress Betty, there is a chamber upstairs. It is yours and know that you will be unharmed."

"I will escort her, Sir Gerald."

Mordaf left, shepherding her up the stairs.

"Well, Jack, we should have brought more men. We cannot tarry here in the north for too long as the summons may come from the king at any time. I cannot expect Hamo and Ralph to form the muster. You and Mordaf take the second chamber and I will hope for nocturnal inspiration."

Jack put the food away and, taking the brand we headed up the stairs. Mordaf was closing the door of the chamber. He shook his head, "How can men behave that way, my lord?"

I shrugged, "They would argue it was punishment for the loss of Berwick but that is not true. They sought a soft target and the fishing port of Beadnell was just such a one. I hope that I have a solution by the morrow."

I had no sooner laid down beneath the sheets, which somehow seemed soiled by the knowledge that the beast had slept in this bed when the solution presented itself. I would leave Mordaf with Betty while I went with Jack to Dunglass. If we found a similar problem then Jack and I would have to deal with it. That thought sent me into a sleep which, after the hard ride, was like food for my aching body. I rose to the smell of ham being fried in a skillet and when I reached the kitchen, I found the other three with smiles on their faces.

Betty patted a chair, "Sit my lord. I cook a fine breakfast and this will begin my repayment to you for ending my suffering."

I ate as the others chatted away. There was an easy atmosphere and I knew that somehow the woman, despite the horrors she had endured, would survive. They bred tough women in the north. I wiped my mouth with the napkin, "Mordaf, Jack and I will ride to Dunglass. Can I leave you here to watch the hall and Mistress Betty?"

I saw that he was torn but he eventually nodded, "Yes, my lord, but you take care."

"I will." I shook my head, "You sound like a mother! I will try to be back before dark but I may need another day in Dunglass. When darkness comes then bar the gates and the door. I will not risk the roads at night."

"Yes, my lord."

As we left the hall, I saw a bonfire burning. I looked at Jack who shrugged, "Mordaf and I did not think that he deserved a burial. This was easier."

We mounted our horses and headed up the coast to Dunglass. As we neared the village I saw, immediately, that it was small in comparison with Coldingham. I saw no stone building. Coldingham had a stone wall and the walls were thick enough to withstand an assault. The largest building I spied on in Dunglass was a wooden building. Whilst it was of a substantial size it had but one floor and I could not see that it was defensible.

"The king, it seems, has given an even poorer prize to Sir Ralph than we expected. I cannot see this land yielding enough to pay for men at arms. Woofferton is a much richer manor."

Arriving in daylight meant we saw the villagers. The houses ran along both sides of the road and appeared to be small farms. Men were toiling in the fields and they looked to be planting winter crops. The largest building looked to be the manor and I reined in outside the door which fronted the road and the small green. We dismounted and led our mounts around the side. The normal detritus of a farm lay all around and when we reached the rear we found a large hogbog with five pigs and a cow byre. The four cows were more than we had seen thus far and I realised then that the manor, whilst lacking a solid building, looked to be well managed. There was a stable too and I saw soiled hay being thrown onto a handcart.

"Hello."

A man and a youth came from the stable and they each held a pitchfork. I was wearing my spurs and the man bowed, as did the youth, "Welcome, my lord, can I help you? Are you lost?"

His English was less accented than Colin of Coldingham. I smiled and took off my gauntlets, "I am Sir Gerald Warbow and the new lord of Coldingham. King Edward gave it to me as a reward for services at Falkirk." I thought it as well to be as open as I could be with the man. I dismounted.

His only reaction was a smile, "Then you must have done something brave, my lord, for such a reward."

I could not tell if he was being sarcastic and, giving him the benefit of the doubt, I shrugged, "I have been Lord Edward's archer for most of my life. I just did what I always did. The king also gave this manor, Dunglass, to my son-in-law, Sir Ralph Fitzalan."

This time a beaming smile filled the man's face, "Then my prayers have been answered." He wiped his hands on his breeks and held a hand for me to shake. It was unusual but I could see no reason that I could not reciprocate. His hand was firm, "I am Stephen, the steward these last fifteen years and this is my son, Luke."

"You do not sound Scottish, Stephen."

"I was born close by Norham and the old lord of the manor, Sir Archibald, hired me to look after his horses. That was twenty years ago and I call this my home now."

"You said that your prayers were answered, what mean you?"

He said, "Luke, take his lordship's horses and tend to them."

I nodded to Jack who said, "I will help you."

As we headed into the house Stephen said, "Since Sir Archibald died ten years ago things have not gone well. The lord of Coldingham was Sir Robert and he claimed the manor as his own. At the time there was so much confusion over who ruled Scotland that none argued, Sir Archibald having died childless. He took all the profits from the manor and returned nothing. It is why just my son and I work the land. It cost my wife her life. She died in childbirth but I blame the extra work she had to do. When Sir Robert died, I was happy but his son is almost as bad. He is just less good at stealing from this manor." He suddenly paused, "Where is he now?"

I said, simply, "Dead. He tried to steal my horse and treasure. He paid the price."

We entered the house and I could see that, at one time, it might have been almost palatial but it was now run down. I could not blame Stephen for the farm itself looked to be well run.

He gestured for me to sit on a wooden chair. He brushed the dust from it and said, "The house is a place where we rest our heads at the end of a long and weary day. We have little time or money to make it comfortable." He poured some beer into a wooden beaker and I drank. "Will Sir Ralph be coming to live here?"

I could not lie to this man and I gave him the truth, "I doubt it but I can promise that it will not be robbed to pay for another's comfort. I came here to assess its worth. You should know that King Edward will return soon and we with him. My son-in-law will visit with you then but I can say that he is an honourable man and it is in his interests to make this farm profitable once more." He looked relieved, "What I can say is that I have taken the treasure that Colin of Coldingham was trying to steal. Before I return to England, I will ensure that you have funds to repair this hall and hire men to work fields."

To my dismay, he grabbed my hand and kissed the back of it, "You are a saviour, Sir Gerald."

I was embarrassed and I pulled my hand away, "And you may be able to help me for Colin Coldingham is dead and I would not trust any man that he hired. So do you know any who might be a good steward for the manor?"

"Perhaps but I have been so busy here that I know not what the farm needs."

"Then I will return tomorrow with the money I promised and I will leave Jack and my other companion to help your son do what is needed here. It means I will have to delay my departure home by a day but it cannot be helped." I stood, "You should know, Stephen, that I am a man of my word and you can trust me. Ask any, even my enemies, and they will tell you that I never break my word."

He smiled, "I knew that when I shook your hand and looked you in the eyes."

On the way back Jack said, "I spoke with the youth. He and his father work every day from sunrise until after it has set. They have to do everything on the farm."

I nodded, "And tomorrow you and Mordaf will do his work while I show him my manor. This is more than a poisoned chalice. It is a millstone that I could do without."

We barred the front gates and stabled our mounts. When we entered the hall, now looking more like a defensible hall than ever having seen Dunglass, we were greeted by the sound of laughter from the kitchen. Mordaf and Betty were preparing food together and laughing. I would not say that I had never seen Mordaf laugh but it was a rare event and even as he began to turn at our entrance, I saw that he looked easier in himself and younger. Betty was good for him.

Betty curtsied and Mordaf said, "We have prepared food and if you would sit in the parlour then I shall act as a servant for you."

"We will sit here, Mordaf, as I have much to impart."

As we drank ale, I recounted the details of our meeting with Stephen of Dunglass. "Mistress Betty, did you know this man?"

She shook her head, "The only folk I saw were the servants from the village."

Mordaf said, "When they turned up for work today, I sent them away and said that they had to wait on your pleasure. They will return at noon tomorrow."

"Good that suits. You and Jack shall ride with me to Dunglass on the morrow and I will fetch Stephen back. I have already wasted time here in the north on something that looks like it will be a drain on my purse rather than fattening it."

Wallace's War

Mordaf shook his head, "Sir Gerald, I took a walk today with Betty and she showed me the land. The proximity to the sea means that there is little snow here in winter or frosts. It is fertile land but badly managed."

I was distracted and I confess that I did not hear his words properly. I heard what I chose to hear and that is not a good thing.

Betty proved to be a good cook and the food was excellent. I insisted that she eat with us and I could not help but notice that the two, Mordaf and Betty, appeared to be drawn to each other. I wondered if Gwillim's changed life had affected Mordaf. Jack and I retired early and Betty and Mordaf cleaned the hall. We rose before dawn. Betty and Mordaf were already up and preparing the food.

"Mistress Betty, will you be comfortable here in the hall alone for a couple of hours?"

She smiled, "The beast is gone and my heart is now more at ease. I will be fine and I will gather some vegetables for a meal when you come." She nodded outside to the bread oven, "Mordaf has lit the oven and when the dough is proved I will bake fresh bread. When you return then there will be plain but homely fare awaiting you."

As we rode, I found Mordaf's silence disconcerting. Never a garrulous man he seemed even more withdrawn, "What is it, Mordaf? I like not this awkward silence."

"I am sorry, my lord, but I was thinking about Betty and her predicament. King Edward should not have bothered with Flanders. The distraction has hurt many ordinary people."

I said, quietly, "Betty was taken before we went to Flanders."

"I know but she was taken when the king left Scotland after Dunbar. Had he been here then Beadnell would not have been raided."

We rode in silence until Jack said, "And you would not have met Betty, Mordaf. Think about that. I would still be in Malton and suffering at the hands of a young noble if Lady Margaret had not been a wilful child. We cannot know what the dropping of a stone in a pond will bring."

Mordaf laughed, "And when did you become so wise?" He shook his head, "You are right and forgive me, my lord, I am not myself. Perhaps I am getting old."

After the steward gave Mordaf and Jack their instructions, Stephen rode Mordaf's horse and we turned around and headed back. "My man, Mordaf, tells me that Coldingham has a good aspect and is free from the frost and the snow that besets other parts of this land."

"Aye, that is true, my lord. It is close to the sea but it is never a warm place. I am not sure what I can do for you. I would not leave

Dunglass as I now have the opportunity to make it the farm I wanted it to be. From your words, I gather that Sir Ralph is a reasonable man and that is all that I ask. I do not know the villagers of Coldingham and I would be loath to choose one who might let you down. You seem like a good man. You have a frightening aspect yet I see a warm heart beneath."

I laughed, "Faint praise indeed. Fear not, Stephen. I need advice from a local on the best way to manage this manor. I will appoint a steward." We were nearing the gates of Coldingham and I reined in, "Before we enter, I should tell you about Betty."

I recounted the tragic tale and Stephen made the sign of the cross, "I had heard tales from travellers but I never believed that they were true. The poor woman."

We unsaddled the horses and I took him around the outside of the building. The smell of freshly baked bread drifted across to us and I saw Stephen smile, "That is a smell I have missed. Perhaps I should learn how to bake bread or, if there are more coins coming into the farm, hire a cook."

Betty greeted us and I saw the surprise on Stephen's face. He had expected, from my words something different to that which greeted us. We ate fresh bread, homemade butter and cheese and then Stephen and I walked the farm. We returned and, after taking a bag of coins from the chest that lay in my bed chamber, I went to make water. I met Stephen at the stables where he had our horses ready for us.

"Betty, if the other servants arrive give them bread and ale and ask them to await my pleasure."

"Yes, my lord."

As we headed back to Dunglass I said, "Well?"

"You have fine animals and the dung has made the ground more fertile than Dunglass. I would happily buy if I had the coins, some of the young from you."

I took out the purse I had taken and tossed it to him. There were silver and gold coins within. Jack and I had sorted out the money and the purse represented one-tenth of the money in the chest. The story I had heard convinced me that Stephen was owed at least that. I would let Ralph have the other purses I had decided were due to Dunglass.

"Thank you, my lord."

He hesitated and I knew that there was more that he wished to say, "Speak, Stephen. I am not Colin of Coldingham and you will not offend me whatever you say."

He smiled, "Thank you, Sir Gerald. I spoke with Betty. She is a good woman with a warm heart. You have a steward but you do not know it."

I shook my head, "If I had then he would now be running the manor. Who is this mysterious man?"

"Your captain of archers, Mordaf,"

His words stunned me into silence. It took me a few moments to regain my voice. "Mordaf is an archer."

"He can learn to be a steward." He shrugged, "It is a suggestion only, my lord. Ask him. I can offer him advice and the two farms are close."

The rest of the ride was in silence. I was thinking about Mordaf, and Stephen was thinking about the spending of his reward.

Luke, Mordaf and Jack had worked hard for the results of their efforts to be clearly visible. Mordaf mounted the saddle as soon as Stephen dismounted. He was keen to be gone. As Jack saddled and then mounted his horse Stephen said, "Think on my words, Sir Gerald. How long do you stay?"

I shook my head, "I had intended to be gone already. I know not."

"I am sorry that I have filled your head with a swarm of bees, my lord, but that does not change my opinion."

"And you are a good man. Whatever I decide I will bring Sir Ralph back with me the next time I come. You shall meet him then."

He held up his purse of coins, "And this will wreak such a change that I am sure Sir Ralph will be a happy lord of Dunglass."

I gestured for Jack to ride behind us and I rode next to Mordaf, "Mordaf, is there aught you wish to say to me?"

His look was one of surprise, "Do you now read minds, my lord, or have you the second sight?"

"Let us just say that some things I saw but did not understand have now been made clear by Stephen of Dunglass."

He nodded and sighing, began to unburden himself, "I am an archer, my lord, and I have served you well. Until Gwillim returned from Wales with Myfanwy and Iago I thought I would end my life as one. Gwillim's joy made me, I know not why, restless, and then when we came here, I found Betty." He looked down at his saddle and I swear he blushed.

"And you are smitten, both of you." He nodded.

"We talked long into the night and I slept barely an hour. We rose and busied ourselves in the kitchen…" His voice trailed off.

"And you would stay here at Coldingham with her?"

His head whipped around as quickly as though we had just been ambushed, "Or take her back to Yarpole."

"You could do that or you could stay here, as my steward."

He beamed, "That would be a perfect answer for me but I would be letting you down, my lord."

I put my hand on his arm, "That, you could never do. We both know that, like me, your strength may desert you and then you would not have your bow as a weapon, it would be a staff. This way you have a chance of the life service with me has denied you and yet you would still be serving me."

"Gwillim could be your new captain, my lord, and William and Edward would make good lieutenants for him."

"Then, as far as I am concerned, it is settled but you will need to speak to Betty."

He grinned, "And I know her answer."

He was right and they hugged and embraced. I was seeing a Mordaf I had never seen before. The dour archer smiled all the time. I let them have some privacy in the parlour while I spoke with the servants who were gathered around the kitchen table. There were four of them and they varied in age. One was a greybeard while the other three looked to be in their mid-twenties. They were meanly dressed. Colin of Coldingham was not a generous employer.

"I am Sir Gerald Warbow and King Edward has made me the lord of this manor. I have to return south but I leave my Captain of Archers, Mordaf of Yarpole, as my steward. He will decide if you can continue to work here at Coldingham. Know that he has my complete confidence." I saw the men's faces fall. "Fear not, like me he is an honest man. We both have humble beginnings and know that if you are retained then you will be paid and treated well."

Mordaf and Betty came back in and she linked my archer's arm.

"Mordaf, I have told them that the decision to employ them will be yours."

Betty looked up at Mordaf and, smiling, said, "And I can help you in your decision."

He looked at me and I sat on a spare chair. I waved my arm for him to hold court. He nodded and began to ask questions. Jack brought me ale and the two of us heard and saw a Mordaf who had been hidden in the garb of an archer. I knew as he finished his talk and the men left that the two of them, Betty and Mordaf, would run my manor well.

Jack and I left the next morning. I left two purses of coins with him and asked him to share his largesse with Stephen of Dunglass. "I will be back in the summer when the king comes north. I will bring more coins with me then."

We faced each other and without a word, clasped arms, "My lord, I will always be your man."

"And I will always be there if you need me, Mordaf. We have buried comrades and stood shoulder to shoulder against enemies. There is a bond between us that distance cannot change. You have a good man here, Betty."

She slipped her arm through Mordaf's, "I know, my lord and he serves a great one. May God watch over you."

We wheeled our horses and headed on the long road south.

N

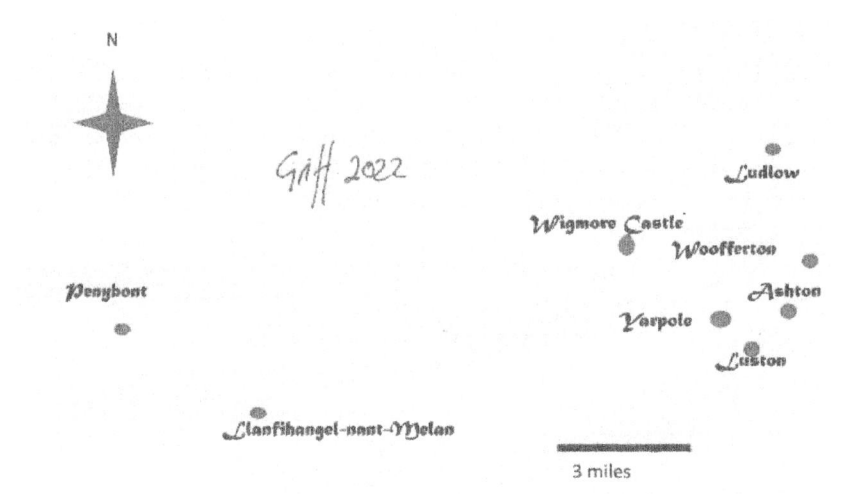

Griff 2022

Penybont

Wigmore Castle
Woofferton
Ashton
Yarpole
Luston
Ludlow

Llanfihangel-nant-Melan

3 miles

Chapter 18

When we rode through my gates without Mordaf, it caused a stir. "Jack, tell the men why Mordaf is not with us and I will tell my family."

There was relief and joy when they discovered the reason he had not returned. Ralph, however, looked disappointed, "So my manor will not yield me the coins I need for warriors?"

"In time it will and there is a purse of coins I brought back that I took from Coldingham. You will like Stephen for he is a good man and he is a good steward. It is your manor but I would nurture him. You have Woofferton and it will yield you the coins that you need. You and Joan are not unhappy living here, are you? You could always move into Woofferton."

My wife said, firmly, "They are happy, my husband, and Ralph should be more grateful for what he has. If memory serves, he had little prospect of anything before he courted Joan. Until the bairn is born then they shall live here." She smiled, "I like being a grandmother."

Ralph dropped to his knees, "I am sorry, Lady Mary, Sir Gerald, I mean no offence but a man likes to take care of his own family and soon we shall be a family."

My wife gave him her stern glare, "And this is the best place for your child to be born!"

That ended the conversation.

Jack moved into Luston. The time he had spent in Dunglass and Coldingham had changed him. I knew that Henry, the steward, would look after him but the hall felt empty without my stepson. Mary was conflicted about Jack's decision. On the one hand, she was sensible enough to know that it was the right thing to do but the mother in her who had cared for Jack as a son did not want to let him go. She went with some of her women to clean the house before Jack moved in. The steward did not live in the small manor house, rebuilt after the Welsh had destroyed it some years earlier. The result was that it was a new building but unlived in. There was no furniture and Mary ransacked our home to give him the start of a home. I knew that she would travel to Ludlow and have new furniture made for us.

That month was a frenetic one but Jack grew into the role every day. He had arrived at a good time. With the main work on the manor done and the harvest yet to be gathered in, he was able to drill and train the men every day. The house had just two servants within but there were half a dozen men who worked alongside Henry, the steward. Jack would not be lonely and he had much to occupy him. He had a manor to manage.

The summons from the king came in the middle of summer. We were warned that King Edward needed the men of Yarpole, Luston, Ashton and Woofferton to be ready to march north to the muster. Alice and Joan were close to their time and I cursed the timing of the summons. We made arrows and found more horses. The actual date for the muster did not materialise and, on the day before Joan gave birth to a daughter, Mary, Geoffrey of Wendover rode into my yard.

"You come to tell me when we march?"

He nodded, "It will not be until next year, my lord." After dismounting he leaned in to speak so that his words would not be heard by another, "Parliament and some of the barons think that without Wallace the Scots have no leader."

I became angry, "The last time the king did not finish the job was his fault and good men died at Stirling Bridge, now it is self-serving earls." I saw his face and I smiled, "I am sorry. I should not take it out on the messenger. Will you stay?"

"Of course."

The result was that Geoffrey the pursuivant saw the birth of the first child of another pursuivant, Ralph and it changed him. He left the next day to inform the other lords of the delay after telling me that he would ask the king's permission to pursue his own life. I was pleased for him. He wanted what Ralph had and I knew that there was a lady he had set his heart upon. Serving the king, as I had found out, meant putting your own desires to the back of your mind.

Alice gave birth to another boy two weeks later. John was a huge baby. Finally, in August, Margaret gave birth to a daughter, Eleanor. Mary and I were delighted. We now had five grandchildren and all had been born healthy. For once I was grateful to the rebellious barons for their selfishness meant we were not going to war, at least not for a while.

It was September when Ralph asked my daughter if he could visit his Scottish estate. Joan showed her maturity by agreeing and Gwillim agreed to give an escort of twenty men. They were the ones who wished to visit Mordaf. They were men like Dick, William and Edward. They had served under Mordaf and wished to say farewell to him properly. We had not heard from him since we had parted but I believed that no news was good news. Jack also went with them. The change from the diffident, shy and almost reclusive boy to the confident man he had become was nothing short of miraculous. He knew the route and he would be able to keep Ralph company. I knew that he wished to question Mordaf about how he had learned to manage a manor and like the others wished a goodbye. I felt sad as they pulled out of my yard. I wanted to be with them. To compensate and to keep myself occupied I had my men build new rooms for my home. The hard physical labour was good training and they enjoyed the challenge. The result was that when, at the end of October, our men returned, the new rooms were finished.

Ralph gushed about his manor when we ate. Since I had left Stephen and Mordaf had begun to help each other. Both manors were in profit. I knew that Mordaf was not a writer. I smiled when Ralph told me that Mordaf was already training the young men of both villages to be archers.

Jack nodded, "Aye, lord, and he has the older men drilling, not with the long spears they used at Falkirk but billhooks. He said that now that the manors were English owned, they should be English armed." He nodded, "I think I shall do the same at Luston. The best archers are here, serving you and the others need better employment on Sunday after church."

I smiled, Mordaf had changed but only in the way he viewed his life and his future. The warrior that was Mordaf was still there and I knew that the men he trained would be good warriors. His influence on Jack was clear. Mordaf had moulded the young man as much as I had.

"And the journey, Ralph, it was not too arduous?"

"It is a long one that is for sure. I cannot see either of us making the journey more than once a year but even that may not be necessary. We have good stewards, my lord. Mordaf told me that your visit to Stephen put new hope into him and his son. The coins you gave to him were the difference between success and failure and he has seized the opportunity to make their lives better." I gave him a searching look and he had the grace to smile, "Aye, Sir Gerald, it has been a lesson for me, too. You make the best of what you have."

After the table was cleared Ralph went to his family and Mary also left the table to help Alice with her charges. It left Jack, Hamo and me sitting before a comfortable fire finishing off the ale and the wine left on the table. Jack would ride to his manor the next day. I saw Jack turn to ensure that the door was closed and then he spoke. His face was serious, "There were two pieces of news I hid from the table, my lord. In fact, I am not even sure if Sir Ralph heard the same whispers as did I." He drank some ale.

"News?"

He shrugged, "Rumours really and they may be nothing but you have both taught me to keep my eyes and ears open. I did so and, well, what I heard disturbed me."

I smiled at my stepson. He had become Hamo's younger brother and showed all the same traits yet they shared not one drop of blood, "Jack, just speak and Hamo and I can judge."

He nodded, "We came back through Galloway and Carlisle."

"Why?"

"When we passed through Newcastle the castellan, Geoffrey of Blaydon, asked us a favour. His daughter had married a knight who now served at Carlisle and he wondered if we might, on our return south drop off a letter. The journey would not be much longer at this time of the year and while it is an impassable route in winter, at this time of the year it is pleasant. Sir Ralph agreed. It was a good journey. We spied many hunting birds on the moors and it was good to see, for the first part of the journey, a different part of the land. We stayed in priories and in the fields of friendly farmers. It was there, in the land that was once Scotland, where we heard of Wallace's origins. His ancestors, a couple of generations back, were Welsh soldiers in the service of a lord who served England. Wallace's grandsire stayed in Scotland and that explains his name and lack of land."

Hamo smiled, "There is irony, a Welshman almost securing the crown of Scotland."

"I am just grateful that his antecedent must have been a spearman for, imagine had he been an archer and trained the men of Galloway to become bowmen, Falkirk might not have been the victory that it was."

I saw my sons reflect on that.

"You said that there was something else?"

Jack nodded, "The information about Wallace was freely given but the other news I heard was caught on the wind. We kept hearing word of Wallace's imminent return. That, perhaps, was to be expected but there were also hints that he had his supporters recruiting an army again. We stayed north of Carlisle in an inn and Sir Ralph had retired early. Gwillim and his archers were drinking and playing nine men's morris. I was not ready for sleep and I went out to see to the horses. You both taught me to ensure that our mounts were well cared for. I was in a stall when I heard two men come in. One was Scottish but one was not, he was Welsh, and they spoke in English. I confess that I did not hear every word but the gist of it was that the Welshman was being paid to recruit more Welshmen for Wallace. I did not hear the purpose of the recruitment but it cannot bode well for England. Wallace's name was mentioned. The Welshman mounted his horse and rode south. I waited until the Scot had left before I rejoined Gwillim. I have pondered the incident ever since and I felt I ought to speak to you about the matter."

"You were right to do so."

Hamo said, "It is like the mist, father, you try to grab hold of that which stops you from seeing and you cannot."

"Aye, and there are many Welshmen still in Scotland." The mutiny in Linlithgow had made King Edward mistrustful of the Welsh he had hired. While the Gascon and French mercenaries had fought hard and well in the campaign, the Welsh spears had been held in reserve at Falkirk until the victory was assured. I wondered if some had stayed in Scotland. "I think that the borders here are safe but it can do no harm if we were to ride a little into Wales and speak with those who are our friends."

Not all the Welsh on the borders saw us as enemies and they might confirm if those who were not the friends of King Edward were joining an army that might threaten King Edward's newly conquered land. I cursed, once more, Parliament. As much as I did not want to go to war, I knew that had King Edward gone when he had planned then Scotland might be secure. As it was his enemies had enjoyed another year to plot and gather men. A campaign this year would have faced less opposition than the one we would have next year.

"Thank you, Jack." He raised his beaker, "You know, you have grown much and, it is right that you now run Luston and have devised new plans for your men. If King Edward summons all the men, then Luston's men will go to war. You will lead them."

I could see that he had not thought of that. He emptied his beaker, "Before I visited Mordaf and Betty I might have thought that it was not time but Mordaf is a man with new energy. I am fearful of the responsibility but I know that it is now mine and I should train the men whom I will lead in battle. How many will King Edward expect?"

I rubbed my chin and tried to remember how many had been asked for the last time. I never took the exact number the king demanded and he had never reprimanded me for any shortfall. Jack would not enjoy the same leniency. "I think it is fifteen archers and fifteen bill or spearmen."

Hamo interjected, "You are right to train them as billmen. The weapons are more expensive but they are a better weapon." He saw the lack of understanding on Jack's face and explained, "It will be the Scots we fight. Their horsemen are not a threat but their long spearmen are. A spear duels but a billhook can chop a spear in twain. It will involve more expense and work for you but I believe it is worth it."

I stood, "Wise words, Hamo, and you should heed them, Jack. We will delay our visit to Wales until you are settled back in and now this old man will retire."

When Hamo and I left for our ride into Wales I was content. We had almost left it too late for our ride. It was November and the nights were drawing in. Wales was not the place to be at night. In addition, the weather in autumn was unpredictable and we could have snow at almost any time. Hamo and I rode with Gwillim, William and Edward. My captain and lieutenants of archers were more than enough to deter any attack. We rose early and we went armed although our weapons were hidden beneath our cloaks. We headed south and west passing through fields whose crops had been harvested. The families of the farmers were gathering any food that might have been missed. The odd bean pod or ears of wheat might make a difference. We knew which farmers we could speak with and we headed for those farms, making the excuse that we would water our horses.

Owen ap Griffith lived just twenty miles from my manor at Llanfihangel-nant-Melan. We had helped him out with food some years earlier when his crops had failed and he still remembered our generosity, "Sir Gerald, I haven't seen you in a long time. Do you still draw a bow or is it now hanging with your sword above your fire?"

I laughed, "Owen, I was a warrior born and I shall die a warrior. I still draw a bow but I fear that my son Hamo is the one who now hits the furthest mark."

Owen was an archer and whilst not as good as the men I led was still a good one. "The only time I draw a bow these days, my lord, is when I hunt the squirrels or the rabbits and more of those survive than end up in a stew."

I nodded, "Then all is peaceful, hereabouts?"

His eyes narrowed, "Have you heard anything, my lord?"

"Just a rumour that men are being recruited to fight for the Scots."

He looked relieved, "No, my lord, no one has asked us for our bows." He frowned, "Although I did hear of a Scot who visited Penybont." He shook his head, "They are a bad lot there, my lord. They are not good farmers and they like to blame everyone else for their ills."

"You say a bad lot. Speak plainly Owen, what do you mean?"

He sighed, "In this village, we have long ago learned to live with England as a master. Your laws are not over harsh and you keep the land free from brigands. Penybont and the men there yearn for the time of Llewellyn the Great. It does not take much to kindle the embers of rebellion that sit in their hearts. If any came here to seek bows and swords they would be given short shrift but Penybont…?"

Wallace's War

The village was just a few miles northwest of Llanfihangel-nant-Melan and, after bidding Owen farewell, we headed there. Gwillim said, "Do not expect cooperation there, my lord."

"And I do not. Just keep your ears and eyes open. What they do not say may be as illuminating as what they do."

The hostility was clear from the moment we passed the first farm on the road that led into the village. There were no smiles and the scowls that greeted us were menacing. I wondered if my decision to bring so few men was a good one. Hamo said, in a low voice, "I am glad that we have time to return to Llanfihangel-nant-Melan in daylight for I would fear a knife between my shoulder blades if we had to travel this road in the dark."

We reined in at the river and dismounted while our horses drank. Some men came from their homes and gathered to watch us. I nodded to Hamo, William and Edward to watch the horses while Gwillim and I walked up the slope to speak to the men. Gwillim could speak the local language but it was many years since I had spoken Welsh and that was the Welsh of the Clwyd Valley. The headman had the look of an archer. He had a squat body but his arms were like oaks. He made no pretence of politeness. "What brings you here, Englishman? You are not welcome." He spoke in English but some of those behind him cursed in Welsh. At least I assumed it was curses. The Welsh dialect I understood came from the north of the land.

My voice was stern and authoritative, "You have no king and your prince bows the knee to King Edward so watch your words, headman. I come to this land in peace for I heard a rumour that men were sought by the Scots to make mischief for King Edward. What do you know of this?"

The grin he quickly hid confirmed the story even though his words did not. "The Scots do not need Welshmen to defeat English knights. The battle of Stirling Bridge should have told you that."

The Welsh laughed and, once more, I heard conversations in Welsh behind the headman. One man nudged a young man in the ribs and the smile left his face.

I nodded, "You have short memories here in Wales. We defeated the Scots at Falkirk without the aid of drunken Welshmen who slew priests."

I wondered if I had gone too far for hands went to weapons. Behind me, I heard the drawing of yew bows as Hamo and my two archers drew back. I held up my hand, "I wish to spill no blood here this day but you know the skill of my men. Would you die this day?" Their

Wallace's War

hands went from their daggers and axes. "Answer my question. Have any of your men been suborned by Scottish rebels to fight in Scotland?"

The look he gave me disturbed me for he had a sly grin on his face, "No, Sir Gerald, we have not been asked to fight in Scotland, that I swear."

His men had also adopted a more relaxed demeanour. I could not understand this.

"Thank you, and we shall leave but know this. If I find, when we fight in Scotland, any Welshmen, then they will lose more than their two fingers. They will die."

Hamo, William and Edward kept levelled bows until we mounted our horses. We rode back down the road but I kept expecting an arrow in the back. That none came was even more disconcerting.

We rode hard and in silence until we had passed Llanfihangel-nant-Melan. The village was almost deserted for men were still in the fields making use of every moment of daylight. We slowed so that we could talk knowing that we were not far from our home.

"Gwillim, what did you hear? I did not like the look on the face of the headman."

"The Welsh are confident, my lord. They disparage us saying that we are weary from war and that our lands could be taken."

"Nothing more substantial than a vague threat?"

He paused and said, "I heard one say, the young cockerel would be the first to taste Welsh steel."

Hamo pulled up his horse, "Jack?"

Gwillim nodded, "I think so, Master Hamo."

"We cannot tarry here. Let us ride home quickly for this is not what I expected. I thought the Welsh might have been suborned to go north to Galloway and fight for Wallace."

Hamo said, "This makes more sense. Since we defeated the Welsh, they have sought vengeance. The men like Owen ap Griffith are not the ones in the majority. Welshmen might be reluctant to march hundreds of miles to fight for Scotland but fighting in England is a different matter. What say you, Gwillim?"

"Your words make sense, Master Hamo, but such an attack would bring the weight of the marcher lords upon them."

I had been reflecting on the words and I said, "Would it, Gwillim? Since the death of Lady Maud, we have become estranged from the Mortimers. From what Ralph has told me neither he nor his family enjoys the support of the Mortimer branch of the family. If anything they are resented. Remember the lords who deserted King Edward so quickly after Falkirk. Parliament has shown us that there are lords who

Wallace's War

no longer put England first, but themselves. They seek to acquire vast fortunes and taking men to serve a king in Scotland or seeking retribution from Welsh raiders might be deemed unnecessary. Let us treat this threat seriously and plan to foil it ourselves."

William was thoughtful, "How many men could they bring, my lord? I counted less than thirty in the village. There may have been others we did not see but I cannot see them bringing more than forty or fifty men. We have more than twice that number at Yarpole."

I nodded, "Aye, but not at Luston. Gwillim, the one who spoke the words was young?"

"Aye, Sir Gerald."

"And he was silenced by another?"

"He was."

"If we take men from Yarpole to defend Luston then what if the Welsh attack Yarpole instead?" Their faces were a mix of shock and mystification.

"But Gwillim heard the words, young cockerel."

"And suppose that is what he was meant to hear? What if the attack is intended for Yarpole and I am the one they really seek to kill? I can see the hand of Wallace in this plan and I have both thwarted and hurt him many times. I do not believe that he has returned to this land yet but that does not mean he has not sent subordinates to do his bidding."

"Then we divide our forces, father?"

"We do and that means that even forty men could hurt us although I believe that there will be more who come. Yarpole still sits close to Wales and they can raid and be back before the rest of the county can react. This will be an old-fashioned vengeance raid. They see us as rich and they would take what we have. This will not be a raid for animals but for horses and treasure. There will be men who come from further afield than Penybont. The riches of Yarpole and Luston will ensure comfort for years to come."

It was beyond late when we reached our home and Mary, Alice, Joan, and Ralph were waiting anxiously for us. As we ate the food they had kept for us, Hamo and I told them what we knew. There was shock on their faces, especially, Ralph's but Mary just nodded. She understood better than any.

"But Baron Mortimer, he could do something."

"He could, Ralph, and whatever we decide to do I would have you ride there in the morning and lay the facts before him. I may be wrong and have misjudged him. If he exercises his authority then this might be stopped before it begins."

Mary said, "But, husband, you do not think so."

I shook my head, "Edmund Mortimer does not like me. He made that clear in the Scottish campaign. He hates the Welsh but a raid by peasants will not have enough glory for him."

Ralph looked confused and Hamo explained, "Edmund Mortimer and his brother Roger were the ones who trapped and killed Llywelyn ap Gruffudd. They sent his head to King Edward. When you have killed a prince then peasants are beneath you."

Mary said, "What about Jack? We cannot abandon him?"

"Nor will we but we must show cunning. I think that the Welsh may have watchers on both Yarpole and Luston."

"Then we find them and hang them!"

I nodded, "We will seek them, Hamo, but these watchers will be the best that they have and we have to plan as though we do not find them. I will reinforce Jack with small groups of archers. We will send them, over the next days, north, in the afternoon. They can sweep around and reach Luston by dark. I intend to send forty men. Luston cannot hide more. I will ride with Edward tomorrow for I would have him as the captain of Luston's men. He is ready for it. I would use William but he has a wife here and the thoughts of his family might distract him." I looked at Hamo's face in case he disagreed with me. He did not and nodded. "We need a signal. I know it is less than two miles twixt the two manors but as we discovered the last time the Welsh came that two miles can be two miles too far for some. I would have a signal beacon built here. I will have Jack build one. Until this threat is eliminated, we act as though we are at war and keep sentries watching every hour of the day and night. The nights are now much longer than the days and that is when I think that this attack will materialise."

Alice had been nursing John and now he slept. "And, Sir Gerald, how long do we have to endure this state of siege?"

I would not lie to her and I said, gently, "Until it is over. I swear, Alice, that you will be safe but I cannot give a time for this to end. The Welsh may come tomorrow or wait until January. We know not and there is little we can do unless Baron Mortimer agrees to intervene."

We all looked at Ralph. A great deal rested upon his young shoulders. Thus far he had not been asked to do anything for his new family but now we did.

Chapter 19

I rose before dawn and I was the one who woke Edward. Hamo roused the other archers for we had much to do. Yarpole's defences needed to be improved and we needed a signal beacon constructed. William came to join his brother as I told Edward of Ware what I intended.

I think Edward was pleased to be given the opportunity to step out of his brother's shadow and lead men of his own. It was well overdue, "This is a good plan, my lord. I am confident that with forty archers we can make Luston strong against the Welsh."

I hoped he was right. "You and I will ride this day and apprise Jack of the problems he faces. Gwillim and William will select the forty archers who will come to you over the next two days. You and Jack will need, without making it too obvious, to improve the defences of Luston. Every day, even an hour that they do not come buys the time that you and Jack will need. You will need two men to guard the beacon that you will build for without that light then no help will be forthcoming."

William smiled at his younger brother, "This is your time, Ned, and I believe that this will be the making of you." Edward appeared to grow a handspan at his brother's praise.

I rode with Edward to Luston. As we headed down the narrow lane, lined with low hedgerows and spindly trees, we saw it not as an idyllic place of peace but as a road filled with danger. It was perfect for an ambush. The two miles a relief force would travel would not seem as short if they were watching for arrows from the flanks. An archer cannot use his bow while mounted and the two miles would be where we were most vulnerable.

We reined in and I saw Jack sparring with one of his labourers. They were using billhooks and I saw that Jack had taken Hamo at his word. The labourer was strong but he had not been trained as an archer. It was too late to do so now and I could see that he would make a good billman.

"Sir Gerald, this is most unexpected."

I dismounted and I saw Jack take note my serious expression, "And it is not a social visit. Edward, you know what to do. Jack, let us go inside. Henry the steward was at the stable and I shouted, "Henry, we need a word."

The main part of the house was empty. The servants Jack employed, two women, were outside at the bread ovens. Without preamble, I told them what we had learned. I watched Henry's face fall. He was not a young man and had been appointed after the last raid when so many from Luston had died. He understood the problem better than Jack.

"Edward is here to help you, Jack, and to command the archers. I have spoken to him and he knows what to do. You must build a signal beacon with a clear line of sight to Yarpole. You will improve the defences. When the archers arrive, they must be hidden during daylight. You have no warrior hall but there are barns and storehouses." I hesitated, "Jack, there will be someone watching your land. While Edward does what I have asked him I need you and one you trust to ride your land and to see if you can either spy or deter this watcher. It would be natural for a young lord such as you to ride his land."

"But I am no lord."

"I am sorry, Jack, but the Welsh think you are. The gift Lady Mary and I gave to you may become a millstone. I am sorry."

He smiled, "This is just a trial, my lord, sent to test me. As yet I have no wife or family. I will make this hall safe so that when I do, they will be able to sleep easy in their beds knowing that I have endured this trial."

When I left, I was still worried and that worry seemed to heighten my senses for as my horse neighed and slowed, my hand went to my sword and I dug my heels into his side. He leapt forward and the arrows that were intended to pluck me from my saddle flew, instead, over my head. I was more than a competent rider and I wheeled my horse with my left hand as I drew my sword with my right. There was a low bush to my right and the hidden bowmen had sent their arrows from that direction. I did what I hoped was the unexpected and I jumped the bush. I knew how quickly Welshmen could draw a bow and I knew that they would not miss a second time. As I landed, I saw the two of them, just twenty paces from my right. My move had confused them and they were still swinging their bows around. They were not at full draw yet. Even the best archer could not hold for longer than a few moments and that would be my only chance to walk away from this encounter and not lie dead.

I rode at them and I lowered both my head and body to make a smaller target. I was risking my horse but that could not be helped. The two men were five paces apart. I had to choose and I picked the one to my right. Brutus was a big horse and would give me some protection from the other warrior. I saw as I neared the Welsh archer, the man draw back his bow. I gambled on the fear of being trampled by a horse and I pulled back my arm. He sent the arrow at me but a combination of a fear of the horse and the motion of my mount meant that the arrow caught the cowl of my cloak and my sword swept across his neck to half sever his head. The other archer sent his arrow, not into my horse but into my left forearm. Such was the power of the blow that the head came through and embedded itself into the leather and wood of my saddle. Ignoring the pain I whirled my horse around and even as the Welshman drew another arrow, I brought my sword to split his skull in two. As much as I wanted a prisoner, I could not risk my life anymore. I tried to pull back on the reins but the pain was excruciating. I sheathed my sword and then broke the shaft of the arrow. Gritting my teeth I pulled my arm from the rest of the arrow. Blood spurted but not enough to suggest that the arrow had struck a vein. As I pulled back on my reins with my left hand, I gripped the hole with my right.

The two men were dead and I needed attention. I gambled that I could make it the one mile or so home before I succumbed to the wound and I rode back to the road and then spurred my horse. The clattering of the galloping hooves on the cobbles of my yard alerted my men who were working on the defences. It was Gwillim who spied the blood and he shouted, "Sir Gerald is wounded. Stand to!"

Hamo raced from the ditch in which he worked as my wife came from the house. Archers began to string bows but I shook my head, "The men who did this are dead. They lie down the road. Fetch their bodies and then…" The blood loss and, I suspect, my age combined and all went black.

When I came to my wife was shaking her head as she bound my arm, "You are getting too old for this, my love."

I was annoyed with myself and I answered a little more gruffly than I intended, "If a man cannot ride a mile away from his own home in safety, then there is something wrong with this world."

Hamo's voice came from behind me, "You are Gerald Warbow and many men wish you dead. We fetched in the bodies and one of them was from the village of Penybont, I recognised him. We were right but that is cold comfort now. You will be laid up until your arm heals."

I swung my legs from my bed, "Nonsense. I cannot draw a bow but I can…" I suddenly felt woozy.

My wife shook her head and placed my legs back onto the bed, "Your head and heart might wish one thing but your body is telling you another. Let Hamo bear some of the burden. Rest this day."

Hamo loomed into view, "Mother is right, father. You have startled two of the watchers and I have men scouring the land for the others. I have sent the first twenty archers to Luston and your wound has alerted everyone to the danger. Woe betide any Welshman they find this day."

They were right and I just wanted to sleep. I closed my eyes and oblivion enveloped me. When I woke it was night and Mary, who must have sat by my bed all afternoon, allowed me to rise. I entered my hall and saw that all were eating. I took my place at the head of the table aware that every eye was upon me. I smiled, "It is but a small wound and struck neither vein nor bone. It will heal." I saw Ralph at the other end of the table.

He saw my questioning look and said, "You were right, Sir Gerald, Baron Edmund does not wish to provoke the Welsh. He says that if they attack then he will punish them but he will not initiate a war."

It was as I had thought. We would be the sacrificial goat that would punish us and allow the baron to make war and increase his lands. It would be up to my men and my archers to defend my land.

As much as I wanted to be up, the next day, to help my men, age had caught up with me and I could no longer shrug off an arrow to the forearm as though it was nothing. I ached and I felt weak. I hated both of those feelings for I was Gerald Warbow, Lord Edward's archer. Mary knew how to deal with me and she ensured that James, Hamo's son was brought to me. The infant occupied me. He could not talk yet but by gestures and looks, he made it clear what he wished. Hamo, for his part, made certain that I was kept abreast of all that I needed to know. When the other scout was hunted, found and then killed I was a little more relieved. It did not mean that the Welsh would not come but merely that they would be in the dark until they had replaced their scouts and have to rely on old information. They would have no idea that there were now forty archers concealed at Luston to augment Jack's men. They would not know of the new ditch that had been dug and filled with stakes. The sentries who surveyed the land around both manors would be hidden from sight but they would give us warning of an approach in daylight. I knew that they would come at night. I had raided enough to know that a night attack suited the attacker more than the defender.

When they had not arrived a day later, I pressed Mary to allow me to walk my manor. She relented if only to stop me from pestering her. I went first to the beacon. It was filled with kindling and two men were in attendance, I doubted that we would need to summon help from Luston but it was good to know that we were prepared. The ditch around my hall had been cleared of the rubbish that always accumulates over time and would be a barrier. My walls themselves were substantial but a night attack meant that unless we had quadrupled the number of sentries we normally used then we might be in danger of men sneaking over the walls.

William visited his brother and returned with the news that all was well and no further spies had been seen. It boded well. However, each night, when I retired to bed I did not sleep well. It was partly the wound but mainly the fear that this would be the night that they came.

Hamo roused me from a fitful sleep. I know he tried not to disturb his mother but it was inevitable that he would. She too was not enjoying rest at night. "Father," he hissed.

My eyes were open immediately and I sat bolt upright. It was a mistake to do so quickly for my wound complained.

Mary asked, "It is time?"

Hamo's voice came from the dark, "The sentry spied the lantern and the men are roused. You need not come, Father. Ralph and I can deal with this."

I swung my legs over the bed, "So long as I still breathe, I can fight my enemies and make no mistake, Hamo, these men come to Luston not because of Jack but because of Gerald Warbow. I have done what I have in the service of my king and country but it has made me a target for my enemies."

Mary's voice was commanding as she said, "Hamo, help your father don his mail." Her tone left us in no doubt that we would not be allowed to question her. It would add time and every second that we delayed increased the chance that Jack and his defenders would be overwhelmed.

When we reached the yard Gwillim, William and the rest of my archers were mounted. Ralph was also mailed and he held the reins of my horse. I mounted and Hamo tossed me the helmet he had carried. I had delayed my men long enough and I kicked my horse to start him. We clattered down the road to ride the two miles to Luston. The beacon burned still and it drew us to the village and the manor. We were less than half a mile from it when we heard the cries and clamour of battle. I drew my sword for Ralph and I would be fighting on horseback for as long as possible. As soon as we entered the yard through the shattered gates then Hamo ordered the archers to dismount. John and his brother James, wearing leather brigandines took the reins of as many horses as they could. If there was a flight then we would need to pursue and we would not have the time to gather horses that had wandered off. A warrior, I assumed he was a Welshman as I did not recognise him, raised his bow to send an arrow at me. I spurred my horse and he leapt forward. The dark, the speed of my horse and my use of the reins meant that the arrow missed. My sword did not and I used the tip to drive into the man's face.

"Ralph, with me!"

I knew the value of two men supporting each other. As my archers' arrows began to fly, heading towards the targets they saw and I did not,

I glanced around the yard at the bodies. To my horror, William's brother, Edward, lay dead at the foot of the beacon. Already we had paid a greater cost than I had anticipated. The Welshmen were using axes to try to breach the solid doors to the hall. I heard them as they crashed and smashed into the wood. We had now been seen and Welshmen turned to aim their bows at us. There were far more of them than I had expected and sprinkled amongst the archers were men at arms in mail.

"Draw!" Hamo's voice commanded.

Welsh arrows flew at us from the dark. One struck my helmet and made my ears ring. One hit Ralph's mail but it was a war arrow and did not penetrate.

"Release!"

The discipline and control of my archers made the difference. While just two of my men fell twelve, at least, Welshmen were struck. Even as a second flight flew from my archers I said to Ralph, "We will charge them."

"Aye, Sir Gerald. You saw Edward?"

"I did and if William saw it then these Welshmen will have to endure his wrath."

The men with the axes had turned, I assumed someone had ordered them to face the new threat, and there was a knot of mailed men protected by their archers. Another shower of arrows made the men raise their shields as Ralph and I covered the last few paces to the Welshmen and their allies.

Hamo shouted, "Draw swords!"

"Wheel Ralph!" I was not a warrior who normally fought on horseback but I had fought enough times to know that a horse will not ride into a wall of steel. I wanted to use the natural reactions of our horses to our advantage. The Welsh still had shields raised and I swept my sword across the tops. My sword smacked into the helmet of one man and my edge must had driven into the metal a little for I felt myself being pulled from my horse. My left arm was complaining and it took all my strength for me to retain my saddle. The sword came away bloody. The man I had struck had to be dead. I pulled back my arm for I saw a face peer over the top of a shield and I thrust, almost blindly. I was lucky and the sword slid into the man's eye. A sword hacked at my leg but my wife's orders to me now saved me from a serious wound. My hauberk took the blow. It might need to be repaired but that was better than a wound.

Having reached the end of the line I wheeled and saw that Ralph was still with me and whole. His sword was bloody and our efforts had broken the shield wall enough to allow my archers to penetrate it. Some still had bows and were sending arrows into the faces and the flesh of men that were busy trying to fight my sword armed archers. Jack had his archers above the Welshmen and protected by the hall. It was their arrows that broke the Welsh spirit.

A Welsh voice called something and then I heard a Scottish voice shout something else. The large numbers were now explained. I wondered if Wallace himself had joined these Welshmen. The thought disappeared as soon as it came into my head for I would have recognised his huge frame. The men who had just been attacking the hall now fled. Some would not be able to do so easily for my men fought them but I saw that there had to be a plan as they all ran for the same place. After running through the shattered gates they headed south down the road.

"After them, Ralph!"

Only Ralph and I were still mounted but I knew that John and James would fetch horses for Hamo and my archers. We had to slow down the exodus. The problem we had was the mass of fighting men between us and those fleeing. It took longer for us to round them than I would have liked. Dawn was not far off and the lightening sky revealed horses. Some of the men who had fled were the mailed men and the leaders. They had horses and were already mounting. There were twelve horses and six men had mounted by the time Ralph and I were close enough to do anything about it. Others grabbed the reins of any spare horse that they could find. One advantage we had was that a man cannot mount a horse successfully whilst still holding his weapon. I slew two by sweeping my sword across the backs of their heads while they were still attempting to mount skittish horses. I heard Hamo urging his archers on and I said, "Ralph, follow me." I knew I was asking much of a man who had fought in just one battle but I had to risk his life. I galloped after the six men who were now heading along the road that led west from Luston. The raiders were heading for home.

My wound was now complaining. I sheathed my sword and took the reins in my right hand. It afforded me a little relief. I knew that the Welsh and Scottish horses had enjoyed some rest while Ralph and I had ridden hard. The sooner we caught them the better. The sky was growing lighter behind us and as I glanced over my shoulder, I saw that Hamo and William of Ware were leading mounted men behind us. Ralph and I, when we reached those we chased, would have support. The road we followed was familiar to me. It twisted and turned and was tree lined. The result was that when one of those we followed turned he saw just Ralph and me, for Hamo and the others were hidden five hundred paces behind us along the road. A command was shouted and the six horsemen stopped and wheeled. They thought to take us.

Switching hands I drew my sword and said, quietly, to Ralph, "Hamo is coming, we just have to hold them."

"There are six of them, Sir Gerald."

"Watch my left side and stay close."

The six men had wheeled their mounts and they rode at us. They had swords as we had but they outnumbered us. I suddenly recognised one of the men. He was a Scot I had last seen after Falkirk, fleeing with Wallace. I almost ignored the others for this one would be the most dangerous of those we fought. He obliged me by coming straight for me. I dropped my reins and although I knew I had little strength in my left hand, drew my dagger.

"You foiled us this night, Warbow, but you and your popinjay will not survive and Sir William will reward me."

His words told me a number of things, as I raised my sword to block his sword swing. He had been sent by Wallace and he recognised Ralph as a pursuivant. Just at that moment Hamo and my archers appeared around the bend. The Scot I was fighting had no chance to escape and he fought on. Ralph had two enemies but my injured left arm meant that I had to fight for my life. He would have to fend for himself.

The Scotsman's sword swept down and was so powerful that it would have either bent most swords or driven the arm down. I was an archer and stronger than any swordsman and my sword was that of a knight. It held and that surprised the Scot. I think he thought to end the fight with the one blow. My left arm was weak but I swung my dagger anyway. Catching the Scotsman's arm it distracted the Scot enough to allow me to swing at his head. He barely blocked the blow and I saw fear in his face as his sword was driven down. In such a fight you cannot allow yourself the luxury of looking around. You have to trust that your shield brothers are doing what they can. I heard cries and shouts but my attention was on the Scotsman. I lunged with my dagger and he reeled to avoid another cut. This time, when I stabbed with my sword, he did not manage to deflect it and my sword went into his thigh. He wheeled his horse and tried to flee. Hamo must have taken men to follow those who had fled because the road was empty save for Ralph and William who were ending the lives of the two men that Ralph had been fighting.

The Scot did not ride down the road but jumped the low bushes that line the road. Perhaps he thought that an archer did not have the skill to follow. I did and my horse began to gain on his as we galloped over the field of stubble. The Scot kept glancing behind him to see where I was

Wallace's War

and that was always a mistake. The next hedgerow loomed up suddenly before him and he had to wheel to the left. I had seen the wall and anticipated his move. He found himself within a sword's length of me and I backhanded my sword across his neck. His lifeless body fell backward and I reined in my weary mount.

Leaving the bodies where they lay, we headed back to Luston, leading the horses. Jack, if he still lived, could send his men to recover and to burn the bodies. I was anxious for my stepson and from William's words, as we rode back, he had not seen the body of his brother.

"My brother did well to hold the attackers."

I glanced at him and wondered if I ought to tell him now of his brother's death.

"How is the arm, father?"

"Complaining but it did not let me down. Nor did you, Ralph, I am sorry for putting you in harm's way."

He laughed, "I am a knight now, Sir Gerald, and part of this family. I was honoured that you trusted me so."

By the time we reached Luston, it was dawn and Gwillim had already begun to burn the bodies of the dead attackers. My stepson's hall would need to be repaired for it had suffered. I was relieved when I spied him with Gwillim. They saw us and walked towards us. Their eyes were on William.

William of Ware said, "Where is my brother?"

Jack pointed to the cloak-covered body, "He was one of the first to fall."

We dismounted and William ran over to look at the face of his dead brother. He bowed his head and I wondered if it was in prayer.

"What happened, Jack?"

"They were cunning, Sir Gerald. They must have watched us and known our routine. Edward and I were doing the rounds when Edward saw that the sentry by the beacon was not there. While I roused the house, he ran to light the beacon. He succeeded but he was cut down before he could make the house. The sentries on the walls had their throats cut. All our plans to hold them at the walls were in disarray and we had to defend the house. Had Edward not lit the beacon we would all lie dead." He pointed to another cloak-covered body, "Henry the steward died valiantly too."

I nodded, "There are two places to apportion blame and neither of them is in Luston. The Welshmen of Penybont and William Wallace are the ones who caused the deaths. We will honour the dead and bury them with honour but vengeance will come to those who thought that they could do this. We will secure this hall and then return to Yarpole. I would ride to Wigmore Castle to speak with Sir Edmund but I need a night of sleep first. My anger might become violent else."

Twenty of my archers had died alongside Edward and Henry. The burnt bodies of the Welsh and Scottish warriors were a testament to the victory but the cost had been too high. Hamo, Ralph and I rode to Wigmore Castle the next day and presented ourselves to Sir Edmund.

"We have come, Sir Edmund, because Welshmen and Scottish warriors attacked Luston."

His eyes narrowed, "And what would you have me do now?" He spread his arms. "I take it that you defeated them?"

I felt myself becoming angry. Lady Maud had raised her children better than this. "We came before to ask you to help and you washed your hands of it. Now I ask again. Punish the Welsh for this attack."

"It is over now and with a war against Scotland looming I would not risk losing warriors to satisfy your need for revenge. Go back to Yarpole, bury your dead and prepare for a war."

"Baron Mortimer, I shall not forget this."

His face became red, "You threaten me!"

I laughed, "I threaten no one. What I do is act. You have shown me this day that you cannot control the border. I shall."

"How dare you! I am the lord of this land."

"Yet you do not act like one."

We were face to face and I saw, in his face and eyes, that he feared what I might do next.

"Go, leave my house. You are no longer welcome and you, Ralph Fitzalan, are no longer part of my family."

Ralph showed how much he had grown since joining my family, "Sir Edmund, the king himself knighted me and I have a title. I would be grateful if you would remember that."

"Go!"

As we rode back to my hall Ralph said, "I have a new family now, Sir Gerald, and a better one I think."

Hamo said, "That is true but this day, father, you have made another enemy."

I laughed, "Gerald Warbow never worries about his enemies. It is they who should worry about me."

Epilogue

It was a week later that I led my archers and the men of Yarpole in a long column back into Wales. We rode in daylight so that all knew we were coming. I wanted the borderlands to know that while Baron Mortimer might squat behind his castle walls we would not. James carried my banner and John the banner of Sir Ralph. We rode in surcoats and Ralph and I were mailed. Even my archers were helmed. The sunlight shone on our metal column as we headed for Penybont. They knew we were coming and the whole village was in uproar. Many took what they could carry and animals that could be driven but others remained to defend their homes.

"Kill the men and let the families go. I would have this village wiped off the face of the earth and let all know that this is what happens if you attack my home." My words carried on the air and I saw men's faces as they realised what punishment was coming their way. They cried out in fear and the last defenders of the village began to run as it dawned on them that this was no idle threat. Ralph, Jack and Hamo, led twenty archers to hunt down the men who had survived the attack on Luston. There were just five. That there were others who had come from other villages meant that many escaped justice but the burning remains of the village would be a reminder that Sir Gerald Warbow now controlled the border. When next I went to war for King Edward those who thought to take advantage of my absence would have to think again.

The End

Wallace's War

Glossary

An Còrsa Feàrna – Carsphairn in Galloway
Banneret-the rank of knight below that of earl but above a bachelor knight
Bachelor knight- a knight who had his own banner but fought under the banner of another
Centenar- commander of one hundred men
Familia- Household knights of a great lord
Hogbog – a place on a farm occupied by pigs and fowl
Centenar – a commander of one hundred men
Vintenar- a commander of twenty men

Historical Note

King Edward's war in Flanders did happen. Men were sent to raid northern France but the main attack was on the port of Damme. Gerald Warbow's chevauchée is my fictionalised account of what would have occurred over a wider front. Damme fell to a mixture of English and Flemish. Its success was marred by Stirling Bridge. The Flemish campaign allowed Sir Andrew Murray and William Wallace to trap and defeat the Earl of Surrey. Although many knights died at Stirling Bridge, it was the loss of archers and spearmen that was the greatest cost.

One incident that has me puzzled was Wallace's decision not to attack Durham but to head for Newcastle. I have travelled that road many times and from Bowes to Durham is a relatively short journey. Newcastle is further away. All I can assume is that the snowstorm stopped east of Durham. His route north was determined by the rivers he had to ford. He was held at Newcastle and then took his army north but Wallace had not been beaten and he retired to Selkirk Forest where he used the archers there to defend the camp while he trained men. He was draconian in his recruitment and men were not allowed to refuse service. His army was largely one of the people. The schiltrons fought in huge circles that cavalry could not penetrate. Wallace had few knights with his army.

When the king came north again to punish the Scots, he did bring Welsh mercenaries, ten thousand of them. His supply ships failed to reach him and the hunger of his men caused the Welsh mutiny. Priests were slain by the drunk fuelled Welshmen and they paid little part in the

Wallace's War

Battle of Falkirk. The incident with the horse and the king's broken ribs did happen. Sir Ralph Basset did insult the Bishop of Durham and caused his men to recklessly charge a schiltron. The account we have of the battle from Guisborough, notes that the retinue of Basset lost not a horse which suggests he took little part in the actual fighting. The English horsemen did drive the Scottish horse from the field but it was the archers who won the battle. Wallace did flee to France to seek help there. William Wallace was part of one successful battle, Stirling Bridge but the architect of that battle, Sir Andrew Murray, died of his wounds. Had King Edward not gone to Flanders but completed the work begun at Dunbar then the land of Scotland might have become English far sooner than it did.

Gerald Warbow will return. He is Lord Edward's archer and so long as the king lives so his archer will serve him.

Griff Hosker
September 2022

Wallace's War

Other books by Griff Hosker

If you enjoyed reading this book, then why not read another one by the author?

Ancient History

The Sword of Cartimandua Series
(Germania and Britannia 50 A.D. – 128 A.D.)
Ulpius Felix- Roman Warrior (prequel)
The Sword of Cartimandua
The Horse Warriors
Invasion Caledonia
Roman Retreat
Revolt of the Red Witch
Druid's Gold
Trajan's Hunters
The Last Frontier
Hero of Rome
Roman Hawk
Roman Treachery
Roman Wall
Roman Courage

The Wolf Warrior series
(Britain in the late 6th Century)
Saxon Dawn
Saxon Revenge
Saxon England
Saxon Blood
Saxon Slayer
Saxon Slaughter
Saxon Bane
Saxon Fall: Rise of the Warlord
Saxon Throne
Saxon Sword

Medieval History

The Dragon Heart Series

Wallace's War

Viking Slave
Viking Warrior
Viking Jarl
Viking Kingdom
Viking Wolf
Viking War
Viking Sword
Viking Wrath
Viking Raid
Viking Legend
Viking Vengeance
Viking Dragon
Viking Treasure
Viking Enemy
Viking Witch
Viking Blood
Viking Weregeld
Viking Storm
Viking Warband
Viking Shadow
Viking Legacy
Viking Clan
Viking Bravery

The Norman Genesis Series
Hrolf the Viking
Horseman
The Battle for a Home
Revenge of the Franks
The Land of the Northmen
Ragnvald Hrolfsson
Brothers in Blood
Lord of Rouen
Drekar in the Seine
Duke of Normandy
The Duke and the King

Danelaw
(England and Denmark in the 11th Century)
Dragon Sword
Oathsword
Bloodsword

Wallace's War

New World Series
Blood on the Blade
Across the Seas
The Savage Wilderness
The Bear and the Wolf
Erik The Navigator
Erik's Clan

The Vengeance Trail

The Reconquista Chronicles
Castilian Knight
El Campeador
The Lord of Valencia

The Aelfraed Series
(Britain and Byzantium 1050 A.D. - 1085 A.D.)
Housecarl
Outlaw
Varangian

The Anarchy Series England 1120-1180
English Knight
Knight of the Empress
Northern Knight
Baron of the North
Earl
King Henry's Champion
The King is Dead
Warlord of the North
Enemy at the Gate
The Fallen Crown
Warlord's War
Kingmaker
Henry II
Crusader
The Welsh Marches
Irish War
Poisonous Plots
The Princes' Revolt

Wallace's War
Earl Marshal
The Perfect Knight

Border Knight
1182-1300
Sword for Hire
Return of the Knight
Baron's War
Magna Carta
Welsh Wars
Henry III
The Bloody Border
Baron's Crusade
Sentinel of the North
War in the West
Debt of Honour
The Blood of the Warlord
The Fettered King

Sir John Hawkwood Series
France and Italy 1339- 1387
Crécy: The Age of the Archer
Man At Arms
The White Company
Leader of Men

Lord Edward's Archer
Lord Edward's Archer
King in Waiting
An Archer's Crusade
Targets of Treachery
The Great Cause
Wallace's War

Struggle for a Crown
1360- 1485
Blood on the Crown
To Murder a King
The Throne
King Henry IV
The Road to Agincourt
St Crispin's Day

Wallace's War

The Battle for France
The Last Knight
Queen's Knight

Tales from the Sword I
(Short stories from the Medieval period)

Tudor Warrior series
England and Scotland in the late 14th and early 15th century
Tudor Warrior
Tudor Spy

Conquistador
England and America in the 16th Century
Conquistador
The English Adventurer

Modern History

The Napoleonic Horseman Series
Chasseur à Cheval
Napoleon's Guard
British Light Dragoon
Soldier Spy
1808: The Road to Coruña
Talavera
The Lines of Torres Vedras
Bloody Badajoz
The Road to France
Waterloo

The Lucky Jack American Civil War series
Rebel Raiders
Confederate Rangers
The Road to Gettysburg

Soldier of the Queen series
Soldier of the Queen

The British Ace Series
1914

Wallace's War
1915 Fokker Scourge
1916 Angels over the Somme
1917 Eagles Fall
1918 We will remember them
From Arctic Snow to Desert Sand
Wings over Persia

Combined Operations series
1940-1945
Commando
Raider
Behind Enemy Lines
Dieppe
Toehold in Europe
Sword Beach
Breakout
The Battle for Antwerp
King Tiger
Beyond the Rhine
Korea
Korean Winter

Tales from the Sword II
(Short stories from the Modern period)

Other Books
Great Granny's Ghost (Aimed at 9-14-year-old young people)

For more information on all of the books then please visit the author's website at www.griffhosker.com where there is a link to contact him or visit his Facebook page: GriffHosker at Sword Books

Printed in Great Britain
by Amazon

11739112R00122